Her scent, the s... curled like breat... his gut.

He didn't know what he'd expected to feel when she opened the door, but this wasn't it, this raw and avaricious need.

Joe had never in his life reacted to Hallie Thompson—or indeed, any woman—like this.

Had never even considered he might.

He drew a harsh, steadying breath. This reaction was enough to warn him that he should run far and fast—and *now*. But then he looked at her, took in all the things that made her Hallie, and knew he was damned.

'Hallie?'

'Joe?'

Numb, he eyed his best friend's defensive stance and suddenly noticed the infant in her arms. Everything inside him lurched and twisted. He had a daughter. He was a father.

And then he heard himself ask, 'She's mine, isn't she?'

Dear Reader,

Silhouette Sensation® delivers six passionate, dramatic novels of romantic suspense each and every month, and this is the spot where we get the opportunity to tell you a little about what's available right now.

Every month we pick one special title with a strong, dangerous, rather special hero for our **HEARTBREAKERS** slot, and this month it simply had to be Joe Martinez from Terese Ramin's *Mary's Child*. He's just the kind of protective, sexy man we love.

Maggie Shayne and Marilyn Tracy continue their popular mini-series, with Maggie's next book about the Brand family being in January 2001, just after Marilyn's *Almost Remembered* in December.

There are also two couples who marry in haste—and then have a lot of talking to do!—in *Midnight Promises* from Eileen Wilks and *Marriage of Agreement* by the well-loved Judith Duncan. All of the above leaves us with *True Lies* from Ingrid Weaver, a classic undercover-cop-falling-for-his-prime-suspect story…

We hope that you'll read and enjoy them all,

The Editors

PS
Do you like to know what other books are on sale this month? Would you rather have something else on this page? Do write to us and let us know; your views are important to us.

Mary's Child

TERESE RAMIN

SILHOUETTE

SENSATION

*All the characters in this book have no existence outside the imagination
of the author, and have no relation whatsoever to anyone bearing the
same name or names. They are not even distantly inspired by any
individual known or unknown to the author, and all the incidents are
pure invention.*

*Silhouette, Silhouette Sensation and Colophon are
registered trademarks of Harlequin Books S.A., used under licence.*

*First published in Great Britain 2000
Silhouette Books, Eton House, 18-24 Paradise Road,
Richmond, Surrey TW9 1SR*

© Terese daly Ramin 1998

ISBN 0 373 07881 1

18-1000

*Printed and bound in Spain
by Litografia Rosés S.A., Barcelona*

TERESE RAMIN

lives in Michigan with her husband, two children, two dogs, two cats and an assortment of strays. When not writing romances, she writes chancel dramas, sings alto in the church choir, plays the guitar, yells at her children to pick up their rooms (even though she keeps telling herself that she won't) and responds with silence when they ask her where they should put their rooms after they've picked them up.

A fully-fledged believer in dreams, the only thing she's ever wanted to do is write. After years of dreaming without doing anything about it, she finally wrote her first novel, *Water from the Moon*, which won a Romance Writers of America Golden Heart Award in 1987. Her subsequent books have appeared on romance best-seller lists. She is also the recipient of a 1991 *Romantic Times* Reviewer's Choice Award. She hasn't dreamed without acting for a long time.

For Sharon, who gave me The Pen:
Love you, my dear, TD
With gleeful thanks to Becky Barker,
who told me about frogs.

'A great lover is not the man who romances a different
woman every night. A great lover is the man who
romances the same woman for life.'
—Ancient Chinese saying

Prologue

January 8—traditionally the coldest day of the year

"Oh, God, I didn't miss this."

Pale and shaky, Hallie Thompson hoisted herself up from her knees in the women's-room stall and fumbled her way across to the sink. The mirror above the stainless-steel ledge designed to hold combs and compacts confronted her with a face that looked drawn and haggard, showed every bit of her thirty-four years.

"I look like hell."

Stiff-armed, she leaned over the sink, head hanging, gathering strength.

"Jeez, Thompson, how stupid are you, anyway?"

Grimacing at her reflection, she yanked a pair of paper towels out of the dispenser and turned on the cold water. In another couple of months or so she would no longer ask herself the "stupid" question, she knew. In another couple of months she would feel healthy as all get-out, full of vim and vinegar—quite literally. Just now, however, in the company of this always-unpredictable afternoon morning-sickness, she felt the way she looked: like death or some of the indecipherable lunches left too long in the squad room refrigerator.

At the very thought of "lunch" her stomach flounced and heaved. Oh, hell, not again, she silently begged. She swallowed back the flex of bile in her throat, dampened the paper towels and dabbed at the perspiration-dotted corners of her mouth, at her throat, at the back of her neck. What in creation had possessed her to suggest to Joe and Mary that she'd be willing to undergo an embryo transfer and carry their baby for them when they'd found out Mary absolutely would never be able to carry a child to term?

Sympathy and forgetfulness, probably, coupled with love, insanity and the certain knowledge that Mary would be the most beautiful mother in the universe, Joe the special kind of father who'd always made such a wonderful extra "uncle" to Hallie's own two boys.

There was also Hallie's treasured mental picture of her oldest, her best friend, Joe, manfully trying on maid-of-honor dresses when they were attempting to decide what he should wear to be her "man of honor" when she'd married Zeke twelve years ago. Her mother had entertained conniptions over the very thought of Joe standing up for Hallie, so the pair of them had decided to, uh, "make Mom happy." Her marriage to Zeke hadn't lasted, but the image of her mother's apoplexy when a straight-faced Joe modeled the dress he and Hallie had settled on for him to wear was something she cherished beyond anything.

Hallie grinned weakly at her reflection with the memory. Knowing that both Joe's loyalty to her and his droll sense of humor made him fully capable of following through on his threat to wear the flamboyantly frothy creation, Hallie's mother had blown a gasket, then backed down immediately.

Joe had looked very nice in his departmental dress uniform holding Hallie's lilac-and-lavender bouquet for her throughout the ceremony.

But that was a long time ago, forever and a day Before. Now was After. After was Mary dead—murdered during a carjacking-gone-wrong six weeks ago, barely three hours after the embryo transfer had taken place, and within two miles of Hallie's house after Mary had dropped her there post-release. After was Joe in a hell so dark, Hallie couldn't reach him; Joe unable to grieve, shattering wineglasses, water glasses within the clench of a fist, punching holes in the thin plasterboard of the run-down old house Mary had loved and insisted they purchase; Joe as Hallie had never seen him—not even when his younger brother had been killed during Desert Storm.

In the blink of an eye he'd become a man she didn't know, a frightening shadow of a beast she'd never have wanted to meet. She'd stayed with him anyway, because he was Joe, her best friend ever—and she had to.

Hallie had made the funeral arrangements, but Joe had arrived late at the memorial-park service where Mary's ashes were scattered beneath the sere prewinter branches of a dogwood slumbering till spring. The Michigan sky had been gray, the ground damp, layered thinly with a light late-November snow that quickly turned to slush. He'd looked as haggard as the sky: hollow-eyed, unshaven, with scarcely banked rage threatening.

The tempest broke back at the office the day after the service.

In the four days since the discovery of Mary's body beside her Blazer, the entire Cuyahoga County sheriff's department had been on twenty-four-hour duty—most of it voluntary—looking for the killer.

With no success.

Raids on each of the county's known chop shops looking for a possible killer had proved unproductive: the coroner could find no fingerprints on the body, and Cuyahoga

County was full of isolated areas that made unwitnessed crimes distressingly easy to orchestrate. Three 9-mm bullets had been recovered from Mary's body, but without a weapon to match them against, they were of little help. Mary's jewelry and purse were missing; the jewelry had not been pawned within the county and the purse had not been dumped or found.

DNA testing of hair and fiber removed from the front seat of the vehicle was inconclusive without a suspect. The Crime Scene Unit was still collecting samples for comparison with those of anyone who might conceivably have been in the vehicle, including Joe, Hallie, Hallie's boys, the garage mechanic who'd serviced the Blazer the previous week, the elderly shut-ins Mary had ferried out to the grocery store as needed.

Bullet and blood patterns indicated the killer had probably stood eye-to-eye with Mary, within five feet, when the fatal shots were fired. No blood or tissue was found under her nails, suggesting there'd been no physical battle.

And that was the thing right there—the puzzle piece that didn't jibe, the thing that none of them could live with: the fact that all appearances suggested that Mary had exited the vehicle, tossed her keys onto the driver's seat where the police had found them, then moved aside to let the carjacker have the Blazer without a fight.

The fact that in order to steal the vehicle, the carjacker hadn't needed to kill Mary at all.

Joe couldn't live with leads that led them in circles to nowhere. He went on a rampage, ransacked his files looking for possible connections to old cases, possible released cons who might have it in for him. He tore Hallie apart verbally in private, publicly castigated deputies who'd already worked every possible lead from every possible angle and had been awake as long as he. He refused to take time off; he wanted results. And he wanted them four days ago, before Mary had died.

He lost it. And the department forgave him, embarrassed but understanding, cutting him slack because God knew how they'd react in the same situation—possibly worse.

Then, suddenly, three days later, it was as if the berserker Joe had never existed; an uncommunicative, lone-ranger ice-Joe had replaced him. In a calm as dead as an ocean's doldrums he'd arrived at the office in civvies and stalked into the sheriff's office. A single jerk of his head when he passed Hallie called her in with him. There he'd handed the sheriff his weapon, badge and resignation. In the sparest possible language he'd thanked Hallie for handling all the arrangements for Mary's funeral; told her to thank the department for everything they'd done to try to catch Mary's killer; said he was leaving town for he didn't know where in an attempt to sort out himself and his future. Then he'd left.

Hallie hadn't believed him for an instant. She'd torn after him to pump the real story out of him, but Joe had shaken her off with a silence as bottomless as his pain. Neither he nor Hallie had mentioned the embryo transfer because, quite frankly, in the face of more traumatic matters, they'd both forgotten it. When he'd handed Hallie the keys to his house, climbed onto his Harley and roared away, she'd let him go even though she'd felt in her gut that he would go underground and do whatever it took to find Mary's killer. Even if "what it took" would cost Joe himself in the process.

He was her best friend. She'd understood and felt his pain. She'd trusted him—wanted to trust him. And that meant she could have done no less.

But of course, that was then and this was now. Now she was six weeks pregnant with his baby—Mary's baby—and he hadn't even called once to say where he was. And so far, because Joe was law enforcement and knew as well as any big-time criminal how to effectively disappear when he didn't want to be found, all the fugitive-finding resources at her disposal hadn't turned him up, either.

Whether or not the infant she carried would ever get to meet its surviving biological parent, Hallie hadn't a clue.

The door to the women's john slammed open hard; Hallie's current partner stuck his head in the door.

"Hey, Thompson, beat feet, will ya? We got a fled, trail's gettin' cold. Let's rock."

"On my way." Hallie grimaced and shoved herself away from the sink. Her stomach objected. Strenuously. She clutched it and headed back into the vacated stall. Strength, someone had once said, came when you were in a very narrow alley and had no way of turning around. Well, she was about to find out whether or not that was true. "With you in a minute, Frank. Get me some soda crackers and I'll meet you at the car."

Hail Mary, she prayed, bowing low to the bowl. Find that bastard Joe fast and let the next seven months be worth this....

Chapter 1

November 25, new moon

He didn't want to be here. He didn't want to feel.

He had to get his keys.

Parked in his weathered truck across the street from Hallie's house, Joe Martinez hardened his heart with the thrust of his jaw and waited—prayed, in fact—for welcome numbness to set in.

He prayed in vain.

Sensation quivered in every nerve, emotion made harsh inroads along every vein and pore. And he'd thought it would be easier to stop by Hallie's first before he had to go by the house that until almost a year ago, he and Mary had called home. Had he been wrong! He should never have come. Shouldn't have let himself get talked into hunting down this particular bail jumper in this particular portion of his past.

Spit, he thought. Friggin' bloody spit.

The house looked the same as ever: medium-size two-story, slightly worn, cedar shingles ragged in spots—welcoming. A pinecone wreath decorated with white fake-snow flowers and bright red berries adorned the front door; a plastic version of a Victorian Christmas village meandered across the wide, single-pane front window. An angel wind sock belled gently beneath the front-porch roof, its golden trumpet extended.

Familiar.

Something wretchedly painful expanded in Joe's chest. Mary had given Hallie the wind sock the Christmas after Hallie's youngest son, Sam, was born. Damned woman always did decorate too early.

Hallie, not Mary. He wondered briefly if Hallie had decorated at all last year.

His mouth thinned. God, he didn't want to be here. But he still had to get his keys.

Could stay at a motel, his mind suggested. Don't let her know you're in town.

Coward, his conscience replied.

Same thing the guys in the FAT squad room had called him when he'd made sure Hallie wasn't there, then gone in to pump them for old favors and information regarding his latest quarry.

"You seen Hallie yet?" they'd asked instead of answering. The Cuyahoga County Sheriff's Fugitive Apprehension Team was a tight unit, they'd reminded him. They took care of their own.

What's that got to do with Hallie? he'd wondered—and ducked just in time when one of his oldest friends suddenly and inexplicably took a swing and threatened to deck him. Then, prevented from following up on the first swing by two other members of the unit, the man who'd succeeded Joe as Hallie's partner cursed the prodigal roundly as a coward who'd get no courtesy from the FAT until *after* Joe saw Hallie—and then, only if she gave the word.

Coward.

Hanging his wrists over the steering wheel, Joe studied the house for an instant longer. Hell, what was he afraid of? This was only Hallie, right? Best friends since kindergarten; best friends for life.

Inside his chest his heart hammered. Only Hallie. Yeah, right.

Folding up his feelings and putting them away the way any cop who stayed a cop was able to do, Joe grabbed the winter flight jacket with the bounty-hunter patch on the sleeve from the bench seat beside him and eased out of the truck. Slid into the jacket and zipped it, then waited for one car, two cars to pass before crossing the street to face Hallie.

The doorbell rang at the precise moment Hallie finally managed to disengage the sleeping-but-still-faintly-suckling Maura from her breast. The eleven-week-old started and reattached herself hard. Hallie winced and swore beneath her breath. With Maura, timing was everything.

There was no question of the infant still feeding; no, this was a question of the colicky, persnickety baby using Hallie as a pacifier.

Downstairs the doorbell buzzed again. Hallie looked at Maura. Sure as sin she wasn't going to answer the door hooked to the infant like this. Not even if she pulled a blanket up over the baby to hide herself. Neither door-to-door salesmen nor religious canvassers required her attention badly enough for her to go to the trouble. And if it was Frank or one of the other guys from the squad, they'd be embarrassed as all get-out, and she'd never live it down tomorrow.

At the back of the second story she could hear her sons, Sam and Ben, ages seven and eight, playing in their room, too far away or too involved to hear the bell. Unfortunately, she didn't dare yell for them and risk waking Maura completely. And they weren't allowed to answer the door by themselves yet anyway—even with the dog beside them—but at least they could look out a window and see who was on the porch. It was probably only their father come to pick them up for basketball practice, but Zeke usually didn't use the front door and only rarely knocked. He simply let himself in.

Another buzz from below, accompanied by an insistent rapping, informed Hallie that whoever was at the door had no intention of leaving without seeing someone. The knowledge rankled: she didn't suffer fools kindly, unexpected visitors who couldn't call first—especially when they interfered with Maura's rare bouts of real sleep. She had half a mind to... Well, never mind. Suffice it to say, the thought wasn't nice.

Still, this time when the baby startled and lost suction, Hallie was ready for her. Quickly she put space between her breast and the infant's questing mouth, pulled her bra up and her shirt down, righted the ready-to-fuss Maura, pulled the baby's bib and blanket to her shoulder and went downstairs to answer the door.

And pity the poor fool who stood on the other side.

His initial reaction when he saw her was depraved and violent, robbed him of speech.

Hunger. Greed. Craving. Want.

Possession.

Now.

He stared at her through the screen she always waited as long as possible to remove from the storm door and blinked, stunned, telling himself it was only Hallie, for God's sake, only Hallie.

But it wasn't. The scent, the subtle essence of her, an undertaste—a call to his senses—of something primal he couldn't identify, wafted gently into the thirty-degree air, filled his nostrils, his lungs; curled like breathable lightning in his gut.

He didn't know what he'd expected to feel when she opened the door, but this wasn't it: this breath-stealing torquing in his lower belly, this shockingly questing *thrust* of his sex against his zipper; this raw and avaricious need.

This base lusting urge to back Hallie against the door and take her like something out of an X-rated movie, have her again moments later on her front hall steps, then on the chair beside her telephone table. And then…again and again and again. Anywhere. Everywhere. Until this hot thing inside him cooled. Until he could see straight and breathe again.

Until he was too sated and too limp for the cruder passions to interfere with what he'd come here to do: pick up his house keys, find his bail jumper and get the hell out of here so he could pick up his body receipt, collect his cash and get on with the process of bringing down his late wife's killer.

He'd never in his life reacted to Halleluia Thompson— or indeed, to any woman—like this.

Had never even considered he might.

He knew the year since Mary died had changed him, but this was the first inkling he'd had of just how savage he'd become.

The first time he'd scared himself.

He drew a harsh, steadying breath. The entire experience lasted less than fifteen seconds, but it was enough to warn him, make him know that he should run far and fast, and now. But then he looked at her, took in the short, straight, uncooperative, almost-too-blond hair, the frank dark blue eyes, the steely "You-have-interrupted-me-whoever-you-are-and-you-are-going-to-pay-for-it" set of her mouth— took in, in short, all the things that made her Hallie, and knew that he was damned. Because in the long run, if his body didn't torture him to death with his first image of her in a year, then his conscience would scourge him for not staying at least long enough to find out why her new partner, Frank Nillson, had wanted to deck him when he'd tried to avoid seeing Hallie at all.

"Yes?" she asked coolly.

He breathed through his nose, expelled a breath of what he might once have identified as regret. She didn't know him. "Hallie?" he asked.

She didn't recognize him at first, he'd changed so much physically.

The product of a Swedish-Viking and Hungarian heritage, at five feet eleven inches and one hundred forty-five pounds, she was not a little girl; delicacy was missing from her genes. But at six foot five and a good two hundred thirty muscular pounds, he filled her doorway, dwarfing her, emanating testosterone and danger.

Her eyes narrowed, and every nerve she possessed stood to attention. Instinctively she turned slightly sideways to the doorway, protectively holding Maura as far away from this black-haired, gray-eyed, heavily bearded stranger as she could. But even then, from underneath her she-bear reflex, something reckless poked out its head, sized up the undeniably hunky creature in her doorway and said *Woof!*

"Yes?" she asked, hoping she sounded cool and coplike, instead of like the dithering idiot inside her who was wondering what he'd look like without the beard and his shirt at the same time she wondered if she could slam the door and lock it, put Maura down safely and get to her gun if he turned out to be as hazardous as he looked.

Then he said her name.

"Hallie?"

She stared at him, did a double take, and stared again, unable to reconcile the voice with the furry face and beefcake body.

The voice was tired and dry, distinctly bass—even

"basso profundo" as their high-school choral director had been fond of stating. A voice able to command attention with a whisper, tumble the walls of Jericho with a shout— or stop a rebellious suspect with a word.

A voice that had destroyed her concentration every time he sang from the time they'd turned fifteen, sent chills down her spine with every confidence they'd shared since. Joe's voice. The voice of the child, the boy, the man she'd loved since kindergarten.

It was only the body that had belonged to somebody else.

Joe's body should be—had always been—lanky to the point of thinness. This man's body was, well, not quite Arnold Schwarzenegger's, but a heck of a lot broader and more muscularly defined than Joe's had ever been.

She swallowed, worked her jaw, put her hand on the door for support. "Joe?" she asked—cautiously.

He nodded, equally watchful.

The baby squirmed under the blanket against her shoulder, drawing his eyes. She clutched Maura tighter, and felt the panic of a mother who fears her child will be taken away from her start to rise.

"Joe *Martinez?*"

He nodded again, eyeing the twitching blanket with bemusement, suddenly impatient. "Yes, damn it, it's me, Hallie. Now open the freaking door and let me in."

Panic risen turned to anger. "Get off my porch, you bastard," she returned, and moved to slam the door in his face.

The movement was too abrupt, joggled the ready-to-fuss Maura from half sleep to thin crankiness to full howl without apparent transition. Hallie automatically let go of the door, put her hand to the infant's back to prevent her from sliding sideways. Joe, who'd already yanked open the screen to catch the inside door before it closed, pushed into Hallie's entryway, head cocked in puzzlement that quickly turned into shock when the blanket covering the dark-haired, brown-skinned baby slipped and dropped to the floor. He stooped to retrieve the covering, held it out to Hallie who backed away from him, clutching Maura tightly, protectively, at the same time she tried to soothe the infant.

"Hallie?" he asked, too dazed to be entirely sure what he was seeing.

A mother cornered with both her maternal heart and her child to protect, Hallie snarled at him, "You're not taking her from me, Joe Martinez, do you hear me? You left her. You left me with her. She's mine! So you just get out of my house now."

Chapter 2

Undone as he was by his initial reaction to the scent and sight of Hallie, Joe couldn't quite get his mind around the implications: Hallie, baby. Hallie, baby. Hallie... *¡Madre de Dios!* Hallie, *baby*.

"You're not taking her from me, Joe. You left her. She's mine!"

But she wasn't.

At least not biologically.

Without a sound he sagged against the wall and slid to the floor, poleaxed. He'd returned to Cuyahoga County for a single reason only: in pursuit of a man who'd jumped bail, then hunted down, tortured and killed his estranged wife and fled with his kids in this direction. There was no indication the guy had harmed the kids—yet—but Joe's goal was to get to him before that happened. Not to mention that the bounty on this particular body would allow him to finance another step in his search for Mary's killer for a while. Maybe even long enough this time. But now...

Numb, he eyed his best friend's defensive, defiant stance,

the infant in her arms, and everything inside him lurched and twisted, the bottom of the universe dropped away beneath him. He had a daughter. Knowing the truth was that simple. He and Mary had a child. He was a parent. A father.

Dios.

In the past year he'd occasionally wondered, but the statistics he'd had to work from were all in the negative: the first embryo transfer usually didn't take; the odds of success of any transfer taking, although greater than they used to be, were still limited; the odds of success would have increased dramatically if he and Mary had allowed the embryo transfer using a donor egg—preferably one of Hallie's—which they hadn't. And on and on.

Disbelieving, he rubbed a hand across his face and stared up at Hallie. So this was what the guys at the department had meant. This was why Frank had wanted to deck him: for deserting Hallie while she'd been pregnant with his baby.

He swallowed, jaw clenched against the urge to self-castigate in favor of self-defense. Who the hell were they to judge him? He hadn't known. How could he have known?

Since he'd successfully gone underground, as it were, and hadn't checked in, he couldn't. It was no excuse, merely the reason. He'd done what he had to do. Was still doing it. Somebody had to relieve his nightmares. Somebody had to lay Mary to rest. And he couldn't do that with an infant strapped to his chest—even if he could find a bulletproof vest that would accommodate them both.

Yet, even as the protests occurred to him he heard himself ask, "She's mine, isn't she? And Mary's? The transfer took."

"You abandoned her. She's *not* yours."

He didn't hear her—or he heard what she said from a distance and ignored her. Even he didn't know which.

"Does she have a name? How old is she? When's her birthday?"

Hallie backed away, protecting both the infant and herself from him with both arms. "None of that matters to you at this point," she said flatly. "You left her, I had her anyway, it's in the courts. I'm adopting her with your family's blessing, Mary's family's blessing and my family's blessing. Even Zeke's family offered their blessing and they don't have a say except for the boys."

The numbness grew to a dull ache at the back of his skull. Family. His family, Mary's family. He hadn't even considered them.

Hadn't considered anyone or lived by anything but guilt, survival and revenge for fifty-one weeks, three days, six hours and ten minutes—give or take.

And now when he'd finally woken up enough to care about finding and protecting someone else's kids, he wheeled back into his past to find a best friend who not only hated him, but whom he wanted to bed and who'd borne him a daughter of his own.

Frank had been right to want to deck him; he *was* a scumbag. He wanted to deck himself, too. But he still had three little kids and their murderer father to find and return to Duluth, and Mary's killer to identify and take down. Personal confusion wouldn't cut it here.

He hauled in air, let it out slowly. Pushed himself to his feet and headed for Hallie's living room. He knew you either dealt with a moment or you let it plow you under.

He had no intention of ever getting plowed under again.

"Shut the door," he said over his shoulder. "We have to talk."

She watched his back—the loose, arrogant, owner-of-the-earth strut—and anger contained for a year pooled and flared in her gut—much the same as it had when they were kids and he'd behaved this way. He was not in charge here.

This was her home, her life—her sons' lives and futures—he wanted to mess with. Allowing him an inch of "in charge" would be unacceptable; much like giving a fugitive the upper hand during the chase and capture. She not only couldn't do it, she wouldn't.

An ache took root in the vicinity of her heart. Not even for Joe.

Or maybe it was especially for Joe.

"No," she told him softly. "We don't."

Then she turned and walked back up the stairs, leaving Joe in the hallway alone.

At the top of the curved staircase she paused, trembling with sudden reaction, holding on to Maura for all she was worth. He was back. He was here.

Oh, sweet heaven, she prayed. *What am I going to do?*

Never in her life had she been more afraid of the possible long-term effects of a single moment, a simple conversation, a man. But then, never in her life before could any of the above have cost her a child. Not even when she and Zeke divorced had custody been a question. They'd been friends before their ill-advised marriage and they'd been fortunate enough to remain friends since. In fact, the only thing that had ever gotten in the way of their friendship had been their marriage. Divorce, friendship and their joint-custody agreement were the things that let each of them—especially the boys—blossom and that now kept their family intact.

But Joe was not Zeke. And for all its longevity and variety, she'd never looked at her friendship with Joe in quite the same light as her friendship with Zeke.

Had never quite had the courage to name the light under which she *did* see her friendship with Joe.

In her arms Maura fussed and squirmed, emitted a pair of fitful cries that quickly turned into full yowls. Her heart torn between anger, pain, not enough sleep and no control over the present situation, between her love for the needy

infant in her arms and Maura's father, Hallie clenched her
jaw against the sudden deluge of hormones and tears. If he
wasn't going to be here that long, why couldn't he at least
have waited another three months before he showed up—
after Maura's adoption was final?

Then she calmed herself by force, shifted Maura in the
cradle of her arms and swayed gently across the hall to put
the fussbudgety infant back to breast. Hallie herself might
have to deal with Joe, but she would do it the way any
other mother would: in her baby's time and in her own
way—after the baby went to sleep. And Joe could just live
with that order of things the way any father who hadn't run
off to avenge his late wife might: he could wait.

Until then, she took what little comfort she could find in
wishing Joe to the devil.

"No," she'd told him softly. "We don't."

Then she'd turned and walked back up the stairs, leaving
Joe in the hallway alone.

Arrested by her tone, the same quietly deadly quality
she'd used, time and again, to bring desperate felons to
drop their weapons in a standoff, knowing that she would
not, Joe stopped and turned. He'd known her longer and
better than any felon ever had; when she spoke this way,
it was faster and less costly to back up, turn and go around
rather than through. After a moment's hesitation, he started
up the stairway after her. He didn't have time to spare for
shock—his or hers.

Didn't have time to waste on emotions he couldn't handle.

He reached the top of the stairs and turned right toward
the master bedroom with its half-open door where he could
see Hallie seated in the low-backed, wide-bodied rocker
Zeke had given her the Christmas before Sam was born.

"Hallie…" he began, unsure what he meant to say, only
that it must somehow make things better.

Or at least approachable.

She turned her head and looked at him with a wordless paragraph full of reproach—and warning.

He misread the warning and didn't heed it.

"Hallie, I—"

Underneath the covering blanket, his daughter broke from Hallie's breast and emitted a thin, coughing cry, struggled against the covering. Even while Hallie sent him a killing glance, Joe saw her shift to soothe the baby with voice and hand, heedless of the fact the blanket had slipped low enough to reveal her breast. He knew the sight shouldn't have been erotic but it was—unimaginably so, leaving him tight and breathless. He caught himself staring and cleared his throat, forced his gaze elsewhere: her bed— No, his mind-of-its-own body advised him, wrong direction; find something else. Wits scattering, he made a visual tour of the safer aspects of the room: the baby's crib, the ceiling, the floor, the toe of his right running shoe. *Dios,* what was wrong with him?

And why was it wrong with him *now*?

When he heard the baby quiet, the rocker's gentle creak resume, he looked up once more; opened his mouth and shut it immediately. He'd already woken the baby twice by speaking; it might take more than one lesson, but he could learn. Instead he gestured back and forth between them, pointed downstairs, then eyed Hallie grimly, the glance between former law-enforcement partners as loud as words: *Now or later, we're going to talk. No way out except through.*

For a moment she studied him, equally determined, hovering between responding *Not a chance* and *Never*. Then her mouth folded unhappily at the corners and she offered him the most clipped of nods before she returned her entire attention to Mary's baby.

Joe's whole heart, lungs, and gut clenched at the sight. Hallie looked so damned natural holding his daughter. So beautiful. He'd bet she'd glowed her way through this pregnancy the way she had when she was pregnant with her boys.

Disloyalty alighted uneasily on the lip of his conscience. It should be Mary rocking their baby in their bedroom, but he couldn't imagine it. Never could. Even when she was alive. It probably didn't mean anything, though, right? It wasn't like he'd actually ever been able to imagine Hallie pregnant or parenting before Ben and Sam were born.

A stranger in this house where he'd always before felt comfortable and welcome, he swallowed, turned and went downstairs to the living room.

Despite their friendship, Mary had both envied and been jealous of Hallie when she was pregnant. Envious of Hallie's healthy pregnancies, jealous of the way Joe looked at his best friend when Hallie was pregnant. And in his own defense, he couldn't help it. All the guys on the squad had looked at Hallie the same way: besotted, protective, enthralled.

The only woman on the team, she'd worked twice as hard as any of the guys to earn her place and keep it. They tortured her incessantly, but she gave back as good as she got—no doubt the result, Joe had often mused, of her lifetime efforts to compete on the same level as "the guys." She fitted into the department as few other women did; the guys accepted her as one of them: a rough-and-tumble platonic playmate, a brass-balls compatriot in the field.

The first time any of them had viewed her differently was at her wedding when their unglamorous, no-frills Hallie had shed her departmental image and become simply, heart-staggeringly beautiful. Certainly at the very least she'd stopped Joe's heart, and left the rest of the guys stumbling over their tongues and feet at the reception. Joe could name at least three of them—probably himself included— who'd fallen half in love with Hallie at her wedding. Like Joe, who'd known her best and longest, none of the guys had ever thought about Hallie having a side to her they didn't know.

It had taken days after she'd returned from her honeymoon and her verbally banging their heads together to finally get the department over the fact that she was literally built differently from the rest of them. On the job she was still Hallie. She just had a private side like any of the rest of them, that was all. The fact that her private side looked a heck of a lot better in satin and lace than any of theirs did was to her credit and their tough cookies.

Still, for all his denials, Joe had never quite gotten over that image of her. He knew it was shallow of him not to have noticed all there was to Hallie before, but sometimes until you saw a thing in a dramatically different light, you didn't *see* it at all. Didn't get it.

In the end, watching her marry Zeke had made him uncomfortable for reasons he'd refused to consider. According to both his ethics and his religion, suddenly waking up and coveting a woman—a friend—who'd given her heart elsewhere was not only wrong, but also unproductive and stupid. So he hadn't done it. He'd found Mary, fallen in love, gotten married and been outrageously happy for all of them.

The status quo had held until Hallie became pregnant with her oldest son, Ben.

He remembered the day he'd known distinctly. It was before she'd even told him. He'd known without being told because he'd had so much practice watching his five sisters and three sisters-in-law blossom, apparently from the moment they conceived. He had thirty-three nieces and nephews, and his entire family lived within the boundaries of Cuyahoga County. Which meant he'd had plenty of practice spotting pregnant women, sometimes before they knew about the pregnancy themselves.

He'd lied.

He'd lied to himself a lot where Hallie was concerned.

With Hallie, knowing had been the same and indescribably, uncomfortably different from recognizing when the women in his family were pregnant. Unfaithful-to-Mary different.

Wishing-Ben-were-his different.

Pregnant Hallie radiated something remarkable, elusive and vital. There was a sweetness in the way the air around her tasted, a glow beneath her skin, a vibrancy of being that was, somehow, not the same to him as the glow his sisters and sisters-in-law got.

He looked around, noting familiar Christmas decorations, the taste of autumn-winter spices in the air. Clove apples in a dish on the mantel over the set of built-in bookshelves that had taken the place of a crumbling hearth. The dolls of the world a favored aunt had made out of note cards and fabric scraps, then given her as a wedding present, and that she brought out only at Christmas. The Advent calendar he knew he'd see if he stepped around the corner into the dining room. The pieces of red-and-green this and that mixed in with Thanksgiving's maize-orange-brown fitted precariously amid the eclectic blend of colors and furniture styles that somehow made this house a home.

Criminy Christmas, how could he have loved anyone as much as he'd loved Mary and still have wanted to father his best friend's children? How could he so fiercely want the woman with whom he'd slept only once—years ago, when they'd lost their virginity together—while he was still mourning his wife, seeking vengeance for her death?

The experience with Hallie had been memorable as a first, but not lightening the way future experience with Mary had taught him lovemaking could be. He and Hallie had been shy and clumsy, working hard at not putting a foot wrong. He'd finished early, she not at all, but she'd held him while he'd shivered with reaction in the cool steamed-up darkness of the back seat of his hand-me-down Dodge and had told him it didn't matter; that from what she'd heard, most girls didn't come the first time because they didn't know how; that now, at least, because of him she understood what went where and why—and maybe a little better what to do with it.

Embarrassed, he had, for the first time in his life, avoided her for days afterward, big macho Mexican stud that he was supposed to be.

Or so his brothers had always said.

Sitting in the privacy of raucous family gatherings, his father, a big soft-spoken man who worked assembly at the local truck plant, used to try to tell him other things. About how being truly a man meant being more than the sum of his parts and physical abilities; that the word *macho* meant more than a man's sexual potency, and was, in his opinion, a word often used by men who were afraid women might be stronger than they; that his brothers had wool between their ears; that it was not only okay to be weak, but *right* to be weak sometimes, with the woman who made you strong.

He'd tried to believe his father. Unfortunately he'd been young enough then to only believe his brothers.

He chose a spot on Hallie's futon and sat. Winced and rose, carefully adjusting himself around the excruciating tightness in his crotch. Removed himself to the front hall and stared through the door glass at his truck. Slid a hand inside his jacket to finger the two packets of photographs tucked into his pocket: first the worn envelope containing the pictures that had lured him away from here a year ago; then the other still-clean folder encasing the photos that brought him back. Funny. It didn't seem like he'd grown up much in the last seventeen years. Seemed he was still relying on his brothers' definition of "macho" to get him through; that he was less a man than a hunger scrambling to find relief, putting the rest of his life on hold until he had.

And now he had a daughter, too.

The simultaneous scuffle of feet on the steps behind him

and the squeaking of the door from the garage into the living room startled him. He turned to find Sam and Ben, his honorary nephews, halted together on the bottom step, eyeing him warily. In another moment, the huge retired Rottweiler police dog who lived with them bounded into the hallway and stopped dead in front of him, ears back, hackles raised; the barely discernible growl coming from its throat caused the floor beneath Joe's feet to vibrate. The boys' father, Hallie's ex-husband Zeke, stepped into the entryway behind the dog. Decidedly hostile, he flicked his eyes to the Fugitive Retrieval patch on the sleeve of Joe's jacket, then back to Joe's face.

"Zeke," Joe said.

"Joe." Zeke made a motion to the dog, who backed up and sat down by his knee, ears at alert. "Frank was afraid he'd wake the baby so instead of calling Hallie, he called me and said you were comin'. I didn't think you'd have the nerve."

Gut twisting, Joe shrugged. "Frank didn't tell me what I'd find, but I always come for what's mine, you know that, Zeke."

What was his... He'd come for Hallie and the boys the night the shouting had gotten too ugly, and the day before Zeke and Hallie had split for good. Divorce had improved the Thompsons' marriage immeasurably, for which they all—Hallie, Zeke, Mary, he, Sam, Ben, and the guys in the department—had been eternally grateful. That time, the definition of what was Joe's was different, of course, but the history existed all the same. And until this moment, friendship had allowed history to live between the men without reminders.

Without macho posturing.

That word again. *Macho.* A muscle jumped in Joe's jaw. Mary used to like his machismo. Hallie had flattened him on his ass once or twice for it.

From the steps Sam asked tentatively, "Uncle Joe?"

Joe nodded. "How ya doin', Sam?"

"You look different." Ben came forward to lace his hand in his dog's ruff, stared him up and down consideringly. "You look mean, sorta like a bad guy. Maybe you should shave."

"'Mean'?" Fingering his beard, Joe looked down at him. Sam was quiet, intense and often secretive, but Ben was Hallie's son, through and through: no minced words, no withheld opinions, no mountain too massive to conquer. Mary had titled him "Mr. 'est" when he was a baby, as in bigg*est,* loud*est,* peski*est,* curious-*est.* The taste of bitter laughter rose in his throat. Trust Ben to spot a truth Joe would have preferred to keep to himself. "You think I'm mean?"

"I said you *look* mean," Ben corrected him, exasperated. "I don't know if you *are* mean—except maybe to bad guys like Mom. I haven't seen you *recently*—"

Word of the week, Joe thought wryly, guessing Ben had the same third-grade teacher he and Hallie had had. Use it in a sentence whenever you have the chance.

"Enough to *know* if you are. I said if you *shave* you'll look different. Maybe not like a bad guy."

"Some bad guys don't have beards," Sam told him.

"Duh." Ben shrugged a face at his brother. "And some bad guys have mustaches and polish their fingernails, but I just said Uncle Joe—"

"Some bad guys don't even intend to be bad guys," Zeke interrupted his sons firmly, eyeing Joe. "They just get hotheaded and make irreversible choices and become bad guys by accident."

Ben nodded blithely, understanding. "Like Uncle Joe did when he left and didn't come back and made Mom cry a lot because she wanted him to be here with Maura and when he wasn't, then she didn't."

"Didn't what?" Joe asked—tightly. Somewhere at the

back of his mind it registered that his daughter's name was Maura, the Irish version of Mary's name.

"Didn't want you to be here anymore," Ben said—matter-of-factly.

"Neither do we," Sam said—softly, intensely, drawing Joe's guarded but undivided attention.

No secrets lay in the seven-year-old eyes staring up at him, only an animosity that shocked Joe more than the adult antagonism he'd already encountered. Ben might be the one who'd verbally knock Joe on his butt, but Sam was the one who would carry his mother's grudge—whether his mother meant him to or not.

He swallowed. "Sam, I—" he began. And stopped. Gestured inadequately. Looked to Ben, the dog, then over their heads to Zeke for guidance. His once-longtime friend shrugged a mocking brow and quirked his mouth: *This is your bed. Lie in it.*

Already awkward, the tableau became unendurable, left Joe involuntarily letting his gaze drift when he could no longer look Sam in the face. Left him feeling like one of the can't-look-'em-in-the-eye bail jumpers he chased for a living. Guilty. Hiding something.

Looking for the way out.

There was a creak on the stairs. Joe raised his eyes to see Hallie descending and knew in that instant there was no way he'd escape. Whatever catharsis or destruction he'd unknowingly set in motion for all of them—regardless of the awkwardness or antagonism holding them hostage—as he'd intimated to Hallie upstairs, there really was no way out of this except through.

Chapter 3

Zeke spoke first. "Sorry, Hal. He went by the department. Frank didn't want to wake the baby so he called me. Hoped I'd get here before he did. Give you some warning he was in town."

Hallie put a hard finger to her lips, pointed upstairs and gave Zeke a teeth-gritted, cross-eyed warning. "Keep your voice down or *you'll* wake her," she commanded sotto voce, making shooing motions toward the back of the house.

When they had reached a distance where Maura was less likely to hear them, she turned once more to Zeke. "Did George get his rabies shot?"

Zeke pulled some papers and a metal tag from his jacket pocket. "Yeah, three-year, here's the certificate. Now, about J—"

Hallie slashed a hand at him, cutting him off at the "J," making a warning motion with her eyes toward the boys. "Whatever it is, I'll handle it." She turned to Sam and Ben, trying to make her voice bright. "You guys ready for practice? Got your homework and anything else you need to spend the night at Dad's?''

Uncertain eyes on Joe, they nodded in unison, indicated backpacks piled together beside the living-room-to-garage door.

"Good." She opened her arms wide and the boys piled into them. "Come give me kisses and hugs, then you guys better get going so you're not late."

"Hallie—" Zeke began, concerned.

She shook her head at him. "You're the coach, you have to go. I've dealt with worse. I'll be fine."

In the circle of her left arm, Ben hugged her quickly, gave her a sloppy raspberry buss on the cheek, and dodged smoothly, laughingly away from her before she could *Oh, yuck!* him and wipe her face on his sweatshirt . "Bye, love you, Mom. See ya tomorrow."

She shook a finger at him. "Behave or I'll get you next time, smarty."

From the safety of distance he grinned cheekily at her, picked up his backpack and headed out the garage door. "See ya later, Uncle Joe."

"Later, Ben," Joe agreed hollowly, watching Hallie.

Not if I can help it, his mother responded silently, glancing up to be sure Joe read that silence on her face. Her more serious, more astute younger son locked his arms around her neck, put his mouth to her ear.

"We don't have to stay all night at Dad's," he whispered, and Hallie's throat closed. He was too young. He shouldn't understand. "We could come home after practice to—" he searched for the word "—protect you and Maura from him."

"Oh, Sam." She hugged him tight. "Sam-I-Am. We'll be all right. Truly. I've been knocking him down since we were five years old, and George is here so don't you worry about protecting us from him tonight."

She turned him loose. He wasn't quite ready to go.

"You won't let him take Maura, will you, Mom?" he asked anxiously. "He wasn't here and he didn't come for her when he should have so she's ours now, right?"

"She's ours," Hallie promised, then added to herself, *at least for now.* "He won't take her." She set Sam away, looked him in the eye. "I won't *let* him take her."

Sam relaxed to the faintest degree. "Okay." He gave her a quick kiss. "Then I have to go. But if you need us, you call." He looked up at his father. "You have your cell phone, don'cha, Dad?"

Zeke swallowed a grin. "I have my cell phone."

"See." Sam turned back to Hallie. "You can get hold of us anytime, anywhere."

She huffed a rueful breath and nodded. "Yeah." So this was what came of having children born into the electronic age. They knew how to keep track of you even as you kept track of them. "If I need you, I'll call. Now go, get out of here, enjoy practice."

Happier now, Sam backed toward the door. "I will. We're havin' pizza and no veggies for dinner, right, Dad?"

"Zeke," Hallie warned—lightly.

Zeke groaned, took three steps toward his son to stage-whisper, "That was a secret. You're not supposed to tell her." He turned back to his ex-wife. "We *usually* have veggies."

"Yeah, yeah." Hallie straightened from her crouch. "Get a bag of those little carrots or a garden salad with ranch dressing. They like those. You won't have to be a bad guy."

"I wasn't afraid of being a bad guy," Zeke lied. The grin playing about his mouth told a different story: caught in the act—again. He closed the distance to the door, paused with his hand on the knob. Glanced back at Hallie, at Joe. "Hal—"

She shook her head impatiently. "We'll be fine, Zeke. Go."

He filled his cheeks and puffed a breath, not quite believing. Hallie pointed an imperious finger at him.

"Go."

"Just checkin'," he said, meaning it. And went.

One of the problems in their marriage had been Hallie neither needing nor wanting him when he'd felt it was appropriate for her to do so. Which meant that now, one of the things that worked best about their divorce was that they accepted each other as they were, and he no longer had the proprietary right to try to tell her when she should or shouldn't need anyone.

But what had or had not been right or wrong in her marriage was neither here nor there at the moment. In fact, the only things here and there just now were the jittery sensation in the pit of her stomach, the tingling of something she refused to identify down the column of her spine, the hard-jawed and intense-eyed man whose presence so unnerved her, and the infant upstairs who lay claim to him and her both.

A lot of baggage to pile onto one frail ten-pound body.

Left to themselves, Joe and Hallie stared everywhere but at each other, let the silence between them expand to encompass the sound of Zeke's car departing, the faint whoosh of traffic along distant streets, the occasional rattle of a vehicle along the street beyond the foot of Hallie's front walk.

So much to say, nowhere to begin, Hallie thought.

Then start anywhere. In her memory, Joe's voice was a husky whisper against her thoughts, a childhood blood-brother promise between them that whatever they said went no further, put no dents in any of the aspects of their relationship: friends and partners; onetime neighbors and long-ago lovers; biological father and surrogate vessel to the implanted seed that had taken root and flourished in Hallie's womb. *You can say anything to me.*

Anything.

She sucked air, spat out the hardest question she'd ever asked anyone. "What are you doing here?"

She didn't ask nicely.

He responded in kind, snapping, "I may be in town, but I didn't come to see you, and I sure as hell didn't come here to screw up your status quo. Circumstances forced me to change my mind."

"You left the living to sleep with the dead. You think this is what Mary would have wanted, Joe?"

"I don't think Mary wanted to die, Hallie. I think she wanted to be here with our baby. You think she'd want you to keep Maura from me now?"

"The boys told you her name." Her voice was flat and unsteady, sidetracking him from a question she couldn't bring herself to answer honestly, if at all. She didn't intend to tell him more about the baby than she had to.

His jaw worked. "You weren't even going to tell me that. You didn't want me to know."

She ducked away from his gaze for a moment, guilty as charged, then raised her eyes to view him straight on. "No."

For a mere instant no hard-case bounty hunter stood before her, simply the old Joe whose emotions were as uncaged and easy for her to read as Miranda rights. "For God's sake, why, Hallie?" The outburst was spontaneous, bewildered.

A piece of his old self awakened for the first time in a year, Hallie guessed sadly. And he looked like the dated suit didn't fit the new frame very well at all.

"Have you found her killer, Joe?" she asked, instead of answering. Hating the steadiness of her voice. Hating the questions she had to ask because she no longer knew who he was. "Is that why you came back? You found him and you killed him?"

Hating the fact that she no longer knew what he was capable of.

His mouth tightened into his beard; he looked away. Not with guilt, she realized, but failure.

Her jaw clenched and cracked, locking on tension, disappointment and anger. "You're still after him, aren't you?"

He didn't answer. She felt color drain, then rise in her cheeks. She'd damn him to hell if she wasn't pretty sure he'd damned himself there already.

"You still think you can find him and bring him down by yourself. Is that what the shield on your jacket's for, Joe? Running down bail jumpers not only gives you traveling money, but the paperwork and a legal excuse if, say, maybe the wrong guy gets in the line of your fire?"

He looked at her finally. "Shut up, Hallie." His voice was soft, hard, full of meaning.

She ignored him. Getting a rise out of him, finding out he still had some…scruples left was what she wanted, after all. "This way, you can say you were on a heavy case, you thought this was the right body. Turns out it wasn't, but before you had a chance to work that out between you, he fired on you, you returned fire, he's dead—"

He took a step toward her. "Shut up."

She lifted her chin, challenging him, and kept on talking. "Oh, and by the by, Cuyahoga County's got a warrant on him for killing an ex-dep's wife. You got that anonymous gun stashed someplace, Joe? The one you can wrap his hand around after you shoot—"

He closed the distance between them, caught her face in a painful grip, brought his down to it. "I said shut the—" He bit off the expletive. His fingers burned where they held her. His spirit burned from the things she'd said, from the loathing he saw in her eyes. His body simply burned.

For her.

He was too angry to let her go, too unwilling to allow desire to dictate his actions. He held on, fought the reflection of himself he saw in her eyes, and burned.

"Just shut up, Hallie. You don't know anything about it."

"Neither do you if you haven't caught him after a year." She yanked her chin out of his hand but didn't back up, didn't allow herself to look away, however much she wanted to.

Told herself not to feel the frisson of anticipation and fear something in his touch engendered.

Told herself not to see the wounds behind his eyes, not to understand his haunted search for peace, not to want to reach out a woman's touch to comfort him.

"Who is this guy, Joe?" She kept her voice and eyes steady, but it was work. "The freaking one-armed man?"

"I don't know who he is. Is that what you want to hear, Hallie?" He swung away from her, paced from the dining room to the adjoining playroom, putting distance between them again. Swung back because the distance made him restless. "That he leads me on and on and I can't stop chasing." He prowled back through the dining room and into the kitchen, wanting to be near her, needing to get away. "That I get this lead or that lead, but he's always steps ahead of me, like he's playing a game with me. And I can't let go." He battered a cupboard with a fist, and Hallie followed him into the kitchen, afraid he'd break a door.

Afraid he'd break her heart.

Remembering he'd already broken it.

"Stop it, Joe."

"*Perdóneme, Dios,* but I can't." He slumped back against the kitchen counter, repeated in defeat, "I can't."

For the first time she reached toward him in sympathy, empathy, pulling her hand back before compassion and touch got away from her. "I miss her, too, Joe."

He grimaced. "That's part of the problem." Again his jaw worked. He turned his back on her and leaned heavily over the counter, closed his eyes and told Hallie the first honest thing he'd said to himself in months: "I don't."

Then he turned and stalked out of the kitchen into Hallie's front hallway, past the basement door, the boot closet, the telephone table, the front staircase, the doorway that opened into the room that had been the parish office back when he and Hallie were growing up and her house had been the priest's residence. He paused. His mother had brought him here once when he was seven and she'd caught him with his hands "down there," and had assumed he must be playing with himself.

"You must confess immediately," she'd told him furiously in Spanish, while towing him up the walk. "You must tell the priest you were impure. If you were to die tonight, you must not go with this on your soul."

When his mother had explained that her son needed immediate confession, the priest had taken him into that room and sat Joe on one side of the screen while he took his place on the other. Joe had repeated the prayer he'd learned only that year, "Bless me, Father, for I have sinned…" and told Father Nelson exactly what his mother had told him to say: "I was impure."

It had seemed to Joe, the father's voice had gotten loud and as furious as his mother's at the admission, and he'd roared, "My child, do you understand that this is a mortal sin for which you could go to hell?"

And though Joe hadn't understood anything about anything of the kind, the frightened answer had squeaked out of him, "Yes."

Father Nelson had asked a second time—to make sure, Joe understood now—and when Joe had offered the same response, the father had lectured him for a moment, then let him go to say his penance—a decade of the rosary.

But it was a long time before the guilt had faded, before he understood that you couldn't sin if you didn't know you had, if you didn't understand what you'd done.

Now was a different time, a different person, similar emotions: guilt and fear. This time, however, guilt and fear were joined by an understanding of the crime, the knowledge that he had, indeed, committed it.

The front door stood in front of him, beckoning. He grabbed its tarnished brass knob and yanked the door open as he had that long-ago night, snapped open the storm door and stepped onto the porch, looking only for escape. The wind skittered leaves along the sidewalk, grazed his face with a light drizzle mixed with snow. Behind him, the doors closed too loudly and he heard the thin cry that told him he'd wakened his daughter.

Again.

His fists clenched, his lip curled back in self-disgust. Damn. He just couldn't seem to get it right, here.

Better, then, to simply leave, he advised himself. Quit screwing up lives he'd left long ago before he made a bigger mess than when he'd begun.

Right?

Yes. He gave the semidarkness of late afternoon a clipped nod. Absolutely right.

Caught with too many puzzles to solve, and too many emotions clouding them, Joe took the front steps two at a time, and ran for his truck.

"Joe?"

Hallie reached to stop him, wanting for the first time since he'd appeared on her porch to listen to what he had to say, but he moved too quickly; her fingers brushed air where his arm had been.

"Joe, wait."

He either didn't hear, or he ignored her, strode away as quickly as he could. Much like, she thought, the day he'd walked away from her, the department, his life, after Mary had died.

She rubbed a hand hard across her chest, trying to ease

the ache in her heart, the trembling uncertainty of a future she'd only this morning thought she knew.

Or at least understood.

Too late and too slowly she turned to the hallway and put one foot in front of the other, letting momentum lengthen her stride before doubt could stop her. By the time she reached where he'd been, he was out the door, rushing away, and Maura was crying.

She listened to the infant while she watched the shadowed hulk that was Maura's father disappear into the pre-streetlight dusk. After his disappearance she heard the heavy sound of a vehicle door slam, then silence.

Upstairs, Maura hiccuped a couple of times and seemed to settle. Torn between pursuing the father farther and checking on his child, Hallie stood still for a moment, pondering the consequences of doing—or not doing—each. Then she sighed, put a hand on the staircase newel post and mounted the steps to check on Mary's child.

Chapter 4

Duty. Honor.

Contracts and promises.

Blood, genes and debt.

Together, all seven, like deadly sins carelessly committed, bound him to the child who whimpered upstairs, and the woman who'd borne and cared for her alone, even when he'd violated her trust.

Fists gripped hard around the steering wheel, Joe sat in his truck in the deepening twilight, trying to sort through the hash Hallie had made of his brain. *Dios,* so many agendas to align, so many lives in balance.

It had been so much easier to think, before he'd set foot inside his old department this afternoon expecting bygones to be forgiven, old trusts to be automatically picked up where they'd been left off.

So much simpler to *be,* before he'd knocked on Hallie's door.

A life lived by the simple rules of numbness and survival was, after all, far less complicated than a life filled with people to whom he owed a certain responsibility; people who'd cared about him once upon a time.

People who'd been as excited for him as he'd been himself the first time Mary had been pregnant, who'd shed tears and condolences with each subsequent loss; who'd rooted for them wholeheartedly when he, Mary and Hallie had made the decision to have Hallie try to carry their baby.

Life had been far less complex when he'd lived only for himself, his lust for vengeance—he sucked air, expelled it in a self-derisive laugh. Jeez, was that only this morning?—dramatically less intricate before he'd seen Hallie and experienced that rush of desire that ran hotter than lust. Before he'd caught sight of his daughter.

Before he'd known he couldn't leave here without her.

He ran a shaking hand through his beard, over his face, through his hair. Damn. What was he thinking? He didn't know the first thing about caring for a baby—not by himself. The person he'd become in the last twelve months was hardly a fit parent, much less a role model. Not to mention the way he lived out of his truck and motel rooms more than half the time—heck, *all* the time, now that he thought about it. How the devil could he possibly reason that the life he led was any kind of life for a baby?

For anybody, in fact, but himself?

Freelance bounty hunters were an endangered breed, but ''freelance'' was the only life that allowed him to travel as he needed to. And he'd quickly gained a certain reputation as one of the best fugitive-retrieval experts available among bondsmen who stood to lose substantial sums of money on higher-profile clients who skipped. That was how he'd gotten this case with the missing kids. It wasn't as though the FBI and local law enforcement weren't involved; because of the wife's murder and the hostage children, all the usual public-paid agencies were on the case. But because the guy was also a high-bond FTA—failure-to-appear—who'd missed his appointed court date, Joe had been hired by the

bond agency to retrieve him before the bond was forfeit.
And the simple statistical fact was that private retrieval
agents apprehended a hefty eighty-seven percent of their
targets, to police departments' twenty-three percent. Bounty
hunters were also legally able to cross lines in the pursuit
of their duties that public servants could not.

The way he saw it, he was duty-bound by the retrieval
papers in his pocket to locate the man, enlisting aid from
the local sheriff's department to make sure the kids came
out of the situation safely. All leads had led him back to
Cuyahoga.

Under normal circumstances this was the sort of job he'd
have taken to Hallie first: the she-bear in her was a for-
midable opponent where child hostages were concerned.
And when it came right down to it, he wanted her help,
needed it. The missing children needed it. But she'd seen
him, he'd seen his daughter, and he hadn't yet talked to
anyone in his old squad about what had brought him here.
They weren't big on bounty hunters in general—bounty
hunters were, after all, to public law enforcement what private outfits were to the post office—but now he knew why
they were even less enthused about him in particular.

He'd burned a lot of bridges when he left Cuyahoga; he
hadn't fully appreciated what that meant until now.

He switched on the truck's interior light and put his hand
inside his jacket, withdrew the envelope filled with still
pictures from his worst nightmares. The packet was warm,
telling him his hands were cold, he noted without surprise.
He'd stopped noticing things like heat and cold, hunger,
pain and thirst a long time ago. Necessity and purpose alone
made him eat and work out to maintain his strength; a lifetime full of women—his mother, his sisters, Mary—relent-
lessly reminded him to put on a jacket because November
was not July.

No matter how old you got, nor how much you thought
you'd outgrown them, Joe knew there were certain things—

like honor, debt, blood, genes and contracts—you never left behind. No matter how badly you might want to, nor how hard you tried.

Honor bound him to his search for Mary's killer—honor, that is, and the envelope of photos in his hands, the shoe box filled with Mary's secrets that he kept hidden behind the seat.

When he'd told Hallie—and himself—he no longer missed Mary, it was the truth. He *wanted* to miss her, but that part of him had moved on, lost in the part of him that lived only for whatever solace he might find in revenge. As far as Mary was concerned, though, he simply wanted her out of his head. And that made him feel guilty. To love and lose and move on so quickly... But the only way he was able to visualize her anymore was bloody and dead. Even when he looked at photographs of her from before she died, he found it impossible to remember her any other way. Lying on the pavement beside the Blazer, eyes wide and blank with death and surprise. Lying in the morgue, gray-blue and pale, bloodless and clean and personless. Grotesque snapshots among ghastly Polaroid photographs in the envelope he held.

He breathed through his nose, slid the envelope back into his inside pocket without opening it and shut off the overhead light. He had, on the other hand, remembered Hallie in all her fearless vitality, her blunt opinions, her uncomplicated companionship. Missed her. Daily. Nightly. Missed her so badly that—

Without warning the passenger door creaked and the overhead light came on.

"Sh—" Startled, Joe lunged sideways out of possible danger, wound up on the floor beneath the dash. It was a tight fit.

From her position in the doorway Hallie looked down at him, picked up a brown envelope from the passenger seat.

"Looking for this?" she asked mildly.

He swore something unprintable in Spanish, levered up and rolled himself back onto the seat with difficulty. "Damn it, Hallie. What the hell d'you think you're doing?"

She shrugged, showed him the weapon she'd hidden along the back of her right thigh. "Checkin' on the strange vehicle parked across from my house. One of the neighbors called and said it'd been there awhile with a guy sittin' in it who was maybe casing the neighborhood. Thought he might be some pervert lookin' for kids out alone. Citizen Watch doesn't like people they don't know campin' out in trucks around here."

"So you left my daughter alone in the house to come out here and see if some scumbag who mighta shot you was casing the area?" Adrenaline made him angry.

"No." Hallie shook her head, slid her weapon into the shoulder holster she wore. "I left the neighbor who called in the house with my daughter, and now I'm goin' back in and send her home. And as far as getting shot's concerned..." She lifted a shoulder, let it drop. "You didn't even know I was here until I opened the door. I'm somebody else, that means you're dead. You're getting slow, Martinez."

Last word in, she slammed the door shut, rounded the front of the truck and started across the street. Joe slid out the driver's door and went after her. Caught her in the middle of the road, grabbed her arm and swung her around. Brought his face down to hers. He'd be damned if she got the last word just because this time she was right.

"You're not keeping my daughter from me, Hallie," he told her fiercely. "Whatever it takes, I won't let you. And I won't leave here without her."

Completely still, she regarded him in the deepening darkness, face shadowed and unreadable. Headlights came toward them down the street, turned into a driveway four houses away.

"Hallie?" a nervous voice called from her porch. "Is everything all right? Is that man still out there?"

Hallie turned her head toward the house. "Everything's fine, Nadie. It's just an old...partner of mine, come to say hello. Joe Martinez. You remember him. Used to live a couple streets over."

"The one whose wife was killed?"

Joe's hand squeezed unintentionally hard around Hallie's arm. God. What an unforgivable way to be remembered. It had never before occurred to him to question how people recollected things. Especially in front of the families of the victims.

"Yes, that's him," he heard Hallie say before she muttered, "Let go of my arm, Joe. You're hurting me."

He loosened his grip, but didn't release her. "Are we going to talk?"

Behind them, Nadie unknowingly concurred with him. "That poor young man. Hallie, aren't you going to bring him in?"

There was no way out of it. She knew Joe when he got like this, and Nadie Kresnak's suggestion was no help.

With a silent prayer that she was doing the right thing, Hallie not-quite-graciously told Joe to park his truck in her drive to forestall further Citizen Watch calls and invited him inside. She was pretty sure she'd have eventually gotten around to inviting him in on her own, but she hated the sensation of being coerced into the decision. Joe got way too smug when he felt he had her at a disadvantage.

And she *was* at a disadvantage. When she'd gone upstairs to look in on the once-again-sleeping Maura, it had been impossible not to see Joe in the infant's face, not to feel something...everything for the man who'd helped give this child life. Not to care...

Index finger hovering above Maura's face, she'd sketched Joe's features in the air where they matched.

There around the baby's eyes, her brows, the promise in the curve of her jaw and chin—all were instant reminders of everything Hallie had ever felt for, or about, Joe.

It didn't matter whether or not she wanted to recall these things, she recalled them. Every moment of laughter, fear, companionship, friendship, love, anger, sorrow and each emotion in, around and between were reflected in Maura's finally peaceful face; forced Hallie to recognize that she couldn't leave Joe out of his daughter's life—at least in some limited capacity. So she would have gone down and called him in, she was pretty sure, but Nadie had phoned about the strange truck first.

And now he was there, his bulk wedged into one of the captain's chairs at the dining-room table, looking more than a little uncomfortable. And she was here in the kitchen, dishing them both up some chili, feeling more than a little uncomfortable herself.

She was also afraid. Of Joe—for herself, for Ben and Sam, for Maura. Because she really wasn't sure exactly what legal or moral right she had to stop him from marching upstairs whenever he chose and simply taking his daughter away from them.

She'd been advised at the time she'd decided to carry Maura despite Mary's death and Joe's desertion, that a case could probably be made in her favor; that by leaving, Joe had voided the contract Hallie had signed stating that the child she carried belonged to him and his wife alone. But for reasons she couldn't name at the time, she'd been unwilling to go that route—and still didn't want to. She wanted Maura, loved her, heart and soul; delighted in having a daughter to fuss over, dress differently than she had her boys. Still, it also seemed wrong to deny Maura her genetic heritage—although there was fat chance of that, the way Joe's and Mary's huge families doted on granddaughter and niece...

Oh, God. She was so damned confused. So freaking, hormonally mixed-up.

So glad to see Joe alive and intact, even if he wasn't quite himself.

And so damn blasted angry with him for running off without her.

For wanting to come between her and her—no, *his,* damn it; she was going to have to start remembering that—daughter.

Seriously grumpy now, Hallie carried the tray of chili, corn bread and Mexican beer out to the dining room, thunked a bowl and a bottle in front of Joe. Settled a little too close to the edge of the table—an accident? if she were to be honest, probably not—hot chili slopped over the side of the bowl and into Joe's lap. The bottle, too, wobbled and sloshed. He snatched it up before it could spill, leaped out of the tight-fitting chair, swearing and grabbing at the close-cut denim to pull it away from his skin when the not only hot-to-touch, but also peppery chili belatedly seeped through his jeans to burn his nether regions—twice.

"Jeez, woman, I know you're ticked, but you don't have to freaking neuter me."

"Ah, c'mon, Joe. It'd take a lot more than some green chilies chili to geld you." Trying hard not to laugh, Hallie put down her tray and snagged a napkin, soaked it in the available beer and tossed it to him. "You might want to get something cold on that, though. I hear if you don't get the burn stopped fast, you can sting like hell for days." She picked a bowl of cut lime from the tray, offered it to him with an innocent grin. "Here, try this. According to your mother, citrus is supposed to help neutralize the pepper."

"Go to hell, Thompson," Joe snarled and headed for the bathroom and the hope of relief.

Unable to restrain herself, Hallie put her ear to the bathroom door and listened to her nemesis curse and dance himself out of his pants. Inside her chest, laughter bubbled up and spurted out in tiny hiccuping explosions. She covered her mouth with her hands, trying to contain it.

To no avail.

It geysered into the open, spilled over in rib-racking, eye-tearing guffaws, a release for all the day's emotions. She leaned her back against the bathroom door, slid down it all the way to the floor when she could no longer stand, laid her face between her knees and let the catharsis come.

Joe yanked the door open, dropping the chuckling Hallie onto the bathroom tiles.

"I did not," he said, as much on his dignity as it was possible to be while wrapping a big bath towel securely about his waist, "come back to Cuyahoga to entertain you."

"But you're doing such a good job of it," Hallie chortled, staring up at him. She pressed her lips together and studied him for a moment, trying to stifle laughter and collect her breath. When she had enough of it, she rolled upright and edged toward the door before musing aloud, "I wonder if Scotsmen wear the same thing under their kilts that Mexicans in bath towels do—"

Loosing a rapid stream of disgusted Spanish, Joe lunged for her. She slid under his hand and danced away, grinning. Hampered by trying to keep the towel in place, he stalked her slowly.

"Uh-uh-uh." She shook a finger at him. "You know what your mother always said. No fair picking on someone who's not your size."

"Don't try that one with me, Thompson." He eyed her grimly, warily, watching for weakness. The trouble with working out, bulking up and being not too small to begin with was that you sometimes paid a price in grace and speed in favor of strength. But the upside was, when he caught her, she wasn't going anyplace anytime soon. "I know exactly what you're capable of, so that size thing doesn't cut it.''

"Oh, now, Joey, Joey, Joey."

She knew he hated that name, equating him, as it were, with a kangaroo's infant joey.

She'd called him Joey a lot when they were kids.

"Yes, Halleluia?" he asked mildly, calling her by her given name—a name she hated due to its history. Supposedly her mother's labor with Hallie had been long and difficult, leading Hallie's mother to exclaim to Hallie's father when it was finally over, *"Halleluia, Fred! She's out!"* Unable to agree to a name prior to her birth, the parents had looked at each other over the squalling infant and christened her then and forever, Halleluia Anne.

"Don't call me that," she snapped now—and stopped backing away from him.

He should have recognized the danger for what it was, but it was so long since he'd played this game with anyone that he didn't.

Instead, he advanced until he was within arm's reach of her. The air around her was warm and spicy, inviting. Intoxicating.

Beneath the towel, he felt it. Arousing. He shook his head, trying to focus.

"Then don't call me Joey," he said. His voice sounded rusty.

The words were childish; the rasp in his throat wasn't.

Something in his tone arrested her attention, halted the game even as it began. The hand she'd been about to use to snatch his towel so she could run with it drifted in the air between them, unused. She saw him reach for her fingers, watched his curl away before they touched hers. She tilted her head back to look up at him, to see the charcoal gray of his eyes deepen to liquid black.

She felt the look in his eyes clear to her toes, a pull like moon to tide: inevitable, unavoidable, potentially destructive. Her breath caught, hung heavy in her lungs.

No, she thought wildly. *I can't. We can't. It's wrong. Not with Joe. Not ever. Not now.*

Not with Joe, what? the nagging demon who lived independently in her brain asked. Not ever, what? Not now, what? Not sex, not trust, not what? What is it you think would be wrong?

"This," she answered herself aloud. "All of this. Any of it."

"All of what?" Joe asked, sliding nearer. He wanted— he could hardly say what, only knew that he was so close he could almost taste what had been missing from his palate for too long. "Did I miss something?"

"I—ah—wha—?" She spread the fingers of one hand across her forehead to massage her temples, backed two steps away from him.

Concerned, Joe followed. "Hallie? Are you all right?"

"Fine." She held up a hand to ward him off. "Don't you need to put some pants on?"

"Yeah, but my duffel's out in the truck."

A nonsensical answer and he knew it. He reached to graze her cheek with the edge of a forefinger. Checking for fever, he told himself.

He lied.

"Are you sure you're all right?" he asked, brushing his finger across her other cheek. "You don't look fine and you feel flushed."

She flinched beneath the caress, then leaned involuntarily into it, caught herself and jerked away. "I told you. I'm—" Her arm swept out for emphasis and dusted the corner of the counter. The brown envelope she'd picked up from the seat of Joe's truck and inadvertently carried into the house slid off the Formica, opened and cascaded photographs onto the floor. She stooped impatiently to collect the pictures, then stopped, gaping, to stare at what she held as the final words tumbled out of her mouth: "I'm fine."

But she wasn't.

Not by a long shot.

Numb, Hallie looked at Joe who'd squatted to retrieve pictures, too.

"What are these?" she asked.

She shuffled through the photos. There was a picture of Sam and Ben holding Maura on Santa's lap at the mall the day after Thanksgiving. Three more of the photos were nearly identical, except for slight changes in the children's expressions and positions. The film was color, but slightly grainy suggesting the photos had been created from videotape. Others were of the boys at school, taken at recess through the chain-link fence surrounding the school playground. There were long shots of them and close-ups. Also pictures of Hallie by herself in uniform and in civvies; putting Maura into her car seat after a trip to the nearby grocery; a shot of Hallie in her office at the department nursing Maura, and another of the same, shot through the filmy curtains at the turreted bay window of her bedroom upstairs.

She viewed Joe with something akin to loathing. "Have you been... What have you been... How long have you...""

Joe barely heard her, he was staring so hard at a pair of photographs of his own: two shots of him on Hallie's front porch. One taken before she opened the door; the other after, where she and the bundle in her arms were indistinctly visible through the screen. Block-printed neatly across the bottom of the second was the legend: Welcome Home, Murderer.

Chapter 5

He breathed, trying to make the fear and disquiet settle in his gut. There'd been—what?—maybe forty-five minutes to a little over an hour between the time he'd first set foot on Hallie's porch this afternoon and the time he'd returned to his truck. Whoever the photographer was, he was bold.

Also pretty damned arrogant if he felt he could hang around and take instant pictures without someone from Citizen Watch noticing.

Disquiet turned into the taste of nausea rising. Too close. Photos, even video, shot from a distance were disturbing enough, but ones of this clarity meant the shooter wasn't worried about being discovered closing in.

Meant that the shooter had, in fact, already closed in.

Madre de Dios. What could he possibly have done for someone to hate him like this? To want to so obliquely threaten him with the lives he valued most above his own in all the world?

It had been almost two months since he'd found the last envelope, placed like this one, on the seat of his truck. The contents of that one had been about what he'd gotten used to with the five prior deliveries, the same old torturous, horrifying scenes: stills from a video someone unknown—the murderer's accomplice?—had shot of Mary's murder.

Of course, none of the frames revealed even the shadow of the killer, but the detail was there. A bit grainy from being shot at dusk, stop-framed and blown up for the stills, but clear enough all the same. Mary with a bag of groceries opening the Blazer door. Setting the groceries inside. Turning in surprise to greet someone from behind. Smiling a little the way she did because she'd decided that part of her job in life was to always make every person who crossed her path feel just a little bit welcome. Smile drooping, eyes widened with what could only be fear at the point when the killer must have produced the gun. Falling back against the side of the Blazer with the impact of the first bullet.

Jaw tight, he stiffened the muscles in his throat, swallowed against rising bile. God. Oh, God, oh God. He couldn't do this again.

He concentrated on the pictures, trying to focus on the similarities between the ones he held now, and the selection in the pocket of his jacket.

To be sure, each new bit of that collection went further than the last, showed a little more of the final moments of Mary's life. But there was something almost desultory, even perfunctory about them—the sense of a lack of imagination at odds with the photographer's apparently insidious intent.

In fact, in retrospect, the deliveries seemed almost more as though they'd been made by someone purchasing time—every packet with its obligatory and cryptic note pointed him first in one direction, then another; drove him to chase leads and a suspect he'd begun to think didn't exist.

But now here was this collection, so similar to the initial envelope, the one he hadn't seen until after Mary's death. Addressed to him in block print, he'd found *that* one in the damnable shoe box now buried under pillows, blankets, maps and whatever other debris he could toss on top of it behind the seat in his truck.

The box itself he'd originally discovered at the bottom of Mary's closet, secreted in plain sight among the other shoe boxes she'd kept in case Sam and Ben needed something in which to build diorama projects for school. The back of the closet was stacked with shoe boxes, empty and full.

Next to her desire to have her own infant at any cost, Mary's greatest vice had been her shoes.

He wouldn't even have found this particular box then if he hadn't, at Hallie's insistence, been looking for a specific pair of shoes to go with the suit nobody had seen on Mary at the funeral anyway because of the closed coffin. But Hallie had been adamant that Mary would want to be as neat and coordinated in death as she'd been in life.

He'd been too numb to think, let alone do, but Hallie had shoved so he'd looked. In looking, he'd found. Things he'd never wanted to know. Things he couldn't reconcile with the woman who'd shared eleven years of his life. Things he didn't think he'd ever be able to bring himself to tell even Hallie.

It was always a bad idea to go rooting around in the privacy of a loved one's life unless you knew in advance what you'd find.

Among Joe's intolerable discoveries had been the snapshots that reminded him of the ones he now held. Pictures of Mary entering and exiting buildings, grocery shopping, getting into the Blazer, lunching with Hallie, with him, with friends from work, at department barbecues. In short, everyday pictures, innocent shots that no one without an agenda would bother to take.

Stalker pictures.

Someone had followed Mary around, shooting videos of her apparently for days, maybe even for weeks or months before her death. Which meant, of course, that the envelope had been left someplace for *him,* but where Mary had found it first, then hidden it from him for some unknown reason.

It also meant the carjacking was never a carjacking in the first place.

And now he was kneeling here in a towel on Hallie's kitchen floor picking up pictures taken by some anonymous person, and the implications behind the scenario and the note scared him to death.

Apparently they did nothing for Hallie, either.

She shoved the photographs she held into his face like someone who'd had enough of trying to get his attention and was now out to simply take it.

"I *said,*" she bit out in the voice no fugitive within hearing, deputy who needed dressing down, or misbehaving kid on the playground would be able to ignore, "where did these come from and what the *hell* is going on here, Joe? You been following me around and taking pictures of my kids? What the—"

He couldn't listen to questions he couldn't answer. Didn't want to look at her and see the betrayal she probably had a right to feel.

Didn't want to experience any more of the guilt that was already settling to irritate and inflame his gut like bad coffee on an ulcer.

As gently as provocation and fear allowed, he interrupted her by catching her wrist and removing the fistful of photos from his face. Even under the circumstances, awareness crackled with skin on skin, briefly drew their rattled attention from one urgent consideration to another.

Desire was mutual. They recognized that simultaneously, shied from it equally quickly. If there had ever been, or would be, a time or place, now with all its attendant complications was not it. But he couldn't look away. Wouldn't. Couldn't-wouldn't-didn't stop himself from imagining what the flare of heat in her eyes would feel like if it sparked all the way through her, then wrapped its fire around him.

He knew the instant Hallie recognized the reflection of his wishes on his face. Her tongue flicked out, touched the corner of her mouth in un-Hallie-like hesitation. Then, for the first time since he'd known her, she blinked startled-doe-lost-in-headlights eyes at him and looked at the floor, giving ground first.

Realization punched him suddenly, hard in the gut. She was afraid of him; he knew it without doubt. Afraid of desiring him, but beyond that, panicked that he had a legal leg to stand on that might allow him to take his daughter from her. Frightened that she could even think—however briefly—that he *might* be capable of hanging around town for a month taking pictures of her and the kids without her sensing they'd been followed.

Scared to death that because he'd changed so much physically, hardened beyond recognition emotionally, she didn't really know him at all anymore.

Sickened by the fact that he couldn't very well reassure *her* when he'd just begun to understand that he had no reassurances either for or about himself, he swallowed once and let go of her wrist; he said quietly, "I didn't shoot these pictures, Hallie. And I didn't shoot the video they were lifted from." He picked up the fallen envelope carefully by its edges, knowing from experience there would be no prints, but hoping. "This is addressed to me, see?"

She moistened her lips; eyed him quickly up and down, probing for possible lies, then looked. Cocked her head suddenly to see what else he held.

Too late he remembered the other instant photographs, tried to palm them away from her. But whether or not she thought she knew *him* anymore, she was still on to his tricks; they'd learned magic together when they were eleven, after all.

She put out a hand. "Let me see."

He shook his head. *Dios,* let him just this once protect her from something. "No, it's nothin'."

She hunkered at eye level with him, afraid, but not about to let fear get the best of her, and said evenly, "You're a rotten liar, Joe. These are pictures of my family we're picking up that fell out of an envelope addressed to you. Some of them were taken the day before yesterday, but some of them had to have been taken at least last month. Now, damn you, show me what the devil you think you're going to protect me from."

He hesitated, studying her face, her eyes in all their fathomless blue storm-tossed depths. It really *had* been so much easier answering only to himself—was that only this morning? Easier to shut off conscience when he didn't have Hallie looking him in the eye.

Easier to hide things from himself, to do the kinds of things he'd never let himself look at by light of day.

Stuff that, if he ever thought about it, he wouldn't be proud he'd done.

Stuff that would, undoubtedly, have made Father Nelson in his homemade confessional throw up his hands and—at the very least—consign Joe to the farthest reaches of purgatory for all eternity.

But he *was* a good liar, damn it, and even better than that, as his bounty record proved. He'd just never been able to lie successfully—even by omission—to Hallie.

Which was why, twelve months ago, he'd had to leave.

Without a word he turned his hand palm up. Equally wordless, she studied the snapshots of her front porch, the message "welcoming" Joe home. Lifted her gaze once more to meet Joe's.

"Get your duffel and put on some pants," she said much too calmly. "You're right. It won't be about you taking Maura, but we have to talk."

* * *

It took a while for him to rejoin her in the dining room over the beer and freshly warmed bowls of chili.

Instead of simply dressing, he took advantage of luxuries he'd grown accustomed to living without and showered, then trimmed his thick beard and shaved clean, turning himself—at least in appearance—as much as possible back into the Joe Hallie remembered.

She recognized the gesture for what it was: an attempt to regain lost confidence by presenting the face she trusted. But she didn't trust this face any more than she had the unfamiliar face of the bearded stranger who'd appeared at her door just a few hours earlier. If anything, she found herself trusting this visage even less. The countenance of this Joe was visibly scarred and vulnerable, whereas the one disguised behind his beard was not, and made her heart pound with recognition, her insides flutter and plummet with the desire to believe him and more.

Especially the more.

His mother's Incan ancestry had given him high, carved cheekbones and a chiseled jawline; the Castilian Spanish mixed with French in his father's heritage had given him the thick black beard, and allowed in part for the gray charcoal rather than black of his eyes. His skin, too, was from his father: a smooth, warm brown with a tendency to show the color of embarrassment that his mother's ruddier complexion frequently denied. His body, encased now in a clean white T-shirt and wear-softened jeans, was hard and sculpted, wide-shouldered, narrow-hipped—designed, she shocked herself by admitting, to fit easily between a woman's thighs for long, full nights of loving.

Embarrassment slid revealingly up the pale skin of her throat and cheeks, while heat hewed a path south along the long overgrown roadways through her breasts and belly. God bless the universe, where had that come from? And why now, when in all the long years she'd known him, she'd never reacted to Joe in quite this way?

Because he *wasn't* the same guy she'd taken for granted, grown up with, seen every day for thirty years. And for that brief period of time in her late teens and very early twenties when she sort of remembered maybe feeling a glimmer of something more than friendly love for him...well, by that time they'd both become sheriff's deputies, often worked as partners and she'd stamped on the hint of unwieldy feelings as unprofessional, a potential conflict of interests. And then, of course, Zeke had come along and found all her hot spots and that was all she wrote.

Until now.

Now Joe was different. Looked different, felt different, seemed different, treated her different. She'd borne his child, for Pete's sake; if that wasn't different, nothing was.

Now was different, too, because she no longer knew if she could quite trust him. And *that* meant she couldn't turn her back on him.

Which meant she had to look at him. And looking at him, gulping in the sight of him after too long without him being around, was driving her crazy.

In short Joe was, as she'd always unconsciously known without allowing herself to acknowledge it, a damnably attractive, frustratingly desirable man. But because he was also a vengeance-seeking vigilante whom she might conceivably have to arrest, as well as the man who could possibly just pick Maura up and take her away, Hallie couldn't allow herself to either simply want him, or to feel anything more for him at all.

Not friendship, not partnership, not anything, but especially not...*that.*

Why couldn't Maura wake up and be cranky now, when Hallie needed both the rescue and the distraction?

She drew breath, expelled it, as she watched Joe come toward her.

He moved easily around the table and sat opposite her, a big, dangerous night creature unconscious of his own grace. She watched him because her rebellious body demanded it, refused to allow her to look away while "videotaping" the images, feeding the fantasy library that would, she knew with dismay, fuel her dreams.

"All right," he said quietly, drawing her attention. "I'm here. Let's talk."

"I—"

Her voice cracked and failed. She swallowed and worked her tongue around her mouth, trying to moisten it. Reminded herself that having the hots for this or any man right now was entirely inappropriate when a person or persons unknown had been out on her street this very afternoon taking pictures of Maura, her, Joe and the house. That the same unseen person or persons had previously followed—and perhaps still followed—her kids and her around, shooting video of them whenever he darned well pleased.

She reminded herself that the only person at this table who seemed to know anything at all about the pictures scattered across the oak surface was Joe Martinez, and she was *damned* sure going to get some answers out of him whether his buff new look rang her body's chimes or not.

Resolved, she picked a lime wedge out of the bowl on the table, sucked the juice into her mouth and cleared her throat. Heat flared in his eyes; she did her best to pretend to herself she didn't see it.

"I want to know all of it, Joe," she said. Her voice seemed a little too hoarse.

She cleared her throat, found a spot over his left shoulder where she wasn't too focused on his face and could ignore his body, and repeated for emphasis, "*All* of it. Start with this—" she tapped the photo with the "Welcome home, killer" note across the bottom "—and bring me up to speed. You know the drill—why'd you run, what couldn't you tell me, why'd you come back, what makes me think this isn't the first batch of pictures you've gotten...."

He regarded her, assessed the deliberate withdrawal of her attention from him. She might possibly want him in the way he wanted her, but she'd never trust him again if he didn't come clean with her. And Hallie's trust had long ago defined his world. He wanted it back now.

"Because it's not the first batch." He eyed her for a moment, got up to retrieve his jacket from the front hallway, took out the envelope and tossed it onto the table in front of Hallie. "This is the first bunch. At least," he amended, "these are the first pictures I saw. There may've been others before 'em, but I don't know."

Hallie opened the envelope and spilled its contents onto the table, sifted through them. Eyed Joe without comprehension. "Mary?"

He nodded. "Yeah. In that envelope addressed to me. I never got it till too late."

"Too late for what?"

"To stop her getting killed."

The words hung heavy in the air—an admission, a confession, a plea. Hallie's mouth opened, closed, instant denial in search of immediate understanding.

"What?" Hallie felt like a monosyllabic moron, but when you were starting to feel a little numb with suspicion, and you were missing information besides, what else was there to ask? she wondered. "You—I—" She looked at the pictures, then up at him. "When—why—how—"

Joe shrugged. "You wanted those damned shoes for her funeral. The pictures were stuffed in a shoe box with a bunch of other junk." He reseated himself at the table, took a pull on his beer, and tapped the table, a study in careful detachment. "You know how she saved every box for every frigging pair of shoes she ever bought. When I couldn't find the shoes you wanted on her racks, I figured she kept 'em in the box to keep 'em clean. Or something."

"But—you—I—" Flabbergasted, she stared at him, her

jaw working. At the bottom of her stomach a kernel of fury blossomed. She held it tightly, encouraged it.

Used it.

"It wasn't a carjacking, was it." Accusation, not question.

His mouth thinned at her tone. Here it came. Shock relieved by the lie discovered. Wrath fueled by both being left out of his confidence and the accompanying sense of betrayal. "No."

"You knew all this time."

He eyed her stonily, but didn't deny it. Couldn't, obviously.

"You *bastard.*" She huffed disbelieving outrage, rose and paced the room, collecting could-turn-out-of-control temper. "You withheld evidence." She came to a halt in front of him, her anger banked but evident. "You deliberately interfered in a murder investigation." She gave him a stiff, two-fingered poke in the shoulder. Okay, so her ire wasn't all that banked. "You thought you'd cowboy it."

He looked away, refusing to respond. It was too late to deny the truth.

She threw up her hands, uncomprehending. "Jiminy Pete, Joe. Why?"

Joe swallowed but said nothing. He owed her something, but not this.

She used the same two hard fingers she'd used on his shoulder against his chin, forcing his attention. "I mean, I kinda understand where maybe there might be some sort of twisted revenge goin' on here from you, but the rest of it—" she shrugged "—doesn't make sense. What's goin' on, Joe, you can't share this with me? I thought the pact was, we could share anything."

"Not this." He looked at her because he couldn't help it. "So please don't ask me, Hallie." His jaw burned beneath her touch. The rest of him ached for seven different kinds of relief. He shut his eyes against the sting of coming home. "This is… It's just…personal."

"Too personal to involve me, Joe?"

He nodded. "Yeah."

"I thought we were family." She swallowed hurt. "I thought we were partners."

"We were. But not for this."

"No," she agreed bitterly, sweeping a hand at the pictures of Sam, Ben and Maura spread across the table. "Not for that. Just for me watching your backside for thirty years and carryin' your baby."

He started to respond to that, saw the look on her face and thought better of it. Yeah, he'd backed her up for thirty years, too, but he was the one who'd cut and run, not her.

"What have you brought to my house, Joe?" She picked up the photo printed with its frightening "welcome home" note. "And if you're not going to give me enough to protect my family—*your daughter,* Joe—from it, why did you come here at all?"

"I wanted to pick up my house keys, Hallie, that's all." He laughed without humor. "I got a case brought me to town, the guys at the department wouldn't even give me the time a day about it before I talked to you. I didn't want to come, but I figured maybe I needed someplace to sleep, keep a base, so I came by to get my freaking keys."

"That's all?"

"Damn straight."

"And instead of your keys you find out I had your and Mary's baby, and you get a packet of pictures left in your truck during—what?—the hour or so you're in here the first time."

"Bingo," Joe said dryly. "Give the detective a prize."

Hallie eyed him, her mouth set in a hard line. "October is national sarcasm-awareness month, Joe. Did you know that?"

"It's November, Hallie."

''Cut the cake, Joe.''

He glared at her for an instant, mouth tight. Then his lips softened, shoulders slumped, eyes closed. ''I'm sorry, Hallie. I don't know what else to say.''

Because she had to, Hallie touched his hand, folded her own about his. ''Then say anything, Joe,'' she urged softly. ''There's too much on the line here to go on keepin' it to yourself. Start with what you know about who killed Mary.''

He worked his tongue around his mouth, opened his eyes to see her. ''I got a man who tortured and killed his exwife and kidnapped his kids to find, Hallie.''

She almost smiled. This Joe she knew. ''You want a shebear to help you, you ought to know damned well that no matter how much I might want to do to you personally, I'll back you up for kids.'' She squeezed his fingers, deadly earnest. ''But you've got to give me what I need to protect mine, too. You have to tell me, why and how could anyone use us to manipulate you?''

For a long moment he simply looked at her and breathed, weighing consequences, decisions, druthers. Then he smiled sadly.

''Yeah.'' He nodded and withdrew his hand from under hers. It was too hard to think with her touching him. Also, he had to be able to say this one to her on his own. ''I suppose so.'' He took a deep breath and spilled it. ''Mary had a lover. The third baby we lost wasn't mine.''

Chapter 6

Once open, the secret he'd kept was both harder and easier to divulge than Joe had thought.

"She kept a…an ovulation diary," he said matter-of-factly. "I don't think she really looked at it as being unfaithful, I think it was more an…experiment. She wanted a baby and it didn't matter whose."

He paused, regrouped against painful history, then went on. "She didn't want to believe it when the doctors told her that even though there wasn't anything wrong with her ability to *get* pregnant, her body was just going to keep rejecting the pregnancies. She thought—probably she hoped—she'd find it wasn't my fault or her fault, but a combination of genes or something that didn't work. That if she just changed the combination a little, maybe it would make a difference.

"So—" he shrugged "—she found a guy who was willing and checked him out—soundness, diseases, all that crap. A big Mexican-American like me, to make sure the physical mix matched. That way, if it worked, I wouldn't get suspicious because the baby was blond or something. They had the affair. She got pregnant, ended the affair.''

He huffed humorless laughter. ''Damned thing is, she charts this all out like it's a biology lab. Guy has no name, he's just a subject with the right look and genetic background. They have sex this date, this date, this date. No pregnancy results, so they try it again during the hot dates next month. Clinical. Six months later, the stars are right, she misses a period. Meets him again in month seven just in case she's getting a false positive. Month eight she tells me she's pregnant and stops meeting him. I'm cautiously happy through month ten when, right on schedule, we lose another baby. Only this one's not mine.'' His laughter was self-derisive. ''Does that make me the biggest chump in the universe or what?''

Hallie ignored the question because she didn't know what to say. What *did* you say when your best friend tells you the woman you thought loved him more than life stepped out to find a breeding stud? Especially since this woman had also been a friend you thought you'd known almost as well as you knew yourself.

Or Joe.

''What has this got to do with the pictures, Joe? I mean—'' She sifted through the disturbing-but-relatively-innocent snapshots of Mary alive. ''I can maybe see what it has to do with these shots of Mary, maybe him stalking and killing her, but the rest of this stuff?''

Joe studied his hands. ''There were other things in the box with the pictures, Hal. A couple of letters, no signature. She ended the affair, but he didn't want to. I get the feeling that he probably wasn't a deputy or a cop, but that he may have been close to the department somehow. She was a social worker. I mean, deps, cops, cons and social services—who else did we know?''

''Her clients?'' Hallie suggested. ''So it'd be someone you wouldn't necessarily know?''

He shrugged. "Possible, I guess, but—"

"Did you go through her files?"

"Are you asking did I break the law and hack her computer at work to get 'em?"

Hallie nodded. "Okay."

Joe looked at her, sidestepped the direct answer. "You don't think it would've been easier for me to go through channels, get help from you guys and her department to get 'em?"

Her smile was grim. "What I think now—same thing I thought then, by the way—and what you were thinking, the shape you were in during and after the funeral, are two different things."

"Yeah." He swallowed and glanced away, feeling not exactly repentant but guilty as charged. He looked back at her. "Put it down to I got copies of her files. She had a bunch of 'em at home. The others…" His mouth twisted. "Let's just say the others came my way. I went through 'em. Found a couple of possibles."

"They didn't pan out." A lament rather than a question.

"No." Joe shook his head. "Plus there were the other pictures. Pretty sophisticated stuff for any of the guys in her files who might've fit my profile. Someone video'd her murder and sent me stills and a chit saying she's dead because of me. That if today were Judgment Day, I'd have to 'fess up. If it'd make a difference, I'm willing, but what to? That because she never intended to do anything but use him and stay with me, I'm responsible for him killing her? Or if he's not the one who actually killed her, somehow it's my fault she died? And the worst of it is, I don't know how long Mary had the pictures before she was murdered. Or if I could have stopped it even if I had. At least I'd have known she needed protecting. Anything."

Hallie ignored the chill that swept down her spine, the abrupt sense of panic that made her want to get up, find a phone and make sure Sam, Ben and their father were all right. But she couldn't let some photographs spook her into scaring the boys or Zeke before she had some real inkling as to what was going on. Her ex-husband had a difficult enough time reconciling her career with their sons' lives as it was. And truthfully, there was no evidence that the person who'd shot the pictures was the same person who'd killed Mary.

"Other than being Mary's husband, you don't know what he's got against you," she said, the lieutenant sheriff sliding into interview mode. It beat the frightened-mom mode all to hell. "What does he want from you and why is it so personal he's started on pictures of us? How could he even know to try to threaten you with us?"

Joe shook his head. "Not a clue. Especially nothing that should begin to involve you. I mean—" He spread his hands, a gesture of frustration. "Hell, Hallie, it's not like we haven't each made our share of enemies over the years. Goes with the job, right? But this… I get little messages and leads that send me running in different directions. I feel like I'm close, then, *bam!* I've got air. He doesn't make any demands so I don't know why he wants me, but I know why I want *him*—" His tone became ugly. "And I want him bad." He looked at her suddenly, his mouth a hard, thin line. If anything, the ugliness in his tone increased. "And now he's stalking you and the kids, I want him worse."

Hallie's mouth quirked at his passion. "I want him pretty bad, too, Joe. I don't want him following and videotaping anybody's kids, but he makes it personal when he does it to mine."

"Tell me about it."

They considered each other for a long moment, old friends whose lives were no longer the open books they'd once been.

Onetime lovers who'd never seen each other in either the

light or with quite the intensity, the unacknowledged and unacknowledgeable desire that they saw each other now.

Hallie drew breath and broke the silence first. "As far as you knew, you were never coming back here, right?"

"I don't know." He looked at her, then away. Turned back and gazed levelly at her. "If those pictures'd wound up in my truck, it wouldn't matter where I was. I'd've turned up on your doorstep like that—" he snapped his fingers "—and you know it."

"I know," she agreed softly. "You'd never let anything happen to the kids."

He snorted an impolite but forcefully descriptive expletive. "And you know damned well it wouldn't be just the kids." His eyes were steady points of deep pewter that commanded her attention. His promise—or was it a threat?—was succinct and definitely *not* comforting. "I'd die before I'd let anything happen to you."

It was too charged an admission for so confined a space.

It wasn't the words themselves: as partners they'd made the same implicit commitment to each other a thousand times and more, every day, every shift they'd spent in each other's company, backing each other up. As friends, too, they'd made the pledge, but tacitly, no verbalization needed. This was different. The emotion was different. The way he vowed it was different. More personal. More explicit.

More exclusive.

More ferocious.

It was also spoken aloud. And the unwritten rule was that there were some things better left unsaid. Some admissions that, if you really cared for your partner, your friend, you simply never made.

Some…awarenesses…you didn't permit yourself to feel.

But after all the time he'd been gone, the infant and the history that stood between them, Hallie wasn't sure she'd ever be able to think of Joe as a trusted "friend" again, and they hadn't been partners for almost a year.

She swallowed and got to her feet. She wasn't a kid; she understood need and desire, want, when she saw it—or when she experienced it. And she'd been fancied and lusted after, liked and courted by enough men not to find the view remarkable. But it had been a hell of an afternoon, filled with too-unexpectedly-much Joe, too many revelations and way more variety of emotions than she'd experienced in, oh, say, ever. And to be perfectly honest, she really wasn't ready to visit this particular feeling now, if ever.

Especially not with Joe.

Even if her body *was* making little please-please-please noises in that direction. She knew her body had a tendency to lie when it wanted things that weren't particularly good for it; to tell her that things like all the french fries, onion rings and chocolate she could eat would make her feel like a million when she was feeling like zero, would never be bad for her, were, in fact, all she needed for a perfectly nutritious anytime-of-the-day snack for any reason whatsoever.

She'd learned long ago that if she wanted to continue to be able to outrun fleeing felons, she couldn't always give in to the things her body said about what she ate.

Similarly she understood that if she gave in to her body's current please-please-please awareness of Joe, she'd never outrun her heart where he was concerned. And if she couldn't outrun her heart...

There were reasons beyond Maura she hadn't even admitted to herself that made her angry with Joe for leaving. Just as there were grounds outside her concern he'd somehow be able to take Maura from her that made her afraid of his coming back.

The need to busy herself, to stop thinking, rose like the tide. She looked down. The table needed to be cleared. She reached in front of Joe to collect his chili bowl. Without warning he caught her hand, and the dish stuttered against the oak, fumbled by fingers she'd always been able to count on to be steady.

"Hallie…"

The sound of a baby waking from sleep came from the direction of the claw-footed buffet set against one dining-room wall. Startled, Joe and Hallie both turned, half expecting to see that Maura had somehow materialized in their midst while their attentions were otherwise engaged. The gurgle, of course, came from the portable half of the baby monitor sitting atop the buffet. For his part, Joe wasn't entirely certain what he felt about the interruption—besides determined to meet his daughter properly at last. Hallie snatched at it with relief.

"I have to go. The baby's up. She'll need to be changed."

When Joe didn't immediately release her, she looked up at him.

"Let me go, Joe."

Still no compliance. If anything, he drew her closer, gripped her hand tighter. A hint of desperation crept into her voice.

"Look, Joe, your house keys are hanging on a hook next to the refrigerator. There's really not a lot we can do tonight. Why don't you get your keys and go home. I'll meet you in my office, say, seven tomorrow morning? Whatever you need to help you trace those kids, you've got it. The guys'll want in on finding whoever took these pictures, too, so—"

Mouth working around ironic laughter, Joe interrupted her. "You're a piece of work, you know that, woman?"

She gave him a look of injured innocence. "Excuse me?"

Through the baby monitor in the background, Maura made noises that sounded like inquiries. Joe glanced at the monitor, then at Hallie.

"I told you," he reminded her, enunciating carefully, "I'm not leaving without my daughter. Did you think I'd forget that?"

"No," Hallie snapped with asperity. "I didn't think you'd forget. I *hoped* you'd forget. There's a difference."

"Ah." Joe swallowed half a grin. At some point down the line, they might come out of this on the same side yet. "That there is."

For a moment Hallie studied him, sized him up, considered what she saw. Then she used his grip on her wrist to yank him down to eye level.

"It seems to me," she said evenly, patiently, and the wink of light Joe thought he'd seen in the tunnel suddenly seemed to have a train whistle behind it, "what you have to remember is that since I currently have court-ordered guardianship of Maura, you have no say about where she goes or what she does. And I say she doesn't leave this house to go out chasing stalkers and murderers with a cork-brained idiot of a bounty-hunter father before she's even three months old."

"And what *I* said," Joe responded, equally patiently, "is that I'm not leaving this house without my daughter. I didn't say anything about taking her anywhere. I said, *I'm— not—leaving.* Ya got somebody I'm after taking pictures of you and the kids, you've got me for company. Get used to it."

Upstairs, all cute-and-happy-baby after a long, crabby day, Maura cooed and oh-ed, oblivious to the pounding din of her surrogate mother's heart.

"You're staying?"

"Yeah," Joe said dryly, dropping her hand and stepping back. "That's what I said."

The thumping racket of Hallie's heart grew louder, moved into her head. She couldn't think. "Here?"

"You live anywhere else?"

"I could." She rubbed her hand where he'd squeezed,

feeling the imprint of his palm and fingers where they'd wrapped around hers. She nodded slowly as her desperation shaped a plan. "Yes. I could—*we,* the kids and George and I—can. Easily. You stay here, we go somewhere else and don't tell you— Hey." She broke off when Joe rolled his eyes and headed toward the front of the house. "Where're you going?"

"Upstairs to check my daughter's diaper and get her out of bed."

"You can't do that."

She charged after him. He was already on the stairs.

"Why not?"

He didn't stop climbing. She took the steps two at a time to catch up with him.

"Because..." He'd discomfragmented her enough, she had to stop and think a minute, wasting time. "Because she doesn't like strangers."

Still ahead of her, Joe turned the corner that led to the second-floor landing.

"She's going to get to know me sooner or later," he said coolly. "And since sooner is good for me, there's no time like the present."

"But you don't know how to change diapers."

"I used to change Sam's and Ben's. Anything I've forgotten, you'll remind me."

He stepped into the combination master-bedroom nursery. Hallie stepped in after him. In her crib, Maura grunted happily, clearly up to something. A cautious sniff of the air in the room told Hallie exactly where the infant's good mood came from—and indicated precisely the best of all possible introductions Joe could have to his redolent little girl.

Apparently too intent on getting a good look at Maura to notice the odor, Joe headed for the crib.

"She's been real colicky lately," Hallie warned him. "If she's feelin' this good, you might not want to—"

"I'll handle it, Hallie."

"I just thought maybe you'd like to know—"

"Hallie." He didn't merely say her name, he commanded it.

"Okay-okay." Hands raised in a gesture of pacification, Hallie backed toward the door. "But remember, I did try."

"Did try what?" He leaned over Maura, started to lift her from the bed. "Hello, darlin', how are you? I'm your dad—oh, *man*." Making a phew face, Joe held his daughter at arm's length. "Thompson!"

"Uh-uh," Hallie admonished from the doorway. "I tried, but you said you could handle it. You *wanted* to handle it."

"Hallie, please."

"Nope." She backed out of the room. "Sorry. Can't help. Not allowed. Oh, by the way—" She stuck her head back through the doorway just as Joe was about to lay Maura down. "You may want to know there are diapers, butt wipes and sheets under the change table, fresh pj's in the dresser, and a baby bathtub in the upstairs bathroom."

She gave Joe a cheeky grin. "Welcome home, Dad."

He sent her a baleful glance over Maura's head. "I'll get you for this, Thompson, if it's the last thing I do."

"You'll try," Hallie agreed.

Whistling cheerfully, she closed the door behind her and went downstairs to call Zeke's and say good-night to the boys.

The job took him a while, but he managed it in the end.

Just as his father used to say about Joe and his siblings when they were under the age of two, Maura wasn't the most brilliant conversationalist he'd ever met. She stared wide-eyed at him while he cleaned her up, supported her head, bathed her, but she was too young to make strange yet as Hallie had told him she might. He was just someone with big, awkward hands who didn't have a clue what he was doing. She started, then squawked and whimpered a bit when he accidentally splashed water in her face in the bath, but she seemed to forgive him quickly enough. She liked the warm water, didn't like to be toweled dry, enjoyed holding and chewing on his fingers and seemed to have quite a number of opinions about diapers and getting dressed.

For his part, he couldn't get over how small she was, cradled in his hands. How frail and strong at once, tying him in knots trying to hold on to her, keep her safe at the same time that he attempted to slide her rebellious and un-coordinated arms and legs into the bunny suit Hallie must have come upstairs and laid out while he gave Maura her bath.

He lifted the soft-bristled baby brush from Maura's dresser, swept it gently through the curly black hair on her head, then caught sight of a pair of cute little infant bar-rettes made of some kind of fabric shaped into tiny pansies. He pinched up some of Maura's hair and made a clumsy attempt at clipping the barrettes into the semifine stuff. Failed. Tossed the pansies back onto the dresser. His fingers were just too damn thick to fuss easily with the tiny things.

He'd always known he was big, but to have it so clearly illustrated by this diminutive being who was literally a piece of himself—the whole idea was incredible, unfath-omable.

Ludicrous.

Even more so than the extraordinary fact that this piece of himself was also a piece of Mary, and had been carried and formed and nurtured inside Hallie.

Strange, because even though Maura's black, black eyes and creamy brown skin were clearly Mary's legacy to her daughter, Joe imagined he saw resemblances to Hallie, and to Sam and Ben, too. *There,* around her nose, and *there,* in the curve of her mouth, the lobes of her ears, the length of her toes and fingers. She was a miracle within herself and she was a part of them all.

Especially Hallie. Because if it weren't for Hallie, there'd be no Maura at all.

The urge to protect and keep rose, savage and unexpected, almost primitive. He would not let anything happen to Hallie, ever. His daughter's life depended on it. And in truth, so did his.

Always had, if only he'd known it.

But he'd never get Hallie to believe that now. Hell, he'd only realized it himself ten minutes ago.

Wondering if he had any chance of untangling then balancing the combination of elements that, in the space of a late afternoon and evening, had overtaken and destroyed the clarity of his life, Joe scooped his daughter close and took her downstairs to Hallie.

Hiding in the shadows, behind doors and bends in the walls, Hallie watched him with his daughter. Just to make sure he didn't encounter problems, she told herself.

She lied.

She wasn't in the habit of lying to herself—except where Joe was concerned. What she really was doing, she admitted, was making sure Joe didn't simply pack a bag and leave with his daughter.

Which, of course, was another lie. She knew he wouldn't leave—with or without Maura; she only wanted him to. Or to at least try to. Hating him was simpler than the confusion of emotions boiling over inside her now.

Underneath the pile of lies she fought to believe huddled the reluctant truth: as much as she wanted to, she couldn't stop watching Joe. Couldn't get enough of the sight of him, the sound of him, the scent of him in her house. Couldn't deny herself the close-your-eyes-and-savor taste that same spice left on the back of her tongue.

Couldn't rid herself of the imprint of his hand on her

wrist, the feel of it wrapped around her fingers. Hard. Strong. Rough-callused. Implacable.

Warm.

Tempting.

She had to watch him with Maura. Her body, her heart demanded it. Had to watch him introduce himself to his baby for the first time, see him discover the wonder of every inch of the minute masterpiece that was his daughter.

She'd done the same watching Zeke with the boys, but something about this was different. Actually, a lot about this was different, from the means of conception, to the actuality that Maura was related to her by the use of an umbilical cord and breast milk; that was all. But the difference also lay in what she saw, how she felt where Joe was concerned; the fact that he needed to be introduced to his daughter at all.

The fact that, with Zeke, Hallie had chosen to have children within their marriage; but with Joe, she'd chosen— no, *petitioned*—to bear Maura *for* him. For Mary, too, granted; but mostly for Joe. And truth be told, while she doubted she'd have been able to get herself to even consider "undoing" any pregnancy once begun, she'd been particularly adamant about not even starting to contemplate undoing this one. She'd wanted Joe's baby as fiercely as some part of her now understood that she wanted Joe.

Appalled, she put out a hand and sagged back against the wall outside her bedroom. Oh, sweet Saint Christopher.

Oh, hellfire and damnation. She wanted Joe.

Wanted him now.

Wanted him bad.

Chapter 7

Except for Maura, the rest of the evening might have proved far more uncomfortable than it did for Hallie.

Before Joe and the baby appeared downstairs, Hallie made phone calls both to the sheriff department's regular and special squads, and to a friend at the local state-police post. From the regular deputies and the state police she asked to have patrolling units do extra drive-throughs in Zeke's neighborhood and her own. From the county's various special squads she requested an early meeting and an undercover baby-sitting-bodyguarding gig at the boys' school, and with Maura at the house.

She also—and she was fairly certain this was to her discredit, but swore her justification was self-defense—phoned one of Joe's sisters to inform the family he was in town.

His sister Gabriella's response to the news was a darkly thoughtful, ''Hmm. Let me see what I can arrange,'' then the line clicked dead.

Joe appeared with Maura as Hallie hung up after Gabriella.

"Patrols?" he guessed.

"And morning meetings." She shrugged. She'd never had any trouble lying by omission to *him*. Mostly because she never looked at it as lying and never felt guilty for it afterward. She simply...put things in motion and let the devil in them catch up with Joe in their own good time. "Cooperation, exchange of favors, a little extortion..." A faintly wicked grin shadowed the corners of her mouth. "Lotta guys remember owin' you this or that when you prod 'em a bit. Anything you need to take down this guy you're chasing, you'll get it whenever you want it. Tonight—"

The hint was broad and Joe didn't miss it. Couldn't have if he'd tried.

"Tomorrow, whenever."

"Tonight'd be better for those kids," he agreed reluctantly. With someone spying on Hallie's house right down to Peeping Tom photos of the interior, he didn't want to leave Hallie and Maura alone here—or anywhere—tonight. Or any night. Still...

He glanced at the spot at the base of the side door where George lay snoring. Hallie had one of the county's finest in retired tracking dogs willing to die for her and the kids. And as she'd illustrated earlier this evening by sneaking up and catching him unaware, she was also perfectly capable of taking care of herself and Maura—and probably half the county—at once if necessary, and the kids he was looking for weren't.

Sure, they had bits and pieces of several federal, state and local law-enforcement agencies looking for them, too, but the public servants were understaffed and overworked and he had fewer jurisdictions to trip him up.

He grimaced. No matter what he chose, his conscience would play him hell. "Long's the dad's still holed up where my info says he is, I can go in tonight, but I'll need some recon first."

"Say where and when. I'll either make a call or we can drop Maura off at Zeke's, and George and I'll go out with you."

Oh, now there was a thought he wasn't sure how he felt about.

Ignoring the stab of unease, he uncradled Maura who was restlessly nuzzling his chest looking for suction and passed her to Hallie. "I think she's hungry."

"Changing the subject, Joe?"

He nodded. "Absofreakinglutely." No minced words there. "But I also think Maura's bathed, powder fresh and hungry."

She viewed him with calculation, not taking the baby. "You think you're ever going to take her out of here and deal with her by yourself, you'll have to learn to feed her."

"I've fed babies before."

"Not this one."

Joe eyed her suspiciously. "She doesn't bottle-feed when you're at work?"

"Nope."

"Then how…?"

She raised a nonchalant shoulder, let it drop. "I've only been back to work a couple of weeks. We tried a bottle the first couple of days, but she absolutely refused it. Wouldn't take one in the hospital the first feedings after she was born, either." Then added earnestly, "And I did try, Joe, just in case. I didn't want either of us to get too attached."

She paused, letting that sink in for a moment, and grimaced. "But then I couldn't stand it. My milk came in and you've come back too late. Your mother, my mother or Mary's mother sits with her and brings her into the office at feeding time. She's pretty much on a schedule and she's started sleeping through some nights, so it's not too bad except on days like today when she's colicky, won't accept a pacifier and there's no comfort but the breast."

The moment the word was out, she knew it was the

wrong one. Seemingly of its own volition, Joe's gaze dropped to her chest, taking with it Hallie's own suddenly self-conscious attention. Attention paid made the area in question tighten up and take notice, too.

"Damn," she swore, turning around to pull her shirt and her bra away from her chest to relieve some of the pressure while at the same time trying to appear as though she were doing nothing of the kind.

It might have been a neat trick if she'd been able to pull it off.

As it was, Joe stepped sideways to keep her in view. He couldn't help himself. "Hallie, what's wrong?"

"Oh, for the love of Pete." Disgusted she stopped trying to hide her predicament and simply held her bra straps away from her chest, vowing to strangle the man the very instant she had a chance.

That is, if she didn't wind up telling him where she really wished he'd put his mouth first.

"José Guillermo Martinez—"

The worst thing about finding yourself somewhat enamored of your oldest, best friend and dearest enemy, Joe decided, was that she knew way too much about you—like the name your mother called you when she wanted to skin you alive—before you could show her you were different.

But God Almighty and he couldn't say why—and didn't care at this point—Hallie sure looked beautiful right now.

"Dammit," he heard her say from the other side of the pulse clanging in his ears. "Hand me that kid, and go away and keep your blasted eyes to yourself."

"Huh?" He didn't mean to appear dense, but really, Hallie's chest could be distracting enough when it wasn't filled out from pregnancy and nursing, and his body and mind weren't engrossed in the increasingly persistent desire to view—and touch and a lot of other things—hers the way they were interested now.

She scooted Maura out of his arms and headed for the

living room. "You looked at me and look what happened, you big oaf."

He heard the exasperated *"duh"* where she didn't say it.

Like he should have known. I mean, it wasn't like he'd ever been around her when they were both, as it were, available and she'd been nursing before. And as far as any other nursing women were concerned, his sisters and sisters-in-law didn't talk to him about such things, and his brothers and brothers-in-law had been grossly negligent about supplying him with the information.

Of course, maybe they would have if he'd been around during Hallie's pregnancy instead out chasing a shadow he'd yet to catch.

Oh good, he thought with resignation. *More guilt.*

A thought occurred to him; he decided to share it with—or perhaps that was poke it at—Hallie.

"You know—" He followed her in and watched as she settled on the couch, unbuttoning her shirt. The sight gave him pause, until his silence dragged too long and she glanced up and glared pointedly at him. He grabbed for control and caught it. Turned his back on Hallie, spotted a baby blanket draped over a nearby chair and picked it up. Moved carefully backward and handed it to Hallie without looking.

What he could see reflected in the blank television screen across the room didn't count—except to him.

Body hungry, lungs tight, and thoroughly envious of his daughter, Joe held his breath and watched until Maura was suckling happily and Hallie had draped the blanket over breast and baby. When he could breathe he cleared his throat and then squatted down, more lazily than he felt in front of Hallie.

"Get over yourself, Martinez," she advised, "because if you think you can just waltz through my door after all this time and play dumb, sexy hunk with me, you're just too full of yourself for words."

He eyed her, amused, picking out the one thing she shouldn't have admitted. "'Sexy'?"

"Dumb," she corrected—but she swallowed, didn't look at him, and seemed nervous.

Good. First time today he'd had *her* at a disadvantage. It was probably evil of him, but he couldn't help himself. He'd witnessed the phenomenon too seldom not to enjoy it.

He crouched lower and canted his head where she couldn't avoid seeing him. "'Hunk,'" he repeated. "'Dumb' might have been in there, too, but 'sexy' and 'hunk' were right next to each other. Those were the positive words. I never listen to the negative, you know that."

Trapped by her own admission, Hallie twisted her neck trying to get away. "Stop it, Joe. If you make me crazy, the mood'll affect Maura, too."

He uncrouched and leaned over her, one hand braced on the sofa arm beside Maura's feet, the other on the back of the couch. "Are you saying I'm making you crazy?"

She tried hard not feel his nearness, not to look at him. To concentrate only on the feeding infant instead of on her entire being's awareness of Joe. "You know that's not what I'm saying."

He bent closer, again forcing her to look at him. Enjoying himself way too much not to end up paying for it later.

But he couldn't think about the piper now. "Then what are you saying?"

Her eyes were wide, her breathing shallow, but it wasn't fear he tasted in the air around her.

It was anticipation.

"Go to hell, Joe," she whispered.

He brought his mouth within sipping distance of hers. "Not unless you come with me, Hallie," he whispered back—and did what he'd wanted to do since she'd tried to slam the door in his face: slanted his head and kissed her just to see if she'd taste anywhere near as good as his body informed him she might.

She tasted better.

Hot pepper and chili, corn bread and lime. The flavors in his own mouth. Then finally, underneath it all, Hallie. Coolness and heat in one. Pliability and strength. Softness beneath the hardness of his mouth, gentling him until he could barely stand.

His arms trembled against the strain of holding himself away from her and the baby, but he couldn't come down on top of them, and he couldn't bring himself to give up this "meal." As greedy as his daughter at Hallie's breast, he wanted more.

His tongue chased the seam of her lips, slid between them and drew the sensitive flesh that formed the heart shape of her mouth below the flume between his teeth to coax, to suckle, to inflame.

Instead a small sound escaped her and her head fell back; she opened her mouth and touched her tongue to his, and he was the one engulfed in lava.

He felt the groan in his own throat before he heard it. Intoxicating. Exactly as he'd known it would be.

She drew his lower lip between her teeth, nibbled, then brushed the edge of her tongue along the sensitized area. He thought he felt his toes curl; his body flooded, drowning in heat; his ears roared. He knew he should—he *must*—come up for air, but his ability to remember *why* was seriously distracted by other needs: the hypnotic throb of his pulse, the crushing urgings of his sex against the button fly of his jeans.

And this from a single kiss. Only think what might have happened on kiss two, three and four.

"Might have" being the operative phrase in that statement.

With an infant's infallible ability to choose her moments

to perfection, Maura chose this one to come up for air on a gasp, suck in two more great bellyfuls of air, then belch loudly.

If he'd an inkling where he was, didn't feel so stunned and wasn't breathing so hard, Joe would probably have laughed. Instead, when he heard Maura through the din in his ears, felt her waving her fists and kicking, and felt Hallie gasp with her own shock, grab the neck of his shirt and push him away, he could only stumble backward and fold heavily into the nearest recliner, dumbfounded.

Kissing her the once or twice he had in high school had never felt like this. In fact, he didn't think kissing anyone had ever felt quite like this.

Scorching.

Underneath his hair, his ears burned and, as hot as his face felt, he wouldn't have been surprised to look in a mirror and find his eyebrows singed.

He stared at Hallie, took in her air of disheveled bewilderment, her kiss-ripened lips and the startled passion darkening her eyes—feasted visually on her once-again Maura-exposed, milk-dampened breast with its pouting nipple. The pinkened tip puckered and lifted under his scrutiny, rose and fell with each shallow breath she drew.

His mouth went dry; with an effort he looked Hallie once more in the eye. Jeez Louise and all her sisters, what had he done? If he thought he—his body—had wanted her before, he'd clearly been mistaken. Beside this desire, that one was nothing, a single drop of rain in a season of monsoons.

He'd known he'd pay for coming home, he just hadn't known how much.

On her side of the equation, Hallie could only gawk and blink, dazed beyond her ability to believe that kissing Joe Martinez could reduce her to *this*—whatever "this" was. Incinerated to ashes and blown away. Kindled alive after a lifeless spell she hadn't realized she'd existed in—thought-less, reckless, starving and unbelievably wet from Maura.

Sighing, she grabbed the cloth diaper she used as a spit bib from her shoulder and tried to cover her breast at the same time she shifted Maura about. Seeing and feeling Joe's eyes on her bared bosom came under the heading of sitting too close to the fire: she ached for the sensation and feared how easily he could use it to rob her blind.

Despite the fact she didn't know him anymore—it had only been an evening, he'd brought danger to her home—she was on some level still angry with him, and he'd al-ready pretty much told her he intended to collect Maura but not stay. Not to mention that somewhere in there she had Mary's less-than-perfect ghost to contend with.

She shut her eyes and let her head drop back, sudden perception getting away from her. "Damn," she said, and meant it.

In her arms, Maura squirmed and patted her shirt, nuz-zling down from where Hallie had half raised her to her shoulder, now looking for Hallie's other breast. There was a crunch and squeak of recliner parts, then Joe knelt on the floor beside her and removed the diaper from her hand.

"Let me," he offered.

"Oh, jeez, just go away, Joe. You're embarrassing me."

He smiled slightly, and as gently and impersonally as possible—*Yeah, right,* his body sneered. *Impersonal. Uh-huh. You keep tellin' yourself that. We'll let you know when you believe it.*—he touched Hallie's breast.

"I don't know what you're embarrassed about, Hallie. It's not like this is the first time I've ever touched you here."

"Yeah, well." She swallowed against unsought sensa-tion. The worst—or best, depending on your point of view—thing about nursing was how blasted sensitive it made your breasts. Idly, he patted the soft cotton around the outside of her breast and across the top. Why couldn't she simply ignore his hand the way she wanted to? It wasn't like he was actually doing anything that should be misconstrued as arousing to her or anything—

She bit back a groan when his thumb grazed her nipple and she knew she'd never be able to ignore Joe Martinez's hands. Which meant she should probably push him away. Now what brain button did you push to do that…?

"The last time you handled this breast neither one of us had any idea what you were supposed to be doing."

He wasn't the least perturbed by her memory of their virgin voyage. "But we know now." A statement, not a question.

"My breasts sure as hell know."

He paused, then held the cloth so it almost touched the tip of her nipple and let it drift lazily up and down. "What about you?"

She looked at him, trying to stay coherent inside exquisite torment. Still, even knowing that she should, she didn't attempt to push Joe away, or the cloth he wielded so erotically.

She couldn't, truth be known.

"However this feels to me, I've got your daughter in my arms and she needs to finish feeding. In the meantime, you're going to quit torturing me and go do your recon. Gil Sanders is catching tonight. I told him you might call."

Thoughtfully, Joe bunched the cloth into his hand and sat back on his heels to regard Hallie. She'd told him physically and verbally that she liked his touch, but he knew her better than to accept her directness at face value. She did her best lying when she was telling him the truth.

"Finish feeding Maura," he agreed neutrally. "I should do recon. Right."

"Exactly," Hallie said, relieved by his easy acceptance. She hiked the nursing-bra cup back over her exposed breast, shifted Maura into her opposite arm, re-covered them both with the blanket, and reached under her shirt to undo the other cup. If she tried really hard, maybe she could convince herself she hadn't felt anything when she'd let Joe play with her.

At this stage of the game, pretense was all.

"Those kids need you to find them," she urged him now. "You've got a job to do. Go do it."

"And take my house keys with me and you'll see me in the morning," Joe suggested dryly.

"Works for me," Hallie agreed.

"I thought it would." He rocked back and got to his feet in one smooth movement. "Trouble is, it doesn't work for me, so I'll go take care of my business and be back." He pulled the blanket aside to smile down at his daughter, trace a light finger over her arm. Thoroughly occupied with her meal, she nevertheless rolled her face as far in his direction as she could without losing suction, found nothing of greater interest and rolled back into Hallie's embrace, mmm-ing her content. "Behave, stinkpot," he told her wryly. "When I get back we'll find out if dads are good for something, too." Then he dropped the blanket into place, leaned over and placed a kiss on Hallie's temple. "I'm takin' *your* house keys, not mine," he said in her ear, "but don't even think about tryin' to get the locks changed while I'm gone. I also want you to get a brown-and-white parked in front of the house until—"

"If you don't leave now and trust me to take care of myself and this kid the way I've been doing since you left almost a year ago," Hallie whispered, interrupting him, "I swear to you that as soon as Maura's done nursing I'll be on the phone with my father telling him where to find you. And believe me when I say, he's a lot less happy with you than Zeke or Frank or your brothers will ever be."

Joe sniffed, thought about it, grimaced.

"Point taken," he said. He straightened, headed for the phone in the front hallway. "Okay, *I'll* call for the brown-and-white, you feed the kid and we'll both get on with—"

The throw pillow she pitched at him caught him in the back as he stepped out of the room.

Chapter 8

It took a while for Joe to make the arrangements he wanted. Hallie watched him covertly as he did it, her mind racing, hormones pumping, thoughts a frantic mess.

Trying to sort herself out, she let Maura distract her.

Unusually obliging, Maura proceeded to be the poster child for why-people-have-babies. She smiled. She kicked her feet and waved her fists, gurgled and was thoroughly engaging.

She lay on her tummy on a blanket on the floor, raised her wobbly head and looked around. She grabbed presented fingers, played startled baby and started to cry when Joe dropped the phone book on the hall tiles; made silly faces and stopped crying when, before Joe could react, George rolled to his feet and plodded across the floor to lie down beside her, snuffling and comforting. In short, she was everything that made women forget why they'd decided not to have another one after the last baby outgrew diapers.

She was also everything that had made Mary envy Hallie, Joe's sisters and sisters-in-law, and any other woman with a child.

In some way, Hallie supposed with regret, Mary's pregnancy envy was only natural. She'd grown up in a small, somewhat-dysfunctional family, had found Joe and married into his large, loving, rambunctious one where the competition, from Mary's point of view, must have appeared fierce. She'd wanted family, needed the unconditional love and support that surrounded him, his friends, and perhaps Hallie in particular. Hallie was, after all, not only his best friend, but his first lover, and his partner, sharing more with him, perhaps, than a wife could possibly share. And while Mary certainly had been part of the society of "significant others" that surrounded the county's deputies and police officers, Hallie was part of the brotherhood.

Hallie was also part of the sisterhood.

Joe's sisters and sisters-in-law got pregnant and dropped babies with astonishing frequency and ease, and so did Hallie. Mary hadn't. The natural functions of a woman's body had eluded her—which hadn't mattered to Joe, as he'd often told her, and tried to show her. It had mattered only to Mary. And Hallie supposed that the year-after-year of teasing and questioning, the When-are-you-and-Joe-going-to's, and then finally the sympathy would have gotten to be too much for anyone, but especially for Mary.

And whether she'd meant to be or not, Hallie had probably contributed her own inadvertent fuel to Mary's desire to have a child at any cost—including betraying Joe.

It didn't excuse her, but no woman—no *person*—needed the kind of pressure Mary must have put on herself to succeed at something that was beyond her biological capabilities. For the first time in retrospect, Hallie saw it clearly: when it came to the ability to have babies, Mary had been as competitive as Hallie had been as a young tomboy around the boys. Surrounded by a growing extended family full of women birthing babies at the drop of a hat, Mary must have felt impotent, less of a woman.

One of nature's freaks.

And if what Joe thought about the pictures and Mary's killing was true, her attempt at finding her own solution to her impotence was the key to her disaster.

But it didn't quite explain the pictures left in Joe's truck this afternoon.

Thoughtfully Hallie picked up Maura and carried her into the dining room. Automatically swaying, she held the sleepy infant to her shoulder with one hand, used the other to sort through the photos on the table, looking for a pattern.

Due to the fact that both sets were primarily stills from video, it wasn't particularly difficult to arrange them frame for frame—which she did: the pictures of Mary alive across the center of table, then the pictures of herself and the kids lined up beneath them. Set out this way, a certain similarity became evident in the kinds of pictures the photographer had chosen to leave for Joe. If there was a picture of Mary loading groceries into her car, there was one of Hallie doing the same. Mary leaving or entering work; Hallie, too. Mary at home; Hallie and the kids at home. And so on. The differences in the groupings lay in the inclusion of Hallie's boys and Maura, the shots that focused on them alone.

Which was, of course, what bothered Hallie most.

She picked up each of the pictures of the kids individually, angled it into the light, studying it. Threat or bait, that was the question. In other words, were the snapshots some sort of concealed warning to Joe against returning to Cuyahoga or, if he hadn't coincidentally turned up, would they have been used to lure him here?

A tempered step on the dining room's hardwood floor brought her around to find Joe standing behind her.

Wondering eyes on Maura's ''oh''-formed mouth and

sleep-peaceful face, he said softly, ''She's beautiful, isn't she?''

Hallie nodded and returned the snapshot she held to the table, smiled a little at his awe. As many times as she'd watched babies sleep herself, the marvel never faded. ''Yeah.''

He glanced once more at Maura, then down at the floor, back up into Hallie's face. And took a deep breath. ''Thank you,'' he said.

Hallie nodded, sadly wary. ''But,'' she said. It might have been a question; it wasn't.

''Yeah,'' he agreed. ''But.'' He took another swallow. When you grew up, became an adult, a parent, things were supposed to make sense, Joe thought. You were, like your parents before you seemed to, supposed to know everything, but especially what to do. Unfortunately, things neither made sense, nor did he know what to do. Not knowing what the future held was difficult enough. And not knowing the future, but knowing that he couldn't have one without considering Maura was downright scary.

Hallie made it easy for him.

''You think you have to take her,'' she told him quietly. ''You don't. And until I can get her weaned, you can't. At least not easily. If you try, I'll fight you.''

''I know. But I can't leave her.''

Hallie looked at him, eyes eloquent and direct. ''Then don't leave her, Joe. Finish the job you came to do and stay. You can always come back to the department, you know that.''

''Easier said than done.'' He swept a hand to indicate the pictures she'd organized on the table. ''And I've got this to handle, too.''

''You think you're going to haul Maura through this, Joe?'' Hallie viewed him, aghast—and scornful. ''Not to mention, you macho jerk, no one said you had to do it alone. I'm involved here, too.'' She poked him hard in the chest, demanding his attention. "So's everybody else in the department. They've all got a stake in your daughter. Cat Montoya almost took a bullet trying to make sure I wouldn't get gut-shot right after I told the team I was pregnant, and never mind I was nowhere near the line of fire at the time. Frank drove me to the hospital when I went into labor at the office. Zeke and your sisters took turns as my labor coach."

She huffed a gee-whiz breath. "Heck, Maura was born in the birthing center, so practically everybody we've ever known—your family, my family, Mary's family, Zeke, the boys, Zeke's family, and over half the department—was either there or stopped in as soon as they heard."

"You want guilt from me, Hallie, because they were there and I wasn't?" Joe waved a hand. "You got it. I shoulda been there, I wasn't. Get over it."

"I don't want guilt from you, Joe. You've got enough on your conscience without me adding to it. No—" She shook her head. "What I want from you is for you to wake up and smell the teamwork. I mean…" She made an earnest but futile gesture in the air between them. "Jeez, Joe. We went out there together, we were magic. We were on the job together, it happened for us. You know darn well it did."

"Yeah, maybe." Joe ran a hand through his hair, caught up in his druthers, in his past—in the things he knew he could live with and those he couldn't. He shrugged. "But that was then, Hal. That wasn't this. It wasn't personal. And I can risk *me* on 'personal,' Hallie. Maura'd be fine without me. Look at her. She's healthy and gorgeous because of you. Which means I can't—and I *won't,* damn it—risk you."

Furious, Hallie retorted, "You don't have a damned choice." Then, when Maura squirmed fitfully against her shoulder, she breathed deep through her nose, blew out the breath slowly, beckoning calm. When Maura settled, she continued quietly, but with no less passion. "Do you ever listen to what you say, Joe? You're not leaving here without Maura, but you know she needs me. You can't risk me because of Maura, but you're going to take her from me if you can. Bottom line here is I'm the only partner you've ever had who knows what you're going to do before you do it *and* I'm already at risk, Joe. So are Maura and Sam and Ben. Which means we bring in the department and I don't stay out of it, understand?"

Momentarily silenced, Joe stared at her. Put like that, it was impossible *not* to understand. It wouldn't matter what he did, she would be there either one step ahead of him taking point, or one step behind, watching his back. And just like always, since the time they were kids, because they were *friends* first, he'd have nothing to say about what she did. And God in heaven, he realized suddenly, clearly, he'd wanted to have something to say about what she did and with whom since the dawn of time. He'd just been uncharacteristically noble—when he wasn't embarrassed by his feelings—and politely put aside what he wanted when Hallie found Zeke.

There was also the point that, since he'd been chasing this cryptic photographer for not quite the full twelve months he'd also been chasing Mary's killer, since he'd seen the pictures that *weren't* on the table....

For reasons beyond those he was prepared to identify, the very thought of Hallie winding up anywhere near this shooter scared him to death.

In the end, in the interests of speed and efficiency, they reached a compromise Joe hated: since fugitives in Cuyahoga County were decidedly Hallie's purview in her capacity as Lieutenant Sheriff Thompson of the Fugitive Apprehension Team, she would leave Maura at the house in the care and protection of Deputy Cat Montoya, who'd sat with Maura on other occasions, and Cat's sometimes-partner Leroy Crompton. Between the two of them and George, Hallie reasoned, the sleeping baby should be better cared for than Fort Knox. That would then leave Hallie free to work Joe's bond-jumper reconnaissance with him and— Joe's demand in this compromise—keep Frank from Joe's throat.

Joe's thought was that with Frank Nillson on board, he'd have at least one other person besides himself determined to keep Hallie out of trouble.

Hopefully, having Frank along would also give them the added manpower to clean up Joe's most immediate job in one night, instead of dragging it out over two or three— and probably increasing the danger to the justifiably paranoid target's children.

While Frank made contact with the unmarked car that Joe had already requested to surveil the area, Joe and Hallie cruised the neighborhood street behind the target's elderly uncle's house taking stock of exits, possible blind spots and danger points. The area was definitely small-town, full of older homes in dissimilar sizes and styles, with garages and sheds, large yards and mature trees—which meant any number of places for one person with a single hostage to hide. Small-town also meant neighbors who'd notice new people or strange goings-on—and be willing to talk about it. Still, of the options Joe had discovered his quarry had, this one had seemed to him the best and most obvious bet.

Let the feds pursue the other directions the guy might have run with his kids; Joe's experience with large families left him with the knowledge that a guy trying to hide three kids would do it in plain sight because there was simply no other good way to do it. People would tend to notice a man traveling with three kids by himself. Matronly women would offer sympathy and help. They'd remember him. Whether he accepted or rejected the offers, women would remember the kids.

And then there was the "reason" this guy had wound

up killing his ex in the first place: because she'd kept his kids from him.

From all accounts Joe's prey—while hardly, uh, mentally fit—was obsessively fond of his children. And Joe's bet was that the guy would want to give those children his own version of a "normal" life: in a small town, and not too far from where Dad had grown up an abused child in a supremely dysfunctional family. Hence, despite more reasonable available guesses, Joe's gut told him to check out the old uncle's home where the father had spent one more-or-less-tranquil summer as a kid.

The fact that the uncle's home was in Cuyahoga County, that the time of year was closing in on the anniversary of Mary's death, both repelled Joe even as it attracted him to the case. But his own possible personal conscious and sub-conscious reasons were entirely beside the point at the moment. The only thing that mattered now—besides the way-too-potent-and-disturbing taste of Hallie in the truck beside him—was locating the kids, making sure they were safe, then taking down their father.

If, that is, Joe was right about where they were.

He was.

The house in question was a small, single-story bungalow with a fenced yard and only two exits from the home: side and front doors. The windows were old-style metal casement and not designed for easy escape by adults—even paranoid self-preservation instincts had their limits.

The plainclothes officers already on the scene had completed a quiet door-to-door across the street and to either side of the house in question, showing photos of both the children and their father to the neighbors. Responses were unhesitatingly uniform: the elderly uncle had canceled calls from his visiting nurse, stopped seeing his neighbors and attending his card club, and essentially quit going out, period. Drapes usually open during the day were now always pulled. Only one person came or went—the nearest neighbors to either side of the uncle thought it was a woman, but couldn't be sure—and this generally occurred at dusk when visibility was at its worst.

The neighbors also reported seeing small children once or twice at windows or doors. They were pulled quickly back into the shadows, but certainly what little these neighbors saw of the kids seemed to match the photos and ages the plainclothes deputies provided. The neighbors were also quite certain they'd never met any of the uncle's relatives in the past, nor had there ever been children in residence at his house before.

While certainly not proof that Joe's subjects were inside the residence, the evidence was plenty enough for him— and Hallie.

Tight-lipped, she eyed the house for a long moment, watching the mere slits of light visible along the edges of the almost too-closely-drawn drapes. Then she moved.

"No," Joe said, a fraction of a second too late, stepping after her quickly and reaching for her arm.

She anticipated the grab and sidestepped him. "You and Frank take the side door," she advised. "Gina and Tom go 'round the back. That's gotta be where the kids and the uncle are. Try to isolate them if you can. Gina's thin enough to fit through those casements, I've seen her do it before. If you can get her inside and get the kids out without waking the neighborhood dogs, do it. Otherwise just try to stay between them and the action. Oh—" A chopping motion of *whoops, almost forgot* in the air. "And dump your badges. We don't have a warrant, but Joe's got retrieval papers. We're his partners on this one, period."

Frank grimaced but nodded. Badging people who didn't know he was the law was one of the small but pleasurable power trips he allowed himself on the job. The plainclothes deputies acquiesced without visible demur.

"Hallie," Joe said quietly.

She looked at him. "I know," she said. "I promised.

But this is what we do, Joe, and we're good at it. We let this go till tomorrow, he's gonna smell something wrong. A man and a woman have already knocked on the rest of the neighborhood doors, why not this one? If he's seen anything at all, we're already in trouble. I knock on this door, a loco lady looking for her cat like maybe the woman who's already been all over the neighborhood was, maybe we got a chance to at least make a positive ID.''

His laughter was wry and silent. Joe shook his head. ''The first time you ever came home from school with me my mother told me to look out, you were hell on wheels.''

''That's all right.'' Hallie grinned, shrugged. ''My mother told me she saw right off the bat we'd be trouble if we kept hanging out together. Now all she does is say 'I told you so.'''

''Oh, good,'' Joe said dryly. ''Always nice to know some things never change.''

''Yeah.''

Silent communion was brief.

''Okay,'' Joe told her finally. ''You play crazy cat-lady at the front door. Just give me enough time to oil and pick the side lock if I have to. If there really is a woman in on this, too, I don't want to get stuck with her answering the door and him having time to get between us and the kids.''

Hallie gave him a clipped nod. ''You got it.''

Then they moved.

Frank and the plainclothes deputies went first, easing up to the chain-link fence on the darkest side of the house, then down through the next-door neighbor's open side yard where they could clip the fence and enter their quarry's yard as silently as possible. Joe moved second, melting from streetlight shadow to streetlight shadow until he could move within the shadow of the bungalow to approach the side door. Hallie gave him thirty seconds before approaching the house herself.

The thing about bringing down fleeing felons was that,

while it sometimes proved a real, physical, adrenaline-pumping chase, the rest of the time it was just *that* easy and *that* anticlimactic. This was one of those times.

Hallie rang the bell and stepped a little to the side, ready for anything. When the curtains to the left of the door moved a bit, indicating someone looking out, she waggled her fingers and looked contrite, a friendly person with a problem. A medium-everything woman wearing jeans and a thick sweater turned on the porch light and opened the inside door, but held the storm closed. Loud enough to be heard through the glass, Hallie did her cat schtick, first milking sympathy from the obviously anxious but painfully lonely-appearing woman, then gradually moving sideways. Drawn in spite of her anxiety, the woman opened the door and stepped onto the porch, pulled deeper into the conversation.

At precisely the same moment that she seemed ready to relax a bit with Hallie, Joe loomed at the front door with his handcuffed quarry, retrieval papers at the ready. In less than a second, Frank hovered into view behind Joe. Then Tom appeared, offering a brief salute to Hallie that stated as clearly as words, "Kids okay, all's clear."

"Call children's services and visiting nurses," Hallie told him. "Get someone down here to pick up the kids and make sure the uncle's all right."

The younger detective nodded and disappeared from sight. Hallie returned her attention to the woman.

Stunned, the woman stared from Joe to the man she'd been living with. "What— Who—" She sucked air, trying to breathe, questions lodged with fear somewhere deep in her windpipe.

Joe showed her his papers. "Fugitive retrieval, ma'am." He jutted his chin at his captive. "Are you related to him?"

"I—" She stopped, swallowed, studied the papers in confusion, looked up at Joe. "I'm his wife."

"Are you aware he's wanted for jumping bond, and also

in connection with his ex-wife's murder and for kidnapping his kids?''

"I—the kids—'' She paused, drew a harsh, frightened breath, then asked, "He killed her? He said—'' She looked at her husband. "You said—you said—it was just the kids. You'd get me the kids, get 'em away from that witch. They'd be happier with me. With us. You said we'd stay here an' she wouldn't find us coz she didn't know about your uncle. You said she'd quit after a while and we'd be able to move someplace safe, change the kids' names before they were old enough for school and—'' She gave a gulp of pure panic. "You *killed* her?''

"She wouldn't give over.'' Guilt made a brief foray across her husband's features before sullen bravado set in. "You an' me, we want them kids, not her. She hated 'em coz they're mine, only wanted 'em to use 'em against me. Control me, she says. Don't matter to her none where they live or with who, 's long's it ain't with me an' she gets her money fer bringin' 'em along. She lef' 'em alone half the time—they're too young fer that. I ain't never hurt 'em, but I got a history with her. Court won't give 'em to me no matter what I tell 'em about her. Don't matter I was gettin' counseling—'' Sullenness and bravado departed in a breath; he sent his wife a genuinely beseeching glance. "You *know* that. You were with me so we could both make sure I wouldn't hurt you. She says things ta me—''

He stopped. Shrugged. "That rage the therapist talks about, it came back. I don't know what all I did, but it was bad.'' Earnest, pleading. "Kids didn't see nothin', though, you gotta believe that. Wouldn't let 'em see nothin' like that, even state I was in.'' Matter-of-factness returned. "When it was over, I didn't even look, just grabbed 'em outta their beds an' ran.'' He looked at her, his face twisted with apology. "Don' mean nothin' now, but I'm sorry it's gonna hurt you.''

Horrified, disbelieving, the woman studied him, her head

canted, tongue working around a trembling mouth. Her throat convulsed, her lips moved without sound; she shook her head, as though attempting to find some better angle to view that which was incomprehensible within her experience and imagination. Then she stilled, stared at her husband, and the knowledge that he was indeed capable of the unthinkable settled on her face.

For an instant, comprehension was everything; in the next, the woman swallowed, her mouth twisted, and anger shaped her features from the inside out. Before anyone could blink, she closed a fist, stepped forward and planted a hard left on her husband's jaw, a knee to his groin, then jerked the same knee into his nose when he doubled over. She was getting set to do more damage when Hallie and Frank hooked her arms and pulled her back, restraining her.

"You bastard," she spat at her husband, struggling to reach him. "You lied to me. You told me you'd get me the kids when we couldn't have our own, then you go and take 'em away from me again. You think they're ever gonna let me near 'em now? I got no legal claims, you flipping idiot. You screwed it up bad, you—"

They didn't wait to hear the rest of what she might have to say. While Gina kept the kids and the uncle in the back bedrooms, and Tom hung on to the wife, Joe hustled his prisoner out to his truck and set off to turn him in. After a brief confab with Hallie regarding the legalities of the situation, Frank handcuffed the man's wife and put her in the back of his unmarked car to take her in as an accessory to the children's kidnapping. After that, Hallie hung around until children's services arrived bearing teddy bears, then she and Gina accompanied the frightened and sleepy children to Children's Village, where Hallie remained until arrangements were made to place all three kids in the same foster home—at least for the night.

When Hallie finally arrived home it was the "wee small hours" of the morning, as Frank's mother would say, and she was exhausted—and incensed and disheartened and too many other things to name. One day—twelve blessed hours, give or take however many minutes—Joe Martinez returned to her life, and her heretofore quiet hormones had turned over a new leaf, she faced a possible custody battle over Maura and she'd been exposed to the lengths two childless women would go to to *get* children in graphic, horrific detail.

There was a lesson in this insanity somewhere, she was sure of it, but at the moment she was having a hard enough time simply putting one foot in front of the other climbing her newly snowy front-porch steps to decide what that Solomon-like wisdom might be. Something to do with Joe, undoubtedly. With surrendering Maura to him out of love for the baby, or finding a way to work *with* him and Maura, rather than dragging them all through a custody battle in which there could truly be no winners. She could hope the entire subject would be moot, that Joe would take his fled back to Duluth, turn him in and keep going, but she knew better than to believe Joe would let go, now that he knew about Maura—especially not with those pictures floating around. No, she had to face it: at best she had a week before he returned. At worst...

She put out a hand to open her front door and he pulled it open for her.

"I turned him over to the local feds and came back," he said without preamble. "Cat said Maura slept through. I just checked on her, she's fine. Milk's in the microwave. You look like you could use a hot nightcap before we turn in."

"We?" Hallie mustered the energy to arch a brow at him. "*We* are not doing anything like turning in. *I* am going upstairs to bed by myself and *you* are going...wherever it is you go when you're not making a mess of my life."

"Your couch will fit me fine," Joe said affably.

"My couch," Hallie countered, "is a little short and narrow for someone of your dimensions."

"It's a queen-size bed when you pull it out. Or I can spread out my sleeping bag on the floor. Doesn't matter which, I'm staying."

"Joe—"

"Losing battle, Hallie." He took her coat and hung it on a peg beside the door. "You're too tired to fight it tonight."

"I'll get you for this, Martinez," she promised, giving in. "You know I will."

"Yeah." His grin was fleeting. "I do. We'll talk consequences in the morning, though, huh?" He caught her hand, pulled her toward the kitchen. "It's been a long night, the milk's hot and Maura's feeding time's what, four hours away?"

"More—" Hallie covered a yawn with the back of her hand "—or less."

He nodded. "More or less. Okay."

He paused to open the microwave, pulled out two mugs of frothy milk, picked up a pint of brandy from the counter, waved it in question at her. It looked good, but she shook her head.

"Nursing," she mumbled. "Gets into the milk."

"Didn't think of that." He unscrewed the cap, poured a dollop into his own mug, closed the bottle and put it into the cupboard over the refrigerator. "Anyway," he said, picking up the conversation where he'd left off, "I'll get up with Maura in the morning. Take care of her diaper. Bring her to you. You stay in bed."

"You don't have to do that, Joe. I have to get up for work anyway, remember? We've got a squad meeting to see about setting up a net to bring in whoever's been taking those pictures."

"Yeah, but you've been back to work for, what did you tell me? Two weeks? Means you're still on postpartum light duty, right? You've got to rest. We'll make the meeting."

"Joe—"

He put a finger to her lips. "Shut up and drink your milk, Hallie. Let me just this once do something for you for a change."

For an instant the craving that had been banked until he'd kissed her earlier flared and curled between them; the finger on her mouth was invitation; the light in his eyes said *please*. Then the "please" faded, his finger withdrew; he brushed a roughened palm across her cheek, bent his head and kissed her temple.

"Drink your milk and go to bed," he whispered.

Both disturbed and tempted by his nearness, a simple human warmth she hadn't known until this moment she'd missed, Hallie swallowed. Only partially of its own volition her right hand lifted toward his mouth. He caught it, trapped it for an instant against his chest.

Time hovered in heartbeats counted beneath her hand, became the air Hallie breathed, the half wish she wouldn't bring herself to name aloud—the ghost of a desire she wouldn't claim for herself, but would give in to if he fed it. She waited, not hoping yet anticipating all the same. Then Joe stirred and sighed, turned and picked up the mug without the brandy, put it into her hand.

"Go," he repeated. "Before we do something you'll regret."

Too tired to argue further, Hallie did as she was told. Twenty-five minutes later she hauled herself upstairs, undressed and collapsed across her bed to fall deeply asleep, uneasily aware of feeling that for the first time in their lives, she and Joe Martinez were really home.

Chapter 9

She dreamed about him, doing there what she would not allow herself to consider when she was awake.

She touched his face, traced his brow, his cheekbones, his jawline; held the well-loved visage between her palms and drew him down, into her kiss.

Their kiss. Fierce and hot, all-consuming and endless, breath on breath, fire fed and exchanged. A fall into a roaring blackness without thought, where the only light was from distant stars.

She woke in the predawn dark—sweating, heart pounding, mouth still reaching for the lingering taste of his lips on hers, body aching for a touch even her dreams wouldn't let her imagine. Across the room Hallie heard Maura stir, turning in her crib; then the soft sound of her night breathing resumed.

No such luck for Hallie.

Closing her eyes returned Joe to her imagination's embrace, took her into his. Staring into the grayness of her room was like standing before a broad canvas upon which the only portrait her mind would paint was Joe's. Instead of him putting his finger to her lips to shush her as he'd done earlier, he put a finger to her mouth and she parted her lips, touched it with her tongue, drew it into her mouth and sucked on it. And around his finger was only the first of any number of places on his body she could envision putting her mouth.

None of the visions allowed her to sleep.

In short, the entire experience gave new meaning to the phrase "no rest for the wicked." She'd used the axiom all her life without ever understanding where it might have originated—until now.

She'd never considered herself a prude—hell, first as a deputy, and now as a lieutenant sheriff in a county where few of the suddenly population-exploding townships had their own police departments, she'd seen pretty much everything, right? Had to. But neither what she'd witnessed as the law, nor encountered within her marriage to Zeke, had prepared her for the limitless—and probably depraved—things she wanted to do with Joe.

Hadn't quite prepared her to comprehend the lengths Mary or the woman she'd taken into custody tonight would go to have children, either.

The thought was a sobering-though-hardly-calming counterpoint to the druthers of her body.

Restless, she rose and checked Maura, then sat on the half-circle bay window seat nearby, blessing and envying the infant's sleep. She turned and pulled aside the heavy shade to look into street below.

The light snow that had accompanied her home a few hours earlier was heavy now, loading trees and bushes. Even as she watched, one of the maples edging the street in front of her neighbor's house lost its main branch to the snow's weight. A small lone pickup with an empty bed inappropriate to the season slewed slowly up the street through the hub-deep snow, searching for unavailable traction.

Already she could see it would be a trying day for the larger part of the department: if the snow continued they'd have to close roads and freeways, deal with fender benders, help emergency medical personnel get to work, rescue stranded motorists and tackle hazardous driving conditions because no matter how many announcements were made calling for people to stay home, too many wouldn't. People who felt they couldn't afford to miss a day regardless of how far they lived from work would still try to make it in. Travelers returning home after an extended Thanksgiving holiday would wind up buried up to their door handles in snow drifts and have to be rescued before they took it upon themselves to leave their vehicles and seek help on their own.

Assuming roads would be cleared as the day progressed, mothers at wit's end because of thrilled kids home for their first snow day of the year would head out for the nearest mall—forty miles away in the next county—by late morning or early afternoon to get the kids out of the house and do a little Christmas shopping. Then, when they wound up stuck in the middle of the street three doors from home in snow falling too fast for the road commission plows to keep up with it, they'd call the sheriff's and complain because even the wreckers would have trouble reaching them.

On the upside, though, the crime and fugitive rates would be down, and Mary's stalker would be as stalled by the snow as everyone else.

Except "whoever" wasn't Mary's stalker anymore; he was Hallie's.

She hissed a breath between her teeth at the thought, rose to prowl impatiently, her mind churning.

After twelve months of digging, she knew there had to be an angle Joe had missed; something he either couldn't bring himself to face or a puzzle piece Mary herself had hidden where he couldn't know to look. Something that wouldn't have come to light during the department's over-time investigation even after Joe had left. Something Joe would have overlooked in his obsession, in his being way too unobjective about this case. He was too good an in-vestigator not to examine the nooks and crannies—unless for some reason he either couldn't, or wouldn't let himself. Heck, why else would he be the one to figure out where to look for his bond jumper when public law enforcement failed to find the guy?

No, there was something about this stalker and those photographs beyond what Joe had told her—both the things he didn't know, and the things she was damn well certain he'd left out. It wasn't reasonable to expect he'd horde this thing to himself since a couple days after Mary's funeral, then suddenly turn up and spill everything to his old partner in one evening.

Especially when that old partner was wet-nursing his child or if he thought that *not* telling her might somehow protect her from God knew what. All of which meant that, in her opinion, Joe had a whole lot more explaining to do. And since he was already keeping her awake…

With one last glance at Maura, Hallie stepped into her slippers and eased noiselessly downstairs to have a serious discussion with Joe about full disclosure of evidence.

He hadn't closed the shades in the living room and by the light from the snow-glow outside, Hallie could see he'd donned a sweatshirt and gym shorts, opened the Hide-A-Bed and stretched diagonally across it. His sleeping bag lay bunched to one side of him, as if he'd used it to cover himself but the slippery fabric had had other plans and had slid away the first time he'd turned in his sleep. He lay almost on his back, legs sprawled so that one foot hung off the mattress; one arm pillowed his head, the other lay draped across his body. Even defined by shadows, his face was more peaceful than she'd seen it since well before Mary's death.

Her determination fled. With a soft sigh, Hallie headed for the linen cupboard to find a flannel-covered quilt, returned to ease it over him. If he could sleep, she wouldn't wake him. Morning would be soon enough to eke more revelations from him—especially since it looked like they'd be stuck here for the better part of the day, at least, without the boys.

She pulled the quilt over his shoulder and her thumb grazed his jaw. Before his eyes opened, his hand snaked out to catch hers.

"Hallie?" he muttered. Something besides snow-light glittered in his eyes.

"It's me, Joe," she whispered, trying to ease her hand out of his grip. "Go back to sleep."

"Not yet." Without letting her go he lifted the quilt. Then, while she was too surprised to protest, he hauled her forward and into bed beside him, tucking the quilt around them both. "I thought I told you to get some sleep."

"I—"

She swallowed. He was much too close, the warmth from his body way too inviting, the blatant and unrestrained reaction of his body to her proximity—even though he did nothing but lie quietly pressed against her—much too intoxicating.

It had been a long time since she'd lain next to a man. Longer since she'd wanted to lie *with* one. Lying next to this man, with whom she knew without doubt she wanted to lie, made it impossible to think. She opened her mouth and tried again.

And couldn't believe what fell out.

"I couldn't. You were in my dreams. I want you, Joe."

He jacked himself up on an elbow and peered down at her, unable to believe it, either. "Hallie?" His voice was rough.

Whatever she heard in his pronouncement of her name, it was enough. She smiled and kicked off her slippers, lifted a hand to cup his jaw. "Kiss me, Joe."

He closed his eyes and sighed, and a shudder ran through him, deep and heartfelt. He opened his eyes and looked down at her. Then he threw a leg across hers and pulled her into him, closer than close, bent his head and met her mouth.

As before, the kiss ran through her, head to toe, zinged along her veins, seeming to change the direction of her pulse, connecting its beat to his; nerve endings flared to life, heat spilled through her, a dam opened.

It was no fluke.

In case she'd wondered, this kiss confirmed the last, verified the message in her dreams: if ever a woman could be truly meant to kiss one single man in her life, it was clear as glass she was meant to kiss Joe.

And *kiss* him.

She angled her head, reaching for deeper access, and he growled low in his throat, drawing her in; she curved her body to fit with his and he groaned into her mouth and arched against her, and she knew she was meant to touch him.

And *touch* him.

She needed to. Wanted to.

Had to.

She freed a hand, slid it up the massive, rock-hard thigh he'd draped over hers, ran it inside the bottom edge of his gym shorts and over his hip, rocked him into the hollow between her thighs at the same time she lifted her own hips to meet him. The statement was shameless, obvious—and one she'd only ever made in quite this way to Joe. And then only the once, a long time ago, when neither of them knew what they were doing except for what *The Joy of Sex* said.

"Hallie…"

His voice was dark with desire and laughter, muted in the hollow of her neck.

"Ah," she said, squeezing his hip. "You remembered."

"Yeah, and thanks a lot for reminding me." His hand skimmed over her pajama shirt to find the curve of her breast, cupped it gently. "I worked damned hard to forget."

"I didn't." She touched his mouth, sighed and lifted her breast into the feather-caress of his thumb across her nipple. The warning tingle-ache that preceded letdown was dull but there; she ignored it. "I never wanted to share that first with anyone but you."

"Me neither, you." The buttons of her pajama top opened without hesitation. The skin of her stomach was silk beneath his touch, the feel of her breast softer still when he moved his hand up to take its freed weight in his palm. *Dios,* Joe wanted to taste her, but he knew if he did, the craving he'd experienced when she'd opened her door to him would return in force; he wouldn't want to stop. Hurting her in any way was out of the question. "I'm a whole lot better at this now than I was then," he said softly. "And I want you, but are you sure you're all right with this...with everything? Okay for it?"

She nuzzled his jaw, liking the graze of overnight stubble under her mouth. "You pulled me into this bed, but I choose to stay. And I don't live on regrets, you know that."

"Good." His eyes closed, stomach muscles contracted when she pushed aside his sweatshirt and ran her fingers inside the waistband of his shorts. "That's..." He sucked air when a fingertip found the head of his sex, traced it gently. "That's good. *Dios,* that's good." He concentrated and gathered his wits with an effort. "But it's not what I meant. At least, not all of it. I mean, it's only been... Maura's only three months old. Are you sure it's okay—*you're* okay to—"

"Yeah, I'm sure." Hallie stroked up his rib cage, his belly, his chest. Sweet heaven, he felt wonderful, lightly furred, tickly if she raised her hand so her palm barely grazed him. Arousing. She wanted to touch all of him, feel that tickly sensation against her bare skin, anticipated the exquisite texture teasing nipples sensitive from nursing. "Not that there was any reason for it, but I got the green light six weeks ago."

"You did? Six weeks. No problems. You're sure?"

"Yeah, absolutely. What about you?" Suddenly feeling a little anxious, a bit careful, she stopped her hand in its exploration of his chest, withdrawing a little. She wanted him, but she wasn't Mary, couldn't be her substitute. "This isn't too soon for you after…after Mary, is it? No regrets for you? You don't really want—"

"No." The word was passionate, definite.

He kissed her, pouring all of himself into it. Lifted his head to look down at her, to run his hand restlessly, possessively up her side, through her hair, over her face, claiming every inch possible. "I loved Mary, but this…this is you. I think I ran partly because I wanted you too soon after—" he stopped, swallowed "—what I found. She betrayed me and I'd have hurt you and… Time's passed. I mean, look at me. I haven't even been back a day, and already I'm touching you because I can't stop myself. Jeez—" He grimaced—a wry, self-derisive twist of a smile—and palmed her cheek. "You talk about dreams… Woman, you've kept me awake practically since I left. Today…you opened the door and I nearly lost it right there. If we start, I don't know if I could stop, and I just don't want—"

"Don't stop." She hushed him with her lips against his. "Don't sto—"

It was all the encouragement Joe needed. Before the word was out, he dipped his head and took possession of Hallie's mouth.

Their kisses were brief at first, circumspect, wondering— a toe dipped in a once familiar creek to test, then to acclimate themselves, to raise the temperature. Then all at once the kisses were dark, urgent, bruised with passion, flavored with the liquor of the night's excess and the morning's second thoughts, potentially costly but unstoppable.

Unthinking.

Hallie was wild, surprising, more passionate—more knowledgeable than he'd remembered. He couldn't seem to absorb her fast enough, and no matter how badly he thought he'd wanted her before, for this *need,* he was not prepared.

It had been a long time, this was Hallie, object of months of dreams, hours of desire, and he was needy and she was willing, and that was all, he told himself.

He lied.

Joe was dark and intense, no laughing eighteen-year-old lover, awkward and tentative and reckless—and fast. Neither was he the temperately thoughtful, considerate lover Zeke had always been; he was frightening, intoxicating, sensual beyond her wildest imaginings.

Hallie couldn't drink him in fast enough, and she was not prepared.

It had been a long time and this was Joe, keeper of half her heart since long before time began, and she recognized what was happening to her the instant it occurred.

She'd never been big on lying to herself, she realized with regret. More's the pity. But because she couldn't deny it, she opened her heart, her hands, her arms, her mouth, her thighs, her body...

And loved him.

Her breasts were tender, tight and full, and she told him, so he left them after first breathing on each a hot promise to return when they were ready for him, and worked his way slowly down her body—ribs, abdomen, belly—inched her pajama bottoms off her, leaving openmouthed kisses and teasing tongue-darts in his wake. By the time he reached her feet she felt like liquid fire, her wakened nerve endings raw with hunger after a long winter's fast.

She held out her arms to him, wordlessly calling him back.

He shook his head and grinned. "Wait," he suggested, and dropped her leggings on the floor, stood and shed shorts and sweatshirt.

"Mmm," she muttered, eyeing him up and down, from the well-defined wall of his chest, to the slim, tight hips, to the muscular thighs—and, of course, to his equally well-proportioned sex jutting out from the dark nest between those thighs. "Mmm-mmm-mmm."

His grin widened; he arched a brow and gave her a variety of weight lifter's poses—offering her the benefit of viewing him from all angles.

She laughed, a little breathless, but unwilling to swell his head to match the, um, *magnitude* of the rest of him. "Not bad," she admitted. She nodded at his erection. "Is that for me?"

"Every bit of it." His chuckle was deep and seductive, suggestively filthy. "As, er, *long* as you want it."

It seemed silly to blush at this point, but Hallie blushed nonetheless. A lieutenant sheriff in a sexual situation of her own choosing, embarrassed? Who would have thought it? But she supposed you had to be there—and, of course, she was.

"Joe, please," she said—or perhaps "demanded" was the word. "I don't think—"

"Wait," he promised again and picked up her foot, starting at the instep and returning back up her body the way he'd come down, only more slowly and far more thoroughly. "I'll get there."

Even with the pleasure seeping into her bones, she tried to twist away, to reach him. "Joe, I don't think you understand. When you've got a baby in the house you don't waste time because there's none to waste. She could get up—"

"I'm not wasting time."

He knelt on the bed and his mouth followed his hand, skimming up her legs, pausing at each raised inner knee, lurking on the insides of her thighs until she thought he'd drive her mad.

"I'm…"

He placed a kiss, dark and wet amid the curls at the apex of her thighs.

"Taking…"

His tongue swirled, gliding, dipping in a quick foray into the treasures hidden below the curls that made her gasp and thrust her hips off the mattress, seeking more of the same.

"Time."

His fingers followed his tongue, sinking into her dilatorily, a little at a time; probing gently, drawing the heat, the wetness from her while she shut her eyes in mindless rapture and concentrated and felt the pleasure begin to burn.

Felt the hard length of his body stretch out next to hers, felt him nudge aside her pajama top, run his tongue up the valley of her breasts.

Felt him pause abruptly when he encountered the scarring left by the gunshot wound that had nearly killed her six years ago; felt him shudder and lift his head when she involuntarily sucked air and stiffened. Then, as though he understood her fear, knew it for his own, he tightened his hold around her, and dipped his head to graze his lips in deep, openmouthed, almost-reverent kisses over the entire extent of the jagged tissue before he moved on.

Felt his tongue, warm and moist, tracing the aching swell of first one then the other of her breasts in ever-tightening spirals until there was no place on them left untouched but the hard, tingling crest that wept for his touch.

And then his mouth was *there*, toying, rolling, tormenting…and his fingers were *there*, just inside her entrance where she was most sensitive, his thumb strumming the pearled nubbin just above…. And she was bowing, gasping, rising up from the mattress, fists and heels dug into whatever support they could find, shoulders and head pressed back, throat exposed, body quivering just this side of release.

He couldn't see her, but he knew what she felt like, knew no one had ever trusted him with as much of herself as Hallie. He wanted badly to be inside her, but this time was all hers—payback, returning a gift she'd given him not quite eighteen years ago.

So he moved his fingers, there and there and *there,* felt her tighten impossibly around them; opened his mouth over her breast and, at the same time he thrust his fingers where she was most swollen, sucked her nipple deep into his mouth. She stiffened for an instant, then convulsed around him, muscles contracting in ever-deepening ripples.

His name was a chant on her lips, a cry for mercy, a plea for more; without releasing her breast he rolled onto his back, pulled her astride him. She balanced her hands on his shoulders and moved with mindless intensity, levering herself onto him, pushing him deep and deeper while he suckled first one breast, then the other, tasting the sweetness of letdown, the heady flavor of passion.

The pleasure was intense, almost beyond bearing; certainly, beyond his experience.

"Don't move," he groaned. "Be still, Hallie. I don't want it over so soon."

"Joe," she whispered. "Please, Joe, not now. I can't… It's…"

She swayed forward, eyes closed, and the fight was surrendered to that place of no turning back. When she rolled her hips, he nearly lost it, hung on long enough to bring a hand down between their joined bodies and touch her.

"Yes," she pleaded, frantic now. "Yes. Oh, please. Oh, there-there-*there.*"

The instant hung suspended in the air…. Then Hallie's breath caught, her head fell back and her entire body con-

tracted even more intensely than before, her muscles
spasming deeply, repeatedly....

Beyond thought and control, he wrapped his free arm
around her waist and surged up into her, pumped hard into
her entreaties and contractions, until his own earthquake
rocked him and he was barely conscious himself when she
collapsed on top of him.

Time passed, a collection of harsh breaths, and wits gathering, and senses returning individually to the moment
where everything between them—in ways known and unknown—lay changed.

"Wow," Joe whispered when he had breath to speak.

Hallie's answering laughter was weak and breathy.
"That was incredible."

"It was more than that."

"Yeah." Too drained to lift her head, she moved her
cheek in a nod against his chest. "What are we going to
do about this?"

Joe rubbed his hands possessively up her back, through
her hair, more grateful than ever that the bullet that had
torn up her chest hadn't gone through and taken out her
spine. "More, I hope."

"Now? Because I don't think I want to move yet. You're
a lot more comfortable to lie on than you look."

He laughed, a low, homey rumble under her ear.
"Thanks a bunch. And don't worry. I don't think I *can*
move yet. But as soon as I can…"

"Mmm," Hallie agreed, yawning. "You…hmm…" Another yawn. "You let me know when you can move and
I'm there…."

Her voice trailed off, her breathing deepened, and she
was asleep.

Trapped but happy beneath her, Joe reached carefully for
the quilt that had fallen to one side and, a little at a time,
managed to twitch it over them. When he had Hallie se-

curely covered, he folded one arm tightly around her, bent the other behind his head. His mind, even muzzy with the best sort of exhaustion, still seethed with turmoil, with the uncertainty of an unexpected physical fulfillment he'd half dreamed about for most of a year, and with fear.

So much, too much, impossibly much to happen in one day. So many thoughts going around and around. So many pieces of the puzzle left to find. So many doubts over what to do about Maura and himself. So many concerns about this thing he had yet to finish that would hopefully lay Mary to rest and protect Hallie, Maura and the boys at the same time...

So unbelievably much Hallie in his arms.

He shut his eyes, let the vision of Hallie lying in the hospital kept alive by seemingly more tubes than he could count come to him. While Frank had stood guard, he'd dealt personally with the bastard who'd put her there that time. And they'd only been colleagues, partners, friends then. Now...

He let himself feel her weight, but shut off the restive stirrings of anticipating what tonight might mean to tomorrow. Even so, the stirrings refused to be ignored entirely.

What did he do about her, about this? He sure hadn't intended... Had hoped, but hadn't prepared—

The thought stuck, slammed him full force with the sensation of the viscous stickiness seeping around the area of their joining. Damn. He *really* hadn't prepared. And although he was certain both he and Hallie were healthy, he was also pretty damned sure she wouldn't be taking anything to prevent pregnancy while she was still nursing Maura.

Now what? He wanted her—how he wanted her!—but he wasn't in a position at the moment to commit to anything or anyone besides Maura beyond this momentary act. Even when the object of his desire was his oldest, his best, his most well-loved friend. He couldn't begin to imagine what she'd expect from him now that they'd made love.

His arm tightened convulsively, unconsciously around Hallie. Here he'd just found her again and already he'd probably gone and—literally—screwed things up. If sex didn't change everything, it sure changed your thoughts.

His jaw clenched, muscles ticked, straining to find the right way to undo or redo what he hoped he hadn't just done wrong.

So many devils on his back and too many druthers driving them. Always thin, the fine line between regret and remorse frayed and began to unravel. A big, macho guy like him, and all it took was one tiny little girl, the woman who'd borne her, and a little—well, okay, more than a little—unprotected lovemaking to bring him to his knees, make him question a lifetime of contradictory beliefs, both sides of which urged him to do what was right to avenge the past, protect the future.

What was he going to do?

He turned his head slightly, looking over the sofa arm beside his head. By rights, he had enough to keep him awake trying to sort through it all that he should never be able to sleep again.

But Hallie's weight was warm and solid, as comforting here in sleep as she'd been their first time together, trying to soothe his bruised I-am-a-great-lover-even-though-I've-never-done-it-before machismo. And even when she was part of what was wrong, it seemed she never failed to make things right—especially now, when she still came to him, loved him, trusted him enough to fall asleep on top of him.

His eyelids flickered shut, open; he offered up The Serenity Prayer and relaxed on a sigh. Amazing woman, his incredible friend Hallie.

Again his eyelids fluttered briefly. Outside he could see

the morning lightening, the snow drifting gently passed the windows…

Then he saw nothing but his dreams because he, too, was asleep.

Chapter 10

Morning came—dull gray light above the bright white ground.

Hallie woke to the scratchy sound of Maura's cry coming through the baby monitor, and the sensation of the earth trying to erupt as quietly as possible both within and beneath her body.

Disoriented, she blinked and raised her head. Still half under her, Joe shrugged and offered up an apologetic smile.

"Sorry. I didn't want to wake you."

"Wake me?" She blinked again. Boy, she felt wonderful, but thoroughly and completely bean-brained this morning. Maura through the baby monitor and Joe in her bed didn't make sense. "Why would you wake me? Why—Ooohh."

He moved slightly and her memory returned, trounced disorientation and raised distraction. No wonder she felt so incredibly relaxed. Heat rose in her cheeks when she looked at him, flashed through her breasts and belly when she felt his morning arousal slide reluctantly from the channel between her thighs; her embarrassment and horniness wrapped in a single package.

"I—you—we...slept like that?" she asked carefully.

"Mmm."

"It's possible?"

He thwarted a grin. "Apparently."

"It...it wasn't...uncomfortable for you?"

"Not till you started wiggling around." The grin turned unruly and escaped the bonds he put on it. Frankness was an interesting commodity when you could afford it. First with Hallie, and second, after last night and its possible unforeseen ramifications, he figured he really couldn't afford anything less. "Then I wanted to dump you on your back and wake you in the best way I could think of."

Deliberately or accidentally, she missed the point entirely.

"I *wiggled* and made you..." Mortification stained her neck. She slid away from him and pulled her pajama top closed. "I can't believe...I didn't realize... Jeez, I'm sorry."

"Don't be."

"I tried to warn you. It's been a long time and I—I've sort of forgotten the etiquette of sex and I'm pretty—"

She didn't hear him—and she was having one of her dense mornings. They happened occasionally to mothers—and to uncertain lovers who hadn't been together for a long time. "—out of practice and—"

"Hallie." He shut her up with tongue and lips and with a hand that glided over her breast, then found her fingers and brought them down to wrap around him. Pulled back slightly to make sure she looked him in the eye. "Does this feel like I think your being out of practice is a bad thing?"

She grimaced, unconvinced but hopeful. "Not exactly, no."

"All right then." His grin was all suggestive bad boy—

and bad all the way to the bone at that. "And anyway, it's my fault. I liked it. You can wiggle against me any time you want."

If he intended to make her feel better—although knowing him as long and as well as she had, altruism was doubtful—he failed miserably. Her blush deepened; she pressed her arms across her chest, trying to contain the refreshed ache for him. "Oh, Jeez, Joe. What are you tryin' to do to me? I've got to get up and take care of Maura in a couple of minutes and all you're doing is making me want to stay here and—"

"Hallie." It was a command to shut up, a plea for relief. He pulled her around to face him where he knelt now at the side of the bed, spread her thighs at his waist and rubbed the hardened length of himself against the roughness of the curls above her mound. "Do you know what you saying that does to me? How hard it makes it—"

"Well, yeah." Hallie's maternal instincts abruptly took over as Maura's pronouncement of wakefulness grew more insistent. She shoved Joe back onto his heels and scooted across the bed. "As a matter of fact, I *can* feel how hard it makes you. But I can't play with you anymore right now, Joe. Your daughter needs breakfast." She eyed him, and from a place of forgotten wickedness she'd only ever used to torture Joe—the ability to needle other people came from someplace else entirely—found herself adding, "If she leaves anything, I'll be sure to offer you the leftovers later."

Mouth agape, he stared at her a second too long. How did she do that, go from shy, befuddled, not-used-to-this-kind-of-thing lover to cheerful, sexy, you're-in-for-it-now, tormenting vamp in the blink of an eye—and in the very instant he thought he had her where he wanted her? Then, before he could recover from his own question, Hallie gave him a grin and winked. He made a lunge for her. The metal edge of the sofa-bed frame caught him where it hurt; he grimaced and swore.

Chuckling without sympathy, Hallie rolled quickly out of reach and off the bed on the other side, stooped to collect her pajama bottoms from the floor. "And let that be a lesson to you," she advised.

"A lesson in what?" he grunted. "How to emasculate a man with a sofa?"

More laughter. "Aw, poor Joey," she crooned. "Want me to kiss it and make it better?"

His pain dulled for an instant, replaced by the sudden burn of an erotic image of Hallie on her knees in front of him "making it better."

"Yeah." One step up took him to the center of the mattress. The next took him off the other side. "I do." He made a grab for her. "If you think you can."

"Oh, I can." Laughing, she dodged him, fled to put the bathroom door between them. "But since I'm not sure you'd survive the experience in your present, uh, *condition,* I'm going to be kind and just send you to get your daughter out of bed while I get cleaned up." Then she shut the door in his face and locked it.

His present Hallie-induced "condition" leaving him at a total loss for dignity and decorum, he rattled the knob. "Hallie."

"Sorry, Joe." Her voice through the wood was breezy. "Can't talk. Gotta get ready to feed the baby." He heard the water start to run in the shower, then Hallie's voice at the door for an instant. "You could go talk to her about it. She's a great listener in the morning. Might even have some advice for you."

"Halleluia, damn it!"

Cursing his frustration, he shoved his hands through his hair. He'd better find some protection or other means of relief soon for the craving she roused in him, or being around her would, much sooner than later, kill him.

"Hallie!"

So much for being in control of the situation, he reflected. But that was the way it had always been between
him and Hallie: one moment he punched her buttons, the
next she dragged him around by the— Well, suffice it to
say it was a lifelong cycle between them. Give a little, take
a little; torture a little, get a little of your own back.

Boy-girl, adolescent-adult. Man-woman, sex-love. Competition that had as little to do with actually competing
against each other as it had to do with the battle—and the
accommodations—between their sexes. His body wanted
hers, his heart reluctantly needed her, and thirty years of
friendship made him feel closer to her, love her in some
ways better than anyone else he'd ever known.

The shower curtain rattled and Hallie's voice came out
of a watery distance, cutting into his thoughts.

"Coffee's in the fridge if you want to make some after
you get Maura up," she called. "Now go away and let me
shower in peace."

"Great!" he shouted through the door. Whatever pride
he'd had in his capacity for self-control had gone the way
of his dignity the moment she'd begun to tease him, tan-
talize him, taunt him. "Just great, Thompson. What about
my *piece?*"

A wicked chuckle drifted above the noise of the water.
"Go away, Joe," he thought he heard her say. "This water's damned cold. So, right now if I have to suffer, so do
you."

The cold-water part of her pronouncement brought back
his sense of humor.

"Just 's long's it's both of us," he muttered. Then, grinning, he released the doorknob and went.

As much as he might *want* her, at the moment he and
Hallie had other responsibilities to see to, he reminded himself. His daughter needed him. Or rather, she needed *Hallie,*

but he was first available and he hoped that counted for something.

But it was another lie. Oh, he didn't lie to himself about Maura requiring attention, or about hoping his attention could substitute even briefly for Hallie's, or even about his sense of responsibility to—his instant and irreversible love for—the incredible little being his genes had helped to create. Or about how it was possible to lose his heart so quickly to someone he hadn't even known existed until yesterday... And he had, lock, stock and solid-gold key.

But Maura and the heart she owned were rather beside the point when it came to his body's hankerings, his spirit's needs, his mind's denials and Hallie.

No, in that respect, it was the reasons he couldn't keep standing outside the bathroom door listening to Hallie—the ones he wouldn't let himself think about—that were his lies of omission to himself.

He left because he was afraid if he stood there any longer he'd find himself admitting something to himself about Hallie that finding the scar on her chest during the night had almost caused him to blurt out right then. A claim she held on his heart that, even after a lifetime and a day of knowing her, he was nowhere near ready to name.

Standing in the shower, Hallie scrubbed the scar she'd all but forgotten about until Joe's intensely wordless reminder that it existed.

She'd been half afraid when he'd found the scarring, holding her breath, wondering if it would cause the same reaction in him that it had in Zeke. Her scars had been a fearful, almost living entity that continually said to him, "My job is dangerous, I might not live to grow old with you."

Zeke had never been able to touch or even accept that, even though her life had been threatened and she'd survived. He'd never made love to or cherished a single portion of her body the way Joe had lavished his attentions on her scar.

The memory brought a lump to her throat. Even if the whole thing fell apart on them in the next few hours or days, she was incredibly glad she'd made love with Joe last night.

She'd also been incredibly careless in loving him. She did figure that, Joe being Joe, she'd nothing to worry about where his health was involved. Not to mention that even to her limited experience he hadn't exactly behaved like a man who'd, um, been, er, regularly *gettin' any*.

Not that she could know with absolute certainty, of course. Hallie had made love with two men in her life, and he was one of them. However, she'd still be willing to bet it didn't even occur to him to keep condoms in his truck, "in case," or that he'd ever particularly considered sex with the single stranger at all in the last twelve months.

He was too much a man on a mission, and Mary had occasionally complained—inappropriately, Hallie had always thought, that when Joe was obsessed with a case, Mary sometimes found it difficult to, well, "get his attention" at all.

One more illustration, Hallie reflected sadly, of how it took two to make or break a marital trust. Zeke had often complained to her about the same thing.

And in the end, despite his ability to trust her not to take another lover, it had taken a whole lot more self-assurance than Zeke possessed to stay married to her.

Especially after she'd been shot.

But that was another thought entirely. The point of this self-discourse being that whether it was her and Zeke, or Joe and Mary, the appearance of perfection in a relationship was a curious phenomenon. It was perhaps not quite a lie, but it was never the entire truth, either.

It was also a good lesson to look to right now while the engram of last night's perfection and this morning's seductive byplay still muddied her senses, Hallie realized. And in consequence, she would be well-advised to consider her mother's favorite bastardized axiom, ''Bed 'im in haste, repent at leisure,'' before she spent any more time throwing herself into Joe Martinez's arms.

Or trying to keep him—wrapped up safely with his daughter—in hers.

In the long run, sex—even when she was sure it was *not* sex, but making love—would hardly be the thing that stopped Joe from trying to take Maura from her. Nor would it be the thing that reminded him to trust her enough to stop guarding whatever secrets he still kept from her about Mary's death.

But on the other hand, loving him physically was an amazing experience, and if the only way she could love him right now was to take him into her bed—when the boys weren't around, she qualified—she'd do it again in a heartbeat.

Or less.

She had—as she vaguely remembered him admitting to her *about* her when he thought she couldn't hear him because she was unconscious and fighting for her life after that nearly point-blank-in-the-chest shooting—owned his beating heart for thirty years, after all.

But the memories from her coma were faint and perhaps only unreliable, six-year-old dreams to which she should never pay attention.

Especially now.

Blowing out a breath of shower spray and unresolve, she swiped the last of the shampoo out of her hair. Cleaned up and—hopefully—back in control of herself, she shut off the water and climbed out of the shower. Toweled off and dug a clean nursing bra out of the basket of laundry atop the dryer. Somewhere the other side of the door she heard Joe descend the stairs, promising an apparently happy Maura the sun, the moon and breakfast in whatever order his daughter preferred. Maura's response was loud and thoroughly engaging, and Hallie listened as Joe laughed and talked nonsense, made wistful wishes about those things he couldn't yet promise Maura.

And made Hallie's heart wrench a little out of place, and start to bleed.

Mechanically she began dressing. Found some purple cotton underpants and pulled them on. Followed the panties with a button-front violet satin camisole, a long-sleeved violet Egyptian-cotton blouse and a pair of women's Dockers pants.

Lord, how would she ever be able to take his daughter from him? Even assuring herself that keeping Maura was well and away the rightest thing to do for the infant, how could she possibly do it to Joe? How could she begin to contemplate the machinations and manipulations of a custody battle—the unwhole truths she'd be forced to speak— if he decided to pursue one?

She couldn't. At this age, it might not be too hard on Maura, but it could destroy Ben and Sam. It wouldn't do much for her, either. And Joe...

Jeez. She blinked, unanticipated emotion cluttering an issue that couldn't be solved by it. She didn't know. Despite their shared years, last night's closeness, she hadn't a clue what warring with her over what was best for his daughter would do to Joe.

Or to their relationship—whatever that relationship might currently be.

From somewhere deep down inside, half a sob rose and got stuck in her throat.

"Hallie?" Joe knocked on the door. "If you're ready for the kid, I'll make Mexican omelettes while you feed her."

"Uh...yeah. Okay." Hallie sniffed, grabbed a hunk of toilet tissue and dabbed at her uncharacteristically weepy eyes and runny nose. Damned postpartum hormones, anyway. Made you cry over anything and everything almost more than pregnancy hormones did. "Sounds good. Be right there."

She gave her nose a final swipe, patted her eyes with a cool washcloth, smoothed down her clothes and took a last look in the mirror. Her eyes looked a little bleary, but they weren't bloodshot and her nose wasn't quite red. So, okay. Not perfect, but passable. Certainly good enough to fake it through breakfast with Joe Martinez.

That was, she reminded herself—and her eyes once more teared up for absolutely no reason she could think of—if she would ever be able to fake anything with Joe Martinez again.

When she opened the bathroom door and joined him in the kitchen, he took one look at her and asked, "What's wrong?"

She ducked her head to hide the latest surge of tears, moved over to where he'd tucked Maura comfortably into her infant recliner on the counter so she could talk to him while he chopped tomatoes, peppers and onions.

"Nothing."

Blast it anyway, she was going to have her damned tear ducts removed if this didn't stop. Lieutenant sheriffs didn't have time to cry—especially not when they had kids to raise and protect, and photographer stalkers-who-might-also-be-murderers to catch.

"Hallie, are you crying?"

"What, me? I never cry." The tears streamed. "Absolutely not."

Joe quit cutting vegetables, wiped his hands on the towel he'd tucked inside his gym shorts as an apron and stooped low enough to get a good look at her.

"You *are* crying."

"No, I'm not." She bent over Maura, playing with the infant's fists.

"Don't lie to me, Hallie." Joe hooked one long index finger around her chin, made her face him.

"Okay." Her temper blazed, brought fresh tears. She shoved his finger off her chin, backed up and, hands on hips, glared at him. "I'm crying, you great oaf. Happy now?"

"No."

He reached for her, uneasy with this never-before-seen view of Hallie, but ready to gather her up and make a difference if he could. She slapped him away, warded him off to a stiff distance.

"It's just hormones. It doesn't mean anything and if you'll quit tryin' to be nice to me, it'll stop."

"What made it start?"

It was the wrong question, but it took a moment for him to realize that.

"You, you big jerk," Hallie said. Then, when she couldn't hold them in any longer, she turned her back on Joe and the sobs poured loose.

"Aw, man, Hallie…"

Again he attempted to touch her; again she yanked away.

"Don't, God bless it, Joe. Don't touch me."

"I'm not going to touch you, damn it, Hallie." He stepped around in front of her and opened his arms. "I'm going to hold you, then I'm going to find out what I did to bring this on."

"No," she insisted, vehemence clogged by tears. "I will not let you do this to me. I won't do it to you."

"Too late," Joe said gently. "Already done."

She watched him through streaming eyes. His shirtfront beckoned, his solidness called, his desire to comfort even though he didn't know why she needed comforting—how could he when she didn't know herself?—undid her. She couldn't bear it.

"Damn you to hell, Joe," she gulped, then walked into his embrace and wept.

He folded his arms about her and hauled her close, pressed her into his shoulder, kissed the crown of her head—and watched his daughter kick her feet and wave her fists, blow bubbles and coo.

And got an inkling of what might be bothering Hallie's maternal hormones this morning: Maura, clean and simple. Him taking the baby from her if it came to a fight. And the trouble was, he couldn't tell Hallie it wouldn't come to that because in all truth he couldn't, with any certainty, tell Hallie anything.

He'd barely been back a day, after all.

So he charged himself with the better part of valor and, in a move of what for him was abnormal wisdom where Hallie was concerned, kept his mouth shut.

For five minutes she dampened his shirt, then she lifted her head, snuffled once and backed out of his arms. He let her go reluctantly. Holding Hallie, he understood with some trepidation, could easily become a vice, a habit, an addiction.

"That's enough of *that*," she said firmly, grabbed a tissue from the counter and blew her nose.

"You going to tell me what brought this on or shall I guess?" Joe asked gently.

She offered him a watery smile. "Neither."

"Hallie." He caught her hand. "Talk to me."

She squeezed his fingers, wiped her nose. "If I can ever make it make sense to *me*, Joe, we can talk about it. Until then it'd be noise. Besides—" her tone grew brisk "—Maura's waited long enough for her breakfast. Come on, Maurie-Mae, let's go eat." She picked the bubble-blowing infant out of her baby seat and headed off toward the living room with her, calling over her shoulder as she went, "After that, I'll call in and see where we stand on the snow, then we'll see what we can come up with on your pictures."

"No," Joe corrected her firmly. "First you feed Maura, then I feed you, then—"

She was back in front of him on his first "then," stopped him on the second when she leaned over Maura in her seat, reached up and gave the dumbfounded Joe a lingering—and thoroughly scorching—kiss on the mouth.

"Then," she agreed softly. "Now is bad, but *then* I can handle."

Then she was gone again, down the hall and around the corner into the living room. Within moments he heard her chatting with the baby, telling Maura stories, singing her a Finnish nonsense song taught to her by her maternal grandmother about a grasshopper combing its hair with a rake, soothing her with a Cajun lullaby Joe had heard her sing to Sam and Ben when they were small.

His jaw set, he looked across the pass-through opening between the kitchen and dining room, found the photos they'd left on the table last night. Some things took no time at all to decide, and this was one of them.

He couldn't take Maura from Hallie.

Emotion stung his eyes, tightened the corners of his mouth.

He wouldn't.

As for himself and the rest of it—he'd taken that vow a long time ago. However long and wherever it took him, Mary's killer would go down. Whatever she'd done to him—hell, for all he knew, whatever she'd done that he himself had driven her to—he owed both her and his sense of duty to her memory; he owed their daughter that much.

But the oath he took now over Hallie's cutting board was different than the one he'd taken at Mary's grave; more selfish, more personal, and potentially more costly because it involved more than his machismo or sense of honor.

It involved knowing exactly how far he'd go, how many laws he'd break without thinking—once, let alone twice—

to make sure no one hurt the only mother Maura would ever know.

The only woman he could imagine wanting in his bed.

The cutting board rattled beneath the furious motion of the knife cleaving neatly, easily through the tomatoes.

He didn't know what promises he could make if last night's carelessness wrought consequences, but he knew this: the guy who'd shot Hallie had only done so because she was the law and he was desperate. But the reasons in that circumstance hadn't mattered to Joe, only the consequence. And Hallie downed for doing her job was unacceptable to all of the codes by which Joe lived, so he'd dispensed his own bruising view of justice in that situation accordingly.

A stalker, however, was different. Stalking took planning, involved studying, learning, becoming intimately—if distantly—a part of your prey's daily life. He understood this from experience; stalking was part of hunting, and hunting humans was what he did.

He also knew that stalkers couldn't maintain their distance, that in order for the excitement to increase, they had to get closer.

And possibly become more dangerous.

Which to him meant only one thing. Whatever it took, Hallie's stalker, like Mary's killer—*her* stalker?—was going down, too.

Guaranteed.

The phones were down, the snowplow came through and pushed the snow out of the street into the driveway, and the snowblower—inanimate object though it was—had apparently decided to give itself a holiday.

Fortunately the power hadn't gone out, but Hallie knew better than to count her chickens over that yet.

Breakfast was strained with silences, filled with the things Joe couldn't decide how to say and the things Hallie chose not to. Yet, in spite of the awkwardness, it was also coated with intimacies: laughter shared over Maura's apparent delight in bouncing in her doorway jumper while George lay patiently beneath her feet cushioning the impact; touches that "just friends" might never note, but that lovers not only noted, but relished, courted and lured.

Glances that measured, made cautious offers, intimated desires.

Kisses that somehow couldn't be avoided, because despite their private thoughts, Hallie knew their bodies were in perfect attunement. Her lips seemed to know exactly when Joe's mouth would be even remotely in the vicinity and how to finagle Hallie's finding and meeting it.

It was during one of these moments that the garage-to-living-room door opened and Zeke stepped into the house.

Startled, Hallie looked away from Joe. Joe rose to stand protectively behind her, his hands on her shoulders.

"Zeke."

"Damn it, Hallie."

Hallie's jaw clenched, a muscle ticked in her cheek. Joe's hands tightened painfully on her shoulders; she glanced up at him, found the same tension reflected on his face that she felt in her own. The look he sent her also suggested he'd be happy to field Zeke right into a snowdrift. She shook her head slightly, warning him not to interfere in her divorce.

"What are you doing here?" she asked. "The roads should be closed."

He shrugged. "They are, but I've got the snowmobiles. Dropped the boys off at your mother's and came by to make sure everything's okay. Your phone's out."

Exasperation made Hallie miss the point. "God bless it, Zeke. We're divorced. You don't get to be territorial—"

Alert to trouble, Joe covered her mouth with a hand. "What'd you mean 'your' phone's out?" he asked. "Isn't everyone's?"

Zeke shook his head. "No. At least," he amended, "not Hallie's parents' or mine or the department's. Phone company hasn't had too many complaints about lines down— none around here. Frank's been trying to reach you—" he looked at Hallie "—since seven. Can't figure why, if you're house phone's dead he couldn't reach your cell phone or your radio. He got worried. I could get here first, but I imagine he and half the department'll be here before long. Said you guys are workin' on somethin' with Joe that can't wait on snow removal—"

He caught sight of the photos on the dining table and stopped. Walked over and touched them almost absently at first, then with growing alarm. He looked at his ex-wife. "What're these?"

Hallie pulled Joe's hand away from her mouth. "Joe's vacation pictures?"

The attempt at humor fell short.

Zeke's patience fell with it. He fingered the picture of Maura and the boys, picked up the one with the welcome home message to Joe printed on it. His jaw tensed and clicked audibly. "Who took these?"

"We don't know." She shrugged her mouth. "It's what we're working on today."

"These pictures of Mary?"

"We, uh…" She glanced up at Joe. His mouth tightened, but he nodded. "We think maybe the same person was taking pictures of Mary before she died."

"I see."

"I don't think you do," Joe began, but Zeke swung on him.

"No, you're the kind of guy who doesn't think," he told Joe angrily. "You're the kind who imagines he's taking care of business when he's running away, who puts my kids in danger by coming back to town—"

"Zeke," Hallie warned.

"And keeps them up half the night askin' me if Maura will still be here when they get home—"

"Zeke, stop it." Hallie rose, moved between her ex and Joe to pick a starting-to-cloud-over Maura out of her jumper. "You're scaring Maura."

"I'm sorry, Hallie." Zeke slumped onto one of the long benches at the table. "It's just he's got the boys worried. And then I walk in here and—"

"Yeah." Hallie grimaced. "I know. Scary pictures and us kissing."

She looked at Joe—a question without words, a suggestion between partners. A smile ghosted his features and faded to something grimmer; he nodded.

"If you don't need me I think I'll go see if I can figure out what's wrong with the phones," he said and disappeared. A moment later the basement door whined opened and closed.

Swaying Maura on her hip, Hallie eyed Zeke.

"Relax, Hallie," Zeke advised. "I didn't expect anything. I just knew that sooner or later…" He paused, shrugged. "Hell, we *all* figured that sooner or later, you and Joe…"

Another pause while Hallie fumed, muttering things like, "This better be good, Thompson. Better be good."

"Okay." Zeke pursed his lips, expelled a breath. "It's like this. Everybody always knew you and Joe had a thing—"

"A what?" Maura startled and began to cry. Hallie swayed again and lowered her voice, repeated, "A what?"

"A thing," Zeke said patiently. "A crush, affection, more than friendship—whatever you want to call it. You just never had it at the same time, and you never let it get away from you, but it was always there. Bothered Mary all to hell."

"It—bothered— What?"

Zeke nodded. "Why do you think she always wanted to

keep you so close? She was never sure she could trust you with Joe.''

''But I—we—never would have even—didn't even realize—''

''*I* know. Knew.'' One shoulder rose and fall. ''Mary...didn't.''

''She talked to you?''

There was a long hesitation, a moment to consider. Then Zeke nodded. ''She was my patient.''

Chapter 11

Hallie stared at her ex-husband. Joe's wife, Zeke's patient. The whole thing got curiouser and curiouser.

Or a lot more tangled, depending upon how you looked at it.

Or maybe not. As a psychologist, Zeke occasionally had members of the local law-enforcement community sent to him for evaluation or referral. The evaluations he made as a courtesy, but even when asked, he generally refused to take on members of the sheriff's department as clients. He didn't, he always said, like to treat friends or people he saw socially. Especially not people who worked with Hallie. Too much possibility, he told them, for conflict of interest.

Hallie would have thought that attitude doubled where accepting Mary as a patient was concerned.

"What do you mean?" she asked carefully. "That Mary asked to see you once in the office? Or that you saw her regularly?"

Zeke's jaw worked; Hallie watched him consider patient

confidentiality, weigh it against the fact Mary had been dead for nearly a year.

"I saw her regularly," he acknowledged finally. "After you and I divorced. The last three, maybe four years of her life—since she lost the second baby."

Hallie looked at him, watched his mouth twist almost defensively under her scrutiny. Then his face relaxed, shrugged philosophically with his shoulders.

"She needed to talk to someone professional and, given her own job, she said she wasn't sure who else to trust. You know Mary. Give the sensible advice to other people, but don't keep it for yourself."

That, Hallie decided, given her unfortunate new knowledge of Mary, would be an understatement. And, although she hadn't seen Zeke's file on Joe's late wife, she'd almost be willing to bet that an overview of Mary's sessions would reveal that her friend had chosen to manipulate—er, "trust"—Zeke because of his own relationship to Hallie and Joe.

Her mouth hardened against her sense of judgment. Sometimes she really hated the cynical, draw-quick-conclusions, cop side of herself.

"How often did she see you?"

Reluctantly Zeke thought back and gave up a little more of Mary's puzzle. "Once a week, occasionally more."

"More than once a week?" Hallie said, aghast. "Things were that bad for her and I never knew? *Joe* never knew? How is that possible?"

"She spent her life in denial, Hallie. She was thirty-two when she died. That's a long time to pretend things are different than your nerves say they are without being able to believe in it yourself. Hell." Zeke gave her his I've-seen-it-all-too-often face. "She only came to me because the depression after the miscarriage was more than she could handle by herself and she didn't want to burden Joe."

He shook his head regretfully. "I told her more than once

that I didn't think I was medically qualified to treat her by
myself. But to her, seeing a specialist would have meant
she was truly sick instead of just—'' he laughed without
humor ''—'depressed.' Like depression isn't its own symptom—''

"You didn't tell her she should maybe talk to Joe or at
least to me?" Hallie interrupted. "Maybe in a session? All
of us together?" She'd heard Zeke's thoughts on the subject of clients who refused to believe the symptom wasn't
the whole disease more than enough. "I'd have gotten as-
signed another partner, transferred departments, anything."

"I know. I told her, Hallie. She couldn't believe...
confronting you or Joe would accomplish anything." He
sighed, a psychologist who couldn't help a patient unwilling or unable to accept what she needed to accept in order
to help herself. "She couldn't believe talking to you didn't
have to *be* confrontation. From what I understood, in her
experience honesty destroyed relationships, so she talked
about everything *but* what she needed to." Behind the an-
alyst's impersonal mask lay sadness. Trying to help Mary
must have cost him more than he'd admit. "I think she
would have played Little Mary Sunshine until it killed her
if she hadn't died first."

Hallie breathed, gathering the reins of knowledge, trying
to ignore the shape the puzzle pieces that made up the other
side of Mary were forming.

"Did Joe know she'd seen you at all? Even once?" The
question was taut with the effort to sound natural, controlled. Sessions with a psychologist that you didn't tell
your spouse about seemed like a lie that could affect the
health and welfare of a marriage deeply.

"I don't know." Zeke shook his head. "She never mentioned telling him, so I don't think so."

"Okay." She nodded, thoughtful, sad, reluctantly aware
of how many other divergent pathways might have led to
Mary's death than even Joe could have guessed. And de-

terminedly mindful of the possibility of how little Joe could be trusted to play it straight in his need to protect Mary's memory among the families. Especially if his need to hide Mary's foibles was as strong as Hallie thought—or until he was given no other choice, or it was too late.

A word she used only when she was out among the guys rose to mind unbidden. One hell of a night had sure turned into one great bitch of a morning—in more ways than one.

Beside her, George rose, thrust his forepaws straight out in front of him in a long stretch, then came over and reached up to nose the bare spot between Maura's hiked-up pant leg and her bootee. The baby jumped excitedly in her arms and Hallie bounced her lightly, absently talking to her about the dog while her mind wended its way elsewhere.

If Joe didn't know about Mary's sessions with Zeke, therein could lie any number more of the needed puzzle pieces that would help them to bring this wannabe nightmare into perspective. She chewed the inside of her cheek. It might also provide her with some idea of what Joe was hiding from her, and possibly from himself.

She glanced through the kitchen pass-through, listened to make sure Joe wasn't yet returning from the basement, and eyed Zeke.

"You think you could step back far enough from the fact Ben and Sam are in some of these pictures to take 'em and give me your professional opinion of who this person might be or what he's capable of?"

"Oh, gee, Hal." His entire face shrugged. "Aside from the kids being some of the subjects, I'm a sit-down-and-I'll-listen-while-you-spill-your-guts therapist, not a profiler. I'd need a lot more information to render a decent opinion than a handful of pictures with a couple of strange notes on 'em."

"Even though Mary was the first subject *and* one of your patients, *and* I tell you everything Joe told me about what he found out about Mary that even as her therapist you might not know?''

"Hmm." He looked thoughtful. "I suppose maybe. I can't guarantee absolute accuracy, but I know a couple of people...."

Hallie nodded. "Just keep it quiet, huh? I've got a strange feeling about this."

"That you won't share with me," Zeke said.

Hallie smiled grimly. The more timid bits and pieces she learned about her late friend, the more it seemed that each of the men Mary took into her life had been given different ingredients of her psyche to hold on to and keep separate from any of the rest. As though perhaps, as Zeke suggested, if they were all put together in one place, an explosion of unwanted proportions might occur.

"That I'm not sharing with Joe yet, either," she said.

"Ah, well." Zeke grinned. "At least then I don't feel so bad."

Hallie laughed, a deep, no-longer-bitter sound of acceptance of the things that had not worked in her marriage. "Did you ever?"

He shook his head. "Probably not. But then, analyzing my way out of every argument—"

"'Argument' was *my* word for them," Hallie reminded him, grinning. "You called it 'discussion.'"

"Fine," he agreed, smiling back. "Every 'discussion' we had was my part of screwing up our marriage."

"Yeah." She nodded. "And wanting to confront and fix everything was mine."

"Joe'd suit you better in that regard."

The remark was offhand, unexpected and took a moment to register.

"What?" Astounded, she stared at him.

Zeke shrugged. "You always argued about everything because you enjoyed the debate. You were honest with each other to a fault, you told each other everything including things most people won't tell their analysts. And instead of making you worse friends and partners, it made you better. Extrapolate the rest of a possible relationship from there. I did.''

''You—what?'' Even more dumbfounded, her mouth agape, Hallie stared at him. ''You *extrapolated* a relationship for me and...'' The question petered out as disbelief flared into outrage. ''Tell me, *Dr.* Thompson, were you still married to me at the time you did this *extrapolating?*''

''Briefly.''

The desire to sink to wronged-fifties-movie-heroine depths and slap the man for his thoughtless stupidity rose in Hallie for the first time in her life.

''You unbelievable bastard.''

He nodded. ''I think you called me that back then, too.''

She gave him ''huffy.'' ''Because it was true, no doubt.''

He grinned. ''No doubt.''

They measured each other in silence for a moment; not for the first time, Hallie was glad that the marriage hadn't gotten in the way of the divorce. Then she drew a breath and shifted gears, returning to her immediate concern.

''I want to look at her file.''

''What?'' It was Zeke's turn to look nonplused. ''Whose file? Mary's? Hallie, you know I can't—''

''Yeah, yeah,'' she agreed impatiently. ''Client confidentiality. Save it, Zeke. You can't break confidence with the dead. And there might be information in it to protect the living. And that includes our sons and this baby, Zeke, so—'' She broke off.

Joe's heavy step sounded on the basement stairs. She swept her free hand at the spread of pictures on the table.

''I'll get copies and fax 'em to your private machine? Nobody sees 'em but you?''

''Sure.'' He nodded. ''But about Mary's file...''

''I've gotta have it, Zeke. If Joe's telling me the truth,

it's taken him a year to come up with practically nothing. I need to see the file.''

The basement doorknob rattled; Hallie watched Zeke, waiting.

He hesitated, breathed deep, and reluctantly, silently assented.

Hallie patted his arm. ''Thanks,'' she whispered and turned to greet Joe.

His face, when he appeared in the dining-room doorway, was somber.

''Your phone line's been cut inside the house,'' he said.

Reconnection was a simple matter of pulling the excess phone wire across the basement ceiling to the wall, poking it through the foundation—and the snow—and hooking it up to the box outside.

With Zeke's I-have-no-idea-what-I'm-doing help, repairs were quick and relatively painless.

Except that even when completed, the phones still didn't work.

It was Hallie's turn, then, to come up with the simple thought of handing Maura to Joe and pulling the kitchen phone off the wall. Sure enough, in the easiest sabotage possible, besides cutting the line near the external source in the basement, the phone had also been unplugged from its wall socket. The same proved true of the phone in Hallie's bedroom, and the one in the downstairs library-cum-office-cum-guest-room.

As far as her police radio and cell phone were concerned, the power sources had been removed from them, too, and the charger for her extra cell-phone battery was also unplugged, the battery discharged. Finding this, a strange and disturbing connective thought occurred to her. Grabbing her jacket, she went out to the garage and lifted the hood of her minivan.

Oh, yeah, there it was. She sucked air between her teeth

and swore under her breath. The distributor cap was missing.

Furious, she spun about, forced herself to examine the garage, and not to succumb to fury's blindness.

Figuring that, like the phones, this would be another of those nasty Halloween-like pranks that would cause frustration at best and time lost in an emergency at worst, she searched up, down, and around the garage for the distributor cap, making herself look and not miss the obvious set-it-aside places just because they were. The cap wasn't far away, merely sitting squarely in the open on the window-sill, not quite hidden by Joe's truck parked in the garage beside hers; but it was out of the van nevertheless.

Anger edging the corners of her mouth, Hallie plucked the cap from the window ledge and turned it over in her hands several times, examining it, before she replaced it in the van. Finished, she turned to glance soberly at Joe, who was standing just inside between the interior house door and the screen door that opened onto the garage landing; Maura sat snugly in the crook of his arm, an afghan covering her against the chill. When Hallie caught his eye, he set his jaw and nodded; handed Maura over to Zeke behind him and stepped into the garage, closing the inside door after himself.

"Everything worked before we left to pick up your man," she said without preamble.

"You had no reason to move the van once you got home from work yesterday?"

"No." She shook her head. "And I didn't use it last night because I was with you in the truck."

"I remember," Joe said wryly. "I was having a hard time keeping my attention on the road because of it."

"Yeah, well, hmm." Hallie looked at him. "We can discuss our mutual distractions at another time, okay? Right now we've got this—"

Sudden noise interrupted her train of thought. From out-

side the garage came the definitive buzz of a multiple-
snowmobile chorus accompanied by the distinctive bass
roar of at least one of the county's four-by-four Suburbans
and the basso-profundo thunder of something that sounded
suspiciously familiar, but which Hallie had no desire to
identify at the moment. The entire orchestra rumbled to a
halt in Hallie's driveway. Zeke opened the living-room
door and poked his head into the garage.

"Company," he announced.

"Company?" Joe looked at Hallie.

She regarded him innocently.

"Hallie…"

"Welll—" She tipped her head, acknowledging his tone.
"Timing's bad, you're right," she said. "But last night,
before… Well, *before,* you made me so mad I couldn't
resist."

Suspicion sharpened his gaze. "What have you done?"

She folded her hands behind her back. "Well…"

"We've covered *well,*" Joe advised her.

She made a face, narrowed her eyes, calculated the moment, the words key to it. Thought of some. Brightened.

"You know that old saying about there being safety in
numbers?" she asked.

"Hallie." Not her name, a command.

She nodded, regarded the exterior garage door, picked
her moment to coincide with its raising and Joe's first view
of a vast array of snow-booted feet beneath it.

"I called Gabriella last night and told her you were
home."

Calling his sister Gabriella, Joe decided not for the first
time, was often tantamount to issuing an open invitation to
be visited at will by the plague or Murphy's Law. You
simply didn't do it unless you really had a grudge against
a man—which he supposed defined Hallie's use of his I'll-
arrange-the-party-just-tell-me-when-and-where-you-don't-

want-it-and-I'll-be-sure-everybody-comes sister to welcome him home in style.

Although he doubted very much that even Hallie would have meant to have Gabriella's sense of the impromptu descend upon them before lunch on a snow day.

He sighed. Family was a wonderful commodity—except when you'd been away too long without either their approval or sending them at least a postcard.... Well, if your family was large and close and you did that, you'd better be prepared to come back and find them all staring you down, waiting for an immediate explanation.

Or most of them, anyway.

Ranged at the yawning mouth of Hallie's garage, he counted at least three of his sisters and their husbands, two of his brothers and their wives, nieces and nephews too many to count, his mother and father, his-uncle-the-priest, Mary's mother, Hallie's mother and Ben and Sam—and Frank and four of the other guys from Fugitive Apprehension, Hallie's captain—hardly a good sign, that—and four deputies, two of whom, Crompton and Montoya, he'd met last night.

"Surprise," Hallie said.

"Oh, it is," Joe agreed darkly—and with some menace. "You planned this."

"Not for this morning, obviously. But since they're here…"

"Communications out from the inside," he mused, nodding, catching her drift immediately. Amazing how rapidly they could fall into the old habit of apparently telepathic exchange without missing a beat, but even for the densest investigator this one had to be a gimme: whoever had cut wires, unplugged phones and removed the distributor cap obviously had easy access to the house. Possibly even while Hallie or the deps who'd baby-sat Maura last night were in it. "Family here, safety in numbers and you get to do a little snooping while I get chewed out by fifty people who just happen to be able to get here even though the rest of the county's shut down because of last night's blizzard.''

Hallie beamed at him, a visual pat on the head if ever he'd seen one.

''Basically,'' she said. ''Aren't snowmobiles wonderful things?''

''Yeah, absolutely,'' he agreed dryly. ''And the fact that one of my brothers works for the road commission and plowed the route is pretty useful, too, huh?''

She fluttered her lashes at him. ''We do what we can.''

''So it would seem,'' he muttered, then bent his head to make sure the threat he was about to make was heard by her ears alone. ''Bat those lashes at me again and I'll back you up against my truck and kiss you so hard, your mother's eyeballs will pop and your clothes will fall off by themselves.''

''That could be interesting,'' Hallie murmured, turned her back and stepped in front of him, brushed her hand surreptitiously over his crotch. His jeans promptly got way too tight; he bit back a groan and contained similar retaliation with an effort. ''But like this,'' she continued without missing a beat, ''hardly useful at the moment.''

Then she stepped forward and braced herself to catch Ben and Sam, who hurled themselves excitedly through the garage to greet her.

''Mom, Mom!'' Sam, rosy cheeked and sparkly eyed, nearly beside himself with eagerness. ''Guess how we got here!''

''In Uncle David's—'' Joe's road-commission brother ''—snowplow!'' Ben exclaimed before Hallie had a chance to guess. ''He stopped at Grandma's and said everybody was coming here—''

''—and Grama made us put on all these clothes—'' Sam indicated the scarves, hats, doubled mittens, snowmobile suits with thermal socks pulled over the legs showing above their boots. Having grown up with her mother, Hallie was pretty certain this was only the top layer; that if she looked, she'd find at least two or three more layers underneath. "Coz she said it's a lot colder riding on a snowplow—"

"So we wore even more clothes than we did when Dad drove us over to her house on the snowmobile—"

"And we're having a family reunion for Uncle Joe—"

"An' Uncle David says maybe he and Uncle Rob—" Joe's other present older brother, Roberto, the family ACLU attorney "—can beat some sense into him about Maura—"

"And we said," Sam finished, "we thought that would be good—"

But as usual, Ben put in the final word. "If you didn't already do it for them." He looked up at his mother, confident in his perception of her capabilities, and Joe's less obvious frailties. "Did you?"

"No." Hallie shook her head. "I did not *beat* sense into him. I never beat sense into anyone. I persuade. Nicely. With words only. You know that."

"Oh, right." Ben nodded, not the least disappointed. "I forgot. Did you *persuade* him, then?"

Hallie glanced at Joe. His eyes were hooded, his mouth hooked slightly upward without telling her anything.

He knew what he'd force himself to say eventually, but he couldn't say or show it now.

She slid her fingers into the crook of his hand and squeezed, offering, he thought—feeling instantly humbled—understanding and comfort without censure or disillusion. Then she returned her attention to Ben.

"We're still talking," she said lightly, and Joe's heart clenched.

"Talking's good." Ben nodded sagely, the eight-year-old son of a psychologist and a law-enforcement officer who'd spent more than a little of her career talking people out of doing things they shouldn't do, or into doing things they should. "Talking means there's hope." He tipped his head back to see Hallie's face. "Right, Mom?"

"Right, sport," Zeke said from the doorway. "Hallie, could I see you a minute? Joe, why don't you and the boys bring the family in and let's get this party on the road."

It was a wonderful way for the kids to spend a snow day.

With plenty of their peers to play with, Hallie's boys were in their element as hosts. Instead of stopping to bring Joe's nieces and nephews—and, he noted, a few neighborhood strays—into the house, they let George out, then, without any urging, led the thundering herd of youngsters straight through the garage's back door and into the yard. Within minutes snow forts, snowmen—and women and other creatures—and snow battles were in progress, divesting the local world of its snow-insulated cocoon of silence.

Joe had a moment's heartbeat-skip when he realized neither he nor Hallie had picked up the pictures on the dining-room table, but when he looked, they were gone. He raised a brow at Hallie and cocked his head toward the table the first time he got her attention. She gave him a quick thumbs-up *Got 'em* and disappeared after Zeke into the room that had once been the parish office and impromptu confessional. Within minutes, Frank and two more members of the FAT squad followed, shutting the door behind them.

Being deliberately left out of the meeting gave Joe an odd feeling—especially knowing that Zeke was part of it. What part, he had no idea, but he really didn't think it would change how he felt about it. Zeke was in, he was out. Territory—for the moment—established.

He didn't have long to contemplate what might be happening behind the closed door, however, before his family pounced on him.

Individually and collectively they cornered him, offering unsought opinions, advice and chastisements, advice on how they felt he should go on from here, condolences he'd never given them a chance to tender in the days and weeks following Mary's death when their sympathy would have been appropriate. In short, without putting it into so many words, they let him know how much he'd denied not only himself but them a year ago. They'd needed the chance to grieve with him, to celebrate with him through their tears when Hallie had learned the embryo transplant had indeed taken and she was carrying not only his, but Mary's, child.

But they didn't know what he knew about Mary, nor would he ever tell them. Kindness, as he'd learned for himself while searching for Mary's burial shoes, often lay in what you didn't disclose, rather than in what you did.

There were other discoveries to be made, by him about his family. He'd missed a lot of events in the last year: confirmations, communions, baptisms....

Maura, of course, was not the only new Martinez to arrive during his absence. Both of the sisters who hadn't made this gathering were home with babies born within the past month; his one absent brother, Luis, and David had little ones six and eight months old respectively. Which meant the conversation turned to labor stories a lot sooner than Joe might have wished—that is, if he'd wished to hear labor-and-delivery stories at all.

The stories were, he decided, gritting his teeth and bearing it—albeit not graciously—just another way to pay him back for not being around to witness Maura's birth.

Everyone got in on the act. His mother, his sisters, sisters-in-law, Mary's mother, Hallie's mother—his father, his brother and his-uncle-the-priest who Joe couldn't fathom why he knew labor stories; the female deputy he hadn't met last night, the male deputy he had; Hallie's captain, noncommittal about everything but this; and the guys from FAT who were out here watching him instead of inside that blasted office with Hallie.

The stories were, naturally, all horror stories of one sort

or another. It was not, in Joe's opinion, an illuminating experience. Until Hallie's mother finally looked him in the eye and told him about Maura's birthday and how Hallie had, for months prior, insisted they videotape the event just in case there came a time when Joe might want to view what he'd missed.

At that point it was all Joe could do to swallow the sudden lump in his throat, to breathe in and out with lungs gone too tight to take in enough air; to try to appear natural when it felt like someone had reached inside his chest, grabbed his heart and squoze it.

Claustrophobia set in. He tried to find space to collect his thoughts, but everywhere he turned, he stumbled over someone else who had something to say to him.

At one point he even found himself turning in a circle, literally head and shoulders above the crowd but unable to spot a direct means of escape.

It felt like he was back in Catholic grammar school, shuffling down the corridor of do don't-do, should shouldn't, seeking footing on the treacherous path of faith and ideals while bearing the weight of his grown-up cynicism. The way here was thick with the stumbling blocks of do-the-right-thing-for-what-might-later-prove-the-wrong-reason.

Someone—Mary's mother? His?—handed him Maura to change. Someone else—Hallie's mother? One of his sisters?—whisked her away, carted her off, saying the infant was tired and needed a nap. He wanted to go after the woman and tell her he'd take care of Maura.

But whoever it was, was gone too quickly, and he was suddenly not sure if he really was capable.

It didn't matter how many nieces and nephews he'd lulled to sleep over the years. This was his own child, but he'd known her for only a day. In too many ways where she was concerned he really was inadequate, and the women had cared for so many babies between them they had to know better than he.

So instead of retrieving his daughter, for her own good—
he thought—he let her go and sought escape. He'd just put
his hand on the garage doorknob, planning to head out and
let the cold clear his brain, when Hallie came up behind
him.

"Hey," she said softly. "You all right? You look like
someone stole your dog."

"Someone did," he said shortly.

She moved around in front of him and leaned back to
look up, surprised by his tone. "What's the matter? Too
much family?"

His jaw tightened and clicked. "That and other things."

"Like what?"

"Like..." He looked around, found no privacy and
grabbed her hand, started to tug her into the garage. "Come
with me. I need to talk to you. Someplace quiet."

She tugged back, urging him in the opposite direction.
"I've got to feed Maura so she can go down for her nap."

"Good enough." He reversed, led the way toward the
front staircase.

She hung back a little. "Joe."

He drew her forward. "Not now, Hallie. Please."

If she'd planned to object further, his "please" stopped
her; she climbed the stairs with him without another word.

It was Mary's mother who'd walked Maura into Hallie's
bedroom, trying to put the unwilling infant to sleep. The
look she gave Joe when he moved to relieve her of her
precious burden was initially refusal, then a sigh that was
more facial expression than sound, then almost...pity. Finally she put the baby into his hands and left the room
without a word.

While Hallie watched, bewildered, Joe raised his sputtering daughter to eye level and told her seriously, "I know
you're hungry and crabby and tired, *m'ija,* but give me a
minute with her first, okay? Then she's all yours."

Maura made a rude sound of what might have been dis-

sent, but amazingly she quit sputtering her discontent. Joe
settled her in her crib on her back, hooked the string of
dangling, brightly colored, different-shaped noisemakers
between the bars above her, wound up the clockwork ones
and bounced the others until they had Maura's attention.
Then he crossed the room, shut the door and turned to
Hallie.

"What?" she asked. "What's wrong? Why are you staring at me like that?"

He moved toward her, silent, catlike, purposeful. She
backed up.

"Joe, what are you doing?"

He reached her. "This," he said. Then he caught her
about the waist, lifted her off her feet, planted her back
against the nearest wall and kissed her. Hard. Deep. Plun-
dering her mouth with his tongue until she went boneless,
moaned once deep in her throat and wrapped her legs
tightly about his waist.

It was his turn to groan, to withdraw from her mouth, to
remember that whatever they mutually wanted, now was
not the time and he had questions he needed to ask.

"Joe?"

Her eyes were very blue from this distance and in this
light, and were filled with unabashed desire. He couldn't
help but notice, sure that what he saw in her eyes had to
be mirrored in his own. He needed something from her, he
understood with resignation, that had nothing to do with
sex. Something that would never go away, that would make
simple *sex* never enough.

"You filmed Maura's birth?"

She nodded, still puzzled.

"For me?"

"Who else?"

"I—" He swallowed. Language was inadequate to the
moment, but it was all he had. "Why?"

"Because." She shrugged, unwound her legs and slid

down to find the floor. "She's your daughter. You might've made me angry enough with you to want your head on a plate, but hating you enough to…" She hesitated. "Leave you out of her life even though I want to keep her…" She shrugged, offered him a wry half smile. "It wouldn't be right. So I asked Zeke to tape her coming-out party for you." She moved over to her closet, walked in and returned with a VHS cassette. "This is it, if you want it."

He took the tape, turned it over, held on to it until his knuckles paled around his grip. "I want it."

She smiled. "Good."

She went to collect Maura, seat herself in the rocking chair, and unselfconsciously open her blouse, camisole, bra, tuck a cloth diaper under her breast and Maura's chin, and bring the baby to her nipple. She glanced up to catch him gazing hungrily at her—not with sexual desire, she realized with unexpected longing, but with the far more complex yearning to be in some way a part of the act of nourishing Maura.

She reached for him with her free hand, gave it an insistent stretch when he momentarily hesitated. Then, when he reluctantly, hopefully crossed to take her hand, she tugged him down to kneel beside the chair, flattened her palm along his cheek and drew him into the simplest, lightest and most dangerous of kisses.

"Stay," she invited.

God, he wanted to. And not only here and now, but later, too. "It won't make you uncomfortable if I…watch?"

"After last night?" She laughed softly. "Being uncomfortable with you after that would be kind of silly, don't you think?"

His entire face twisted in a lopsided grin. "Probably. But I was thinking more about not wanting to embarrass you, considering how many other people are in the house and Sam and Ben are downstairs…. And maybe you—we both—should think about appearances for a change."

More quiet laughter. "The man who got fitted for a pink maid-of-honor dress in order to blow my mother's mind telling me to think about appearances? You're years too late for that, Joe."

He smiled, finding relief in history. "Maybe."

"No 'maybe' about it." She rubbed her thumb along his cheekbone, leaned over to blow a single whisper across his lips. "Stay."

He opened his mouth once, shut it, knelt up straight and took Hallie's face in his palms. Slanted his head and gave her back, kiss for gentle, perilously intimate kiss, what she'd given him.

Then, without further argument, he made himself comfortable where he could see both her and Maura.

Allowed himself the luxury to simply *be* for the first time in months.

Let himself stay.

Chapter 12

The day progressed.

It was an unusual grouping, to be sure, especially for the before lunch crowd, but the community was small, with fingers reaching into most of the surrounding neighborhoods and farms. What affected one of them, affected them all. Ties were close—a sizable portion of the community was related by marriage; friendships were decades old. And with the exception of blood and genetics, everyone had ties to Maura that Joe lacked: they'd been there; he hadn't.

Hell of a thing to realize: his daughter had a bigger family than he did himself. They each had a stake in her existence; her tiny fingers had more hearts than Joe could count wrapped securely around them. And whether the members of the sheriff's department in particular had children of their own at home or not, by virtue of circumstance and conception, Maura was different, special. Community property, community pride. She belonged to them all.

And one by one, they all—family members, old friends,

peers—took him aside and told him so. Made sure he knew
that if he fought Hallie for custody, he fought them all.

Which was why, Joe realized belatedly, amused and angry at once, the captain was here. Not only did she intend
to be on the scene to coordinate the search for the stalker,
but she was also here to send Joe a message that people in
high places were on Hallie's side. They'd vouch, if needed,
that she'd make Maura a better and more stable parent.
Why—as she off-handedly pointed out—only a phone call
away, the captain's good friend the local family court judge
waited. Heck, if someone sent out the plow for her, the
judge would be at Hallie's for lunch herself. Always did
like a good party, not to mention Joe's mother's paella, the
judge.

Especially a party that hosted a lot of *happy* kids—which
Hallie's impromptu Gabriella-planned parties always did.

It was hell being the current number-one pariah in a
small-town county seat where everybody knew who you
were, what you'd done and why—and didn't like it that
you'd done it to your best friend for exactly that reason.

The cause for the number of deputies in attendance was
less subtle. They were here to supply security for Hallie
and the kids, keep an eye out for trouble—and generally
give Joe a hard time. Not difficult to accomplish under the
circumstances, chiefly because Joe was already giving himself the crash course in hard times.

Sometimes, he thought, guilt was a damned fever blister
on the lip of creation: the minute you thought you had it
under control, the blasted thing spread.

Naturally, Joe's family and the rest of the blood relations
just thought the captain, FAT and the deps were on tap for
the food and games because it was a slow crime day.

On the other hand, having the deputies around would
give Joe—as soon as he could corner them alone, that is—
an opportunity to question the ones who'd baby-sat Maura

the prior evening. He could ask about anyone else who might have had access to the house during their tour.

In the meantime, he had his own questions to answer. Such as, who else might have been in the house after he'd arrived yesterday afternoon? Only Hallie, himself, Zeke, the boys... Frank, the two deputies.... His eyes narrowed with the automatic sense he'd left someone or something out. No. He relaxed, counting. Make that *four* deputies who'd come to the house with Frank. Crompton and Montoya who'd stayed, and Tom and Gina who'd gone out with them.

Hallie's neighbor, Nadie Kresnak, had been in, of course, but that was before.... Then there were the two detectives who'd helped with last night's reconnaissance, but they'd met Hallie and Joe at the scene.

He sucked a sound of frustration between his teeth. He supposed two of Hallie's phones could have been unplugged at some earlier time, leaving the one in the front hall that Joe had used to make his calls last night still functioning.

Leaving one phone working reduced the culprit's risk immeasurably, made it far more difficult to pinpoint when the others might have been unplugged. And it was possible, if someone knew the layout of Hallie's basement, that the wires that appeared to have been cut inside the house might actually have been pulled through, cut outside and carefully shoved back in.

But that would have required the vandal knowing Hallie had an excess of phone wire rolled into a loop at the foundation.

With a crawling sense of unease, Joe stood back and watched Crompton and Montoya and wondered. Crompton was older, had been around awhile and Joe had known him long before Mary was killed. Montoya was younger but seemed familiar. Still, Joe didn't think he'd ever worked with her as a deputy. Frank... Well, Frank was about as

straight and protective of Hallie as they came. And as for
the other two deputies… Joe didn't *think* they'd been out
of sight the entire few minutes they'd been at the house
last night.

Then there was Hallie's ex-husband. But Zeke as Hallie's
stalker made no sense to Joe—not that that was any crite-
rion for dismissing him, only that Joe could see no obvious
reason for Zeke to stalk Hallie. As far as he knew, Zeke
bore no grudge against either Hallie or Joe. He had as much
access to her and the boys as he could want; no need to
stalk. Nor was he the type to suffer a grudge quietly. Zeke,
as the saying went, was not prone to the ulcers silent
grudge-bearers got.

Not to mention that Joe had no idea how, without an
accomplice having been *here,* Zeke, Frank, the deputies or
anyone else with regular routines in Cuyahoga—city or
county—could possibly be connected, when he'd received
batches of photos for the past year from someone who'd
found and followed him—and/or possibly *led* him—about
when Hallie hadn't.

Or hadn't bothered to.

The thought brought him up short. Had he really been
so difficult to locate over the last year? He'd taken some
pains to cover his trail, but he hadn't gone to the extraordinary efforts that, as one of law enforcement's finest, he
certainly knew how to employ. Hadn't changed his social-
security number or his name. Hadn't set up blind paths to
hidden post-office boxes. Hadn't, in short, done anything
that should have prevented an investigator of Hallie's tal-
ents from finding him if she wanted to.

Wanted to being the operative phrase in that thought.

His jaw tightened against the notion. It wasn't, he decided, as if she'd spent the year sitting on her hands, after
all. Still, while she might not have thought to consider looking for him as a bounty hunter, private freelancing was a
fairly obvious step. And even at that, he'd merely moved

around a lot, chasing, as he'd told Hallie, one freaking lost lead after another.

And now all leads had led home.

His unease and paranoia grew with the scent of his mother's paella filling the house, compounded by Hallie's laughingly serious view of security-in-numbers.

A draft of cool air from the front door arrested his attention. He turned to see Zeke and one of the deputies slip back into the house, each man carrying two cardboard file boxes. They disappeared into Hallie's library-office with them, reappeared moments later. Joe thought Zeke regarded the door he closed behind him with mulish uncertainty, but that might have been applying his own questions to the situation. He drifted closer, hoping to overhear what Hallie's ex told the deputy before the officer disappeared into the crowd. Around him voices rose and fell—laughter quickly muted out of respect for Maura and other short preadults asleep upstairs; snatches of conversation half-heard.

"Naw," his brother David told someone. "Crews were out all night moving this stuff. Long's it stays stopped, road's oughtta be cleared by late afternoon...."

"...glad all the new power lines have gone in underground. Lot fewer houses without it..."

"...seems like a lot of money to put into one bond issue."

"Yeah, but if the schools and the library need it..."

"You children have to play more quietly—" Ears instantly attuned to the once-familiar, he picked out the voice of his former mother-in-law talking with a group of the younger crowd that included Sam and Ben. "Otherwise you'll wak—" Her voice went abruptly hoarse. She coughed and tried again. "Otherwise you'll—" No better. In fact if anything, worse. She choked and coughed, waving a hand at the children.

"Mrs. Montalban," Sam asked, alarmed, "what's wrong?"

Another headshake accompanied by hand waving that was obviously a request. Joe turned to see if he could find a glass of water or other handy liquid, spotted Hallie already weaving her way toward Maura's grandmother, glass in hand.

"Mrs. Montalban, are you all right?" It was Ben this time, and as always, he was more curious than worried.

"Fine." She coughed, sipped the water Hallie pressed into her hand, cleared her throat. "I'm fine, dear." She still sounded a little hoarse but better. She took another sip of water, shook her head and sighed. "There, that's better." She looked at the children. "Just a little frog in my throat."

To a youngster, Joe's nieces, nephews and the neighbor kids accepted this explanation and went more quietly on their way to the playroom at the back of the house. Sam and Ben, however, stared at Mary's mother, bug-eyed and fascinated.

"You have a *frog* in your throat?" Sam asked. He sent his own mother a priceless look of total, horrified mystification. Joe watched Hallie swallow and cover her mouth, trying not to laugh. The boy turned back to Clara Montalban. *"A frog?"*

"How did it get there?" Ben, as usual, was more direct. He pulled a folding chair over, climbed up onto it and studied Maura's grandmother's throat with a scientist's excitement. "Can I see?"

Taken literally aback and not knowing what to say, Clara took two steps back. Looking ready to explode with mirth, Zeke stepped out of the crowd and hoisted Ben off the chair, grabbed Sam up under his other arm and headed quickly for the hallway.

"C'mon, guys, I'll explain it to you later."

"But, Dad, how can she have a frog in her throat if—"

The front-hall bathroom door shut behind them, cutting off whatever "if" question Ben might have had.

Eyes bright with thwarted laughter, Hallie soothed Clara with a vague explanation of how literal boys of a certain age—especially if they had Zeke as a parent—could be. She waited until Clara, suspicious but almost mollified, moved off to find someone more obviously sane to speak with, then she fled. Joe grabbed her arm, bringing her to a halt.

"What's up?"

Nearly choking with laughter, she gasped, "I can't right now, Joe, really."

"Hallie..."

Sputtering with mirth now, she peeled his fingers from her arm and begged, "Later, I promise. Really, please, Joe. Gotta help Zeke." And she was gone.

Joe watched her meet Zeke and the boys, swallow her laughter long enough to ask her disgusted-looking boys something, and when they nodded, send them on their way. Then she and Zeke took one look at each other and collapsed together, howling but trying to hide it, over some private joke.

Jealousy struck without warning, stopping Joe in his tracks. Hell in a handbag, had she already reduced him to this? One night and...

But it wasn't merely one night. It was thousands of them, shared before she'd ever met Zeke—thousands of them afterward spent in patrol cars and on stakeouts, sharing their own private jokes.

Sharing everything, Joe used to think, without ever wondering why he'd done so. Even though he himself had never shared quite everything with Hallie, especially after Zeke and Mary had entered their respective lives. And since every marriage had its moments, of course she'd have private jokes with Zeke; she'd been married to him for nearly eight years, after all.

But that didn't mean Joe liked either what he saw or what he understood of it. High-school of him in the extreme, no doubt, but there it was. Emotion that overwhelmed but that also remained undefined and therefore uncommitted was like that. Especially for a guy who had the funny feeling that in a single night he'd found everything he'd ever been looking for but now that he'd found it, he had no idea what to do with it.

Particularly when it—*she*—had been under his nose for thirty years.

Cursing the vagaries of his sense of duty versus his responsibilities and his desires, Joe turned around to avoid watching Hallie with Zeke and nearly ran into Montoya.

"Sir," she said, startled, snapping back out of his path and nearly, Joe thought, saluting.

Which, given the circumstances and the fact that he no longer had rank nor had he even—as far as he knew—been her instructor when she was in training, seemed odd to him. Given it was a day full of oddities, however, he dismissed this one as unworthy of note.

"Talk to you, Montoya?" he asked.

She cast a glance over her shoulder—no doubt looking for rescue, Joe thought—then nodded.

"Hallie—" He paused. No, too personal. Better to keep this official-sounding in spite of the party atmosphere. He corrected himself. "Lieutenant Thompson mention to you the way we—*she*—" Yeah, he'd been the one to send Montoya and Crompton home last night, but no sense advertising he'd also spent the night. "Found the phones this morning?"

"No, sir."

Too formal. Uncomfortable with him. Possibly been told to hold her distance, damn it. By whom? Frank? The captain? Hallie...

"That'd be Sergeant Nillson."

Frank, Joe thought. "He ask you if anybody stopped by?

You saw or heard anything? Make or get any calls last night?''

"Yes, sir."

Yes, sir, what? Joe wondered, exasperated. *Yes, sir,* all three, or only the first. No, she definitely was not comfortable with him. He contained impatience with an effort. "And?"

"Oh, of course, yes, sir."

She expelled a breath and drew herself up, a young dep in report mode. Except she wasn't all that young. And regardless of his former department status, he was the last person in the house to whom she'd have made a report.

"It was late, sir. No one stopped by. Leroy—Deputy Crompton, that is—made rounds outside when we thought we saw a vehicle stop in front of the house. We didn't think to check the phone wires, sir, and the vehicle moved on before we could get a license on it. We figured it was probably all right."

She shrugged her mouth, a move uncharacteristic with the rest of her presentation, and continued. "There was enough snow by then, too, sir, that Deputy Crompton would have found footprints if anybody'd been up next to the house. We didn't take any calls for Lieutenant Thompson, but I believe Deputy Crompton phoned his wife when he came back inside after his rounds."

Joe nodded. "You make any calls yourself, Deputy? Use the lieutenant's police band at all?"

"No, sir. No need, sir. Had our own unit with us."

Another nod. "Thank you, Deputy." The dismissal, *That'll be all,* rose in his throat; he bit it back. He turned away, saw Montoya's posture relax out of the corner of his eye; turned back as a sudden thought occurred to him. "One other thing, Montoya?"

Stiffness returned. She viewed him guardedly. "Yes, sir?"

"Do we have a problem here I don't know about?"

She paled. "Pardon, sir?"

"A problem, Montoya." He was patient, circumspect, trying not to spook a less experienced investigator with his need to know something she might not be supposed to reveal to him. "You seem familiar. Have we met before last night?"

She hesitated. Her cheek worked, back teeth chewing it from the inside.

He wanted to be kind, but sometimes kindness was more hindrance than help. "Spill it, Deputy."

She inhaled deep, expelled the breath. "Yes, sir."

"Yessir, what?" Impatience getting the better of him. In his opinion, hesitation in a deputy was not a good thing. Another dep's hesitation had once gotten Hallie shot. "Yes, we've met before, yes, we have a problem, yes, you seem familiar. Yes, what?"

Her mouth thinned, lip curled briefly and was controlled; she drew herself up. "Yes, sir, all of it, sir. We've met before, we've had a problem, you make me uncomfortable, I'll live."

"Refresh my memory. I'm older'n you, I've got a lot on my mind right now and time's short."

"'Bout two years ago, sir." Her tongue shoved out her lower lip from the inside, stiffening it, then relaxed. "I was a state trooper then. There was a domestic at my house—my boyfriend was out of work and drunk. I was dressing for work. He got hold of my weapon. My daughter and I…we were hostages. He threatened us…threatened *her*. Neighbors heard us yelling. He fired a shot. They called it in. You were first on the scene." She swallowed, wet the inside of her mouth, her lips. Looked at Joe, recognized the dawn of comprehension. Nodded. Continued. "Yes, sir, that's it. Bullet ricocheted, turned my daughter into a vegetable until she died a little over a year ago. He saw you and panicked, put the gun to my head, took it away and started firing at the neighbors. You had no choice, you put him down.''

Joe nodded, remembering the time with revulsion. All shootings were subject to internal investigation, but this one had been worse than most. Montoya had pushed the matter with IID and it had gotten ugly. Despite all her boyfriend had done, Montoya had wanted Joe charged with her boyfriend Tomas's murder. She'd claimed that what had happened to her daughter was an accident and that if then Sergeant Martinez had handled things properly, the entire matter might have been resolved without further shooting.

Even when he'd finally been exonerated by internal investigations, Joe had questioned his actions for months after. Still questioned them, truth be known. When you were by yourself out there and an incident occurred, all you had was your own judgment, your own perceptions of the situation to back you up. And in Joe's perception at the time, Montoya's boyfriend had been begging to go down. Joe had held off, trying to talk to the man, but the situation went downhill faster than fast. When he'd begun firing wildly about the neighborhood, there'd been no other choice; Joe had taken him out.

When there were no amends to be made, he'd tried hard to put it behind him, had only succeeded when Mary's death blasted everything else from his mind. He should have remembered Cat more clearly, though. Her name, her appearance, something. She'd changed a lot physically, true, but that was little excuse when you'd been the instrument by which another person's life changed forever. He could only imagine it was the change in her uniform that did it: she'd shed the navy blue of the state police for the county's beige and brown.

"You left the troops after the investigation because of your daughter." A statement of memory, not a question.

She nodded. "They gave me an extended mourning, then I took a leave. When she died six months later, I, uh, I

came back for a while. It didn't work out, so I went home
to Texas until...until things...'' She hesitated. ''Until
things felt better. Then I came back here again and hired
in as a dep.'' There was another hesitation. Then she lifted
her chin and looked him in the eye. ''I wanted to tell you
I'm sorry for everything I put you through at that time, sir.
I wasn't myself. You did what you thought you had to. I
accept that.''

Joe swallowed regret. ''Thank you, Montoya. That, uh,
that— Thank you. It means a lot. I never got a chance to
tell you then how very sorry I was for your loss. I still am.
And I appreciate you being willing to work with me, look
after my daughter the way you did last night despite our
history.''

''No problem, sir.'' Montoya's eyes were neutral dark
brown pools in her face. ''Lieutenant Thompson's baby—''
her very lack of emphasis on changing Maura's parentage
from his to Hallie's supplied the italics for her thoughts
''—wasn't even a breath on the wind. She didn't have anything to do with it. And anyway, the past is dead. It's the
future we have to pay attention to.''

''True,'' Joe agreed. ''But thank you anyway, Montoya.''

She gave him a clipped nod. ''Is that all, sir?''

''That's all, Montoya.''

He would have sworn she ducked by him and fled.

When Joe finally had a chance to talk with him later,
Crompton verified Montoya's story—although in his version, it was Montoya who'd noted the vehicle out front,
pointed it out to him. The only time the two deputies were
out of sight of each other was, as Montoya stated, when
she was upstairs with Maura, or when Crompton went out
to look around.

By the time he was able to catch up with Hallie again,
lunch was ready. Eager to sample the first real food he'd

had since he'd been gone—Hallie's burn-your-mouth-and-privates chili didn't count—he forked up a mouthful of paella the moment his plate was passed. With barely a pause in dishing out, his mother reached over and rapped his hand with the flat of a spatula and sent him a quelling glance.

"Grace first," she reminded him.

Feeling like a chastised little boy despite his age, Joe gulped his mouthful of rice, put down his fork and waited. Although he rarely prayed anymore himself, he'd forgotten what it was like to be "home," with all its rules and entanglements.

In the serving line ahead of him, he saw Hallie glance over her shoulder at him, eyes bright, shoulders shaking with silent laughter. It was a sight he knew and relished. Part of Hallie's charm was that regardless of almost anything he'd done or felt bad about, she was able to laugh at him, point out whatever it was he needed to see to laugh at himself.

She was also singularly able to understand when laughter was not the key; when silence, darkness and arms wrapped around him were all that would keep the hounds of hell at bay. He'd done the same for her.

They'd shared any number of those nights: all of Mary's miscarriages; the night Zeke finally left. The day he'd shot Montoya's boyfriend and the weeks after, when hell was his own self-doubt.

The afternoon she'd nearly died and he'd held her, covered in her blood, begging her to live. She'd even been there when he'd finally broken down and wept over that at her bedside later, alone except for the faces of the other deputies and detectives peering through the wall of glass surrounding her room in intensive care. Then she'd come out of her coma to squeeze his hand, touch his cheek—tell him in a voice that was barely a whisper that he'd better quit soaking her bandages or the nurses would pin back his ears.

And had made him laugh in spite of himself then, too.

Now, when she took her plate through to an almost-quiet spot in a corner of the playroom at the back of the house, he followed. His entire life, it seemed, he'd never been able to do anything less.

Had never wanted to.

"All right, it's later," he said without preamble. "What's so funny about Clara having a frog in her throat?"

Hallie's lips compressed around laughter. "That's driving you crazy, isn't it?"

"Unfortunately."

Laughter escaped. "You really need other things to think about, Joe."

"True, but that's never stopped me before."

She gave him grinning-but-earnest. "I can't tell you here. Really, Joe. It's the wrong place and time. Later, I promise. After everybody's gone. Truly."

"Hallie..."

"Okay. I'll give you a hint." Her eyes danced with mischief. "I won't only tell you about it later, I'll demonstrate."

"Thompson—"

"Think about it, Joe. That's all you're going to get."

He made a face and swore under his breath, ready to grumble, but accepting there was no way he'd get anything further out of her now, so he changed tactics—and subjects. "How'd the huddle go?"

She shrugged, not bothering to pretend she didn't know what he was talking about. "Not sure yet."

"What's Zeke got to do with it?"

Amusement formed her mouth again, teasing him, tempting him, taunting him. He wanted to wipe the grin away with a kiss she wouldn't forget. All in good time, he promised himself. All in good—

"Jealous?" she asked, interrupting his promise to himself. The question was sophomoric, she knew, but she needed to distract him until later when she could explain...what she'd done—and was about to do—and why.

"Damn right," he said.

Shocked, she studied him.

It was his turn to let his shoulders rise and fall, to look away. "Sorry. You've never included Zeke in an investigation and left me out before. With the frog stuff, that's twice today. A lot's happened and I'm curious and insecure, sue me."

Emotion swamped her at his admission. She touched his face and sighed. Sometimes male egos were a thorough pain in the butt. "I'm not all that secure about what's happening here either, Joe, but Zeke saw the pictures. They freaked him a bit. Can't blame him. They freaked me, too. So even though it's not really what he does, I asked him to try to profile the shooter. Keeps him out of our hair and gives him something to concentrate on that might actually help."

"And?"

"Jury's still out. I told him not to broadcast them, but he's got a friend who does profiling for the Minneapolis PD when they need it. They'll consult and let us know ASAP."

"Okay."

They sat in silence for a bit, enjoying the paella, beans and fruit salad, watching the children eat, giggle, play. Awareness was an invisible line between them tying them together beyond where their knees touched, their shoulders met where they sat close together on the small sofa.

It was also comfort and discomfort at once: if Hallie turned only slightly away from him, it would have been easy for Joe to wedge her into his side, against his hip; slide her under his shoulder and slip his arm around her, across the top of her chest—or inside her shirt where the cool smoothness of her camisole seemed to beckon him to skim his hand down to find her breast. Or he could cup her chin and turn her face into his kiss, lose himself in hers.

In her turn, Hallie knew his warmth along her side and found herself craving his heat, as well. It was not in her nature to back away from anything, but especially not from Joe. So she let sitting beside him bring them closer by hauling one of his younger nieces up onto the couch on her other side, forcing herself to lessen what little distance there was between them. Then she canted her head to listen to something the little girl was trying to tell her, exposing her neck to Joe—making herself vulnerable and flirtatious at once, reminding him of other things she'd learned from him.

Smiling at the ploy, Joe slid his arm across the back of the couch and waited for Hallie to send his niece on her way and straighten quite conveniently under that arm. He bent his head to breathe, "Careful there, woman, you're playing with fire."

She slid her near hand up his thigh. "And if I want fire to play with *me?*" she murmured back.

His arm convulsed around her shoulders, his belly tightened. With mouth and tongue he made quick, spine-tingling love to her ear. "Where and when?"

"Hmm?" She leaned into his clandestine caress, unable to think. Unable to *want* to think.

Able only to want to be part of him again as soon as possible. "Joe..." His name was a breath, a whisper on her lips as she turned her face toward him.

Across the room someone male coughed discreetly, arresting the movement. In concert, as fluid as a waning wind, they separated. Hallie looked at Frank, who motioned her out of the room with a slanting of his head. When Joe moved to follow, she stayed him with a hand on his thigh.

"Not yet," she told him quietly—although the expression she turned on him was more plea than request. "Later."

He looked at her, measuring his desire to leave her out of this completely, against the wisdom of the moment. Then, because he trusted her, he unwillingly let her go.

She got up and walked across the room without a backward glance. Afraid that if she turned her head, he'd see the lie on her face.

Knowing that because he trusted her, the things she wouldn't tell him were the lies.

Chapter 13

Though insulated, the garage was cold. Hallie grabbed the jacket she kept hanging beside the door to the house, slipped it on, pulled it up around her ears and zipped it. Then she eased quietly down the landing steps to the garage floor and around to Joe's truck.

She felt like a perfect heel spying on Joe instead of asking him what she wanted to know straight out, but a quick glance through Zeke's file on Mary had convinced her to move first and apologize later. Clearly her late friend had not been a woman to keep two truths in the same barrel; even if Joe had the answers he needed to put the puzzle of Mary's killer and Mary's stalker together, he might not realize it. And truth be known, Hallie wanted to protect Joe as much from Mary's duplicities as she wanted to know what Joe himself was hiding about Mary. Finding out, solving the riddle, freeing Joe from his quest… It was the only way she could think to have a custody battle over Maura end happily.

It was the only way she could think of that might allow

Joe the freedom to choose to stay in town. And selfish or not, after last night, this morning, the discovery of the emotion that had brought her willingly into his arms in the first place, she wanted very badly to have Joe around. To have him *want* to stay.

Permanently.

If, when he discovered what she'd done, he didn't hate her for the rest of his life, that is.

But that was later's concern. Now her only worry was moving quickly enough so Frank and company wouldn't have to keep Joe occupied for long. Sometimes the man could be just too damned prescient for her good.

Not that he'd yet exhibited that particular talent since he'd been home. She made a face, puffed air through one corner of her mouth. *Give him time and a toothpick,* she thought. It wouldn't take more than that.

Which meant she had to move.

The passenger door of his truck was farthest from the house; she slipped around, found the door locked, swore. The driver's side was also locked. Okay, no problem. A little time wasted, but no big deal. Since they'd had to stop using them to help stranded motorists due to insurance considerations, she had her handy-dandy keys-locked-in-the-car tool at home.

Not that unlocking Joe's truck would have been difficult anyway; he'd shown her how to do it when they were kids. But the right tool was always more effective and quicker to use than one—like a coat hanger—that was jerry-built.

It was also easier for her to disguise its use because she was less likely to miss and scratch the paint. Now all she had to do was slip the flat metal between frame and door in the right place and...

Voilà! A satisfying clack announced success.

Quickly she popped open the door and slid into the truck; let her hands glide swiftly above the sun visors and beneath the dash and front of the seat, the inside door pockets before she turned her attention to the glove box. For a moment it stuck and she thought it, too, was locked, but it was simply overfull. When it opened, half the contents dumped onto the floor: pens, pencils, notepad, microcassette recorder; a small high-tech 35-mm camera with telephoto lens...

For a moment all she could do was stare at the camera, her jaw painfully clenched against a suspicion she couldn't begin to reconcile—and didn't want to entertain. Then she forced herself to relax, to think, to behave like a detective rather than an automatically distrusting, uncertain lover.

Though a few of the photos she'd seen yesterday were indeed 35-mm, most were either Polaroids or stills from videotape. Which meant that finding a single camera in Joe's truck meant nothing. No doubt he occasionally used a camera in his work, she told herself. Surveillance, same as they did on the job. Or maybe it was a tourist thing—although she didn't remember Joe Martinez ever in his life having a proclivity toward photography in any form whatever. Still, it was what she wanted to believe; to trust Joe was who she'd always thought he was.

Her lower jaw working, she laid the camera on the seat and sifted through the remainder of the glove compartment's contents. Truck owner's manual, a copy of his registration, proof of insurance, upkeep records, a pair of socks, an unopened package of plaid boxers, a box of condoms...

The double take was immediate and painful. Condoms. Joe had *condoms* in his glove box? Damn it to hell, and she'd thought...assumed...

She shut her eyes against the nauseating taste of jealousy on the back of her tongue. How could she even have considered he wouldn't...? It had been nearly a year, after all. It probably wasn't reasonable to think...

Damn. This was worse than discovering the camera. She

didn't want him sleeping with anybody else. Having sex
with anyone else.

Making love to anyone but her.

As Zeke had seen, whether Hallie had ever chosen to
admit it or not, it had been difficult enough sometimes
watching Joe with Mary when they were couples, let alone
imagining—

"Find anything interesting?" Joe's voice was deliberate,
quiet—anger waiting for a good explanation.

Hoping for one.

He didn't get it. Instead Hallie flinched, startled, and
swung on him; initially guilty, then defensive. Then any
pretense at guilt disappeared, was replaced by wariness—
and, Joe thought, surprised by the un-Hallie-like character-
istic, pique. When she shoved the box of prophylactics at
him, he understood perfectly.

And started to laugh. Unquestionably the wrong thing to
do, but he couldn't help himself. For the first time since
he'd turned up on her doorstep yesterday he knew exactly
what she was thinking. Here she was, searching his truck
for whatever he might have hidden from her, and the thing
that ticked her off was the last thing that should. The very
thought of her getting sidetracked from anything at all by
a box of condoms he'd never used...

The concept and the result were simply too funny and
too terrifyingly wonderful for words. So he laughed.

"You have condoms in your truck, Joe."

It was an accusation if ever he'd heard one. "Yes." He
laughed harder. "I do."

"This is *not* funny, Joe."

"Oh, but it is, Hallie." His sides hurt; it had been a long
time since he'd laughed like this. Hallie had been there
then, too. "If only you knew."

"Enlighten me," she snapped.

"Hallie..."

Still laughing, he attempted to gather her up, draw her

in, but it was like attempting to embrace the thorn-apple tree in her backyard. She shoved him away.

"I mean—" She waved a hand, stamped the length of his truck and back. "I don't *do* this. I don't sleep casually with men who need to keep condoms in their trucks 'just in case' even if they do practice safe sex. The whole idea is they have to practice it at all. I mean it's not like the ability gets rusty if you don't use it. And honest to John, if I'm any judge—and I'm probably not, but there we are, it's what we're stuck with—*my* abilities haven't gone bad from disuse. And I don't sleep with anyone like I did with you, period. Who has time? Not to mention there're the kids, and I mean really, Joe, I thought…and you could have said…and…" She stopped and looked at him, eyes deeply blue and bewildered. "There're condoms in your damned truck, Joe."

"Hallie." Amusement lessened to a chuckle. He caught her wrists, held her still when she would have wrenched away. "Pay attention to me. I'll explain."

"You don't have to justify yourself to me, Joe," she said sadly, contradicting her previous request. "I don't own you." Her mouth twisted. "Heck, it's obvious I don't even *own* myself. And it's not like I wasn't the one who got carried away, who didn't even think— I mean, it's my body, my protection, right? But I don't know. I guess I thought…or didn't think— And it was *you,* damn it. It's been forever since anyone…since I wanted…and my period should start in the next couple of days and—"

"Hallie."

She looked at him. "What?"

He sighed. Then he slid his hands up her arms, sandwiched her face between his palms and kissed her hard, pouring everything he'd ever felt for her—or thought he might ever feel for her—into it.

"Shut up a minute," he said.

She bit back whatever else might have blathered out of

her. The fact that she'd blathered at all was a bad sign. Lady lieutenant sheriffs did not blather about anything, ever. Especially not to best friends named Joe with whom they'd slept the night before. They couldn't afford blathering. It gave best-friends-named-Joe far too much information and put lady-lieutenant-sheriffs—well, *any* lieutenant sheriffs, if you wanted to quibble, which she didn't, since quibbling at this point could be construed as part of the blathering—at a disadvantage, set a precedent. And not a good precedent at that.

"Okay."

A smile ghosted his mouth; he let it go. How could she be so smart, know him better than he knew himself and be such an idiot about him all at the same time? How could she be the brightest investigator he'd ever met, yet fail to miss the obvious when it came to one simple box of contraceptive devices?

How could he have known her for thirty years and only now realize that when he measured beauty he measured it against Hallie. Always had, forever would.

He took the condom box out of her hand, held it in front of her face. "I bought this box six months ago and it's never been opened, Hallie." He showed her the sealed ends. "See?"

She took back the box, turned it over in her hands. It was, indeed, unopened. She looked up at him. Bit the inside of her cheek. Opened her mouth.

What she *meant* to say was an almost-contrite-but-mostly-sarcastic *"Gee, Joe, that's nice, but I already told you, you don't owe me any explanations. I was out of line."*

Instead, what she said was a tad furious and more than a little nose-in-the-air-haughty. "If you weren't going to use them, why the devil did you buy them in the first place?"

She was instantly mortified by her temerity.

It wasn't as though the question was one she'd never

consider asking him. She'd asked him that very type of
question often in the past; that was what friends did. But
last night had changed the import, had changed what was
allowed—particularly since she didn't yet know where she
stood either with him, or with herself.

"I'm sorry," she apologized. "I didn't mean to say
that."

Joe snorted. "Yes, you did. You always mean what you
say, Hallie."

She shook her head. "No. Well, yes, you're right. I mean
what I *say* when I say it, but I really didn't mean to say
that. I meant to think it and say something else."

Again laughter swelled and burst its seams. "Damn,
lady, you are something." He looked behind her, spotted
the camera on the seat, stilled. Tapped the box she held.
"You found that—" he gestured toward the camera
"—and all you're worried about are these?"

She made a face. "You think my priorities are skewed?"

"I think you need your head examined."

"Naw." She grimaced and shook her head. "Zeke already did that once today. For what it's worth, I don't think
he found anything worth keeping."

"His loss," Joe said softly.

His eyes on her face were gentle, searching, open. Uncomfortable, Hallie ducked her head.

"What are you looking for in my truck, Hallie?"

"Not what I found." Then, honestly, "The way it…*we*
felt last night, I didn't think you'd bothered to consider
keeping anything like this in your glove compartment 'just
in case.'"

"Just like you, I don't sleep around, Hallie." His tone
was quiet, unapologetic, decisive. "But just because I've
never needed to use them doesn't mean I don't know myself well enough to go unprepared. So 'just in case' I walk
into a bar and get too loose to say no, I keep 'em around

like part of my shaving kit, make sure I get a fresh box every so often. Just in case.''

''Last night—''

He hushed her with a brush of his mouth across hers. ''Last night it was you. Seeing you blew me away. I wanted you so badly I didn't—couldn't—think. Not even—'' his mouth twisted with belated apology ''—long enough to remember to protect you.''

Her hands went to his chest, gathered his jacket in her fingers, unflexed and smoothed it aside. Slid inside to brush a line down the center of his T-shirt, to still along his ribs. ''Joe.'' It was a whisper, a request, a promise.

He let out a shuddering breath. His eyes were deep and hungry, his hands skimmed restlessly down her arms, around her back to her hips, her rump, fitting her intimately to him. ''God, what you do to me, Hallie,'' he muttered, and crushed her mouth beneath his.

Wild and uncharted, the kiss lasted a mere heartbeat, long minutes, forever—left them both gulping for reason and unfulfilled.

''We can't,'' Hallie gasped, unzipping his jacket so she could fit her arms around him inside it. ''Can we?''

''No,'' he agreed, but his fingers brushing open the buttons of her jacket, blouse, camisole were unconvinced. When he undid the cups of her bra and grazed his nails over her already distended nipples, she was lost.

''Joe.'' Her own frantic fingers skated under the waistband of his jeans to the button fly, stumbled to open it. It occurred to him briefly that he should maybe try to stop her, but then she freed him, pushed aside his briefs and skimmed her own nails down his length, cupped him in her palm and he, too, was lost. ''Joe, please. I need…I need…''

His body jerked and trembled, already almost beyond his control, thrusting into her hand. ''Hallie, wait.'' He tore open the box of condoms, yanked out a foil packet and mashed it into her hand. ''Put this on me.'' Then he had to grit his teeth against the primitive urge to simply take her when she followed directions and tore the envelope open with her teeth, rolled the bit of latex over the head of his sex and down.

Encouraged by Hallie's soft pleas and his own matching cravings he made short work of her trouser fastenings. Shoved underwear and trousers down to her calves in one quick movement. Fit a foot between her knees and stepped her pants the rest of the way off her at the same time he tucked his hands beneath her buttocks and lifted her out of them. She wrapped her legs around his hips on a moan; straining, sweating, holding back as much as he could, he centered her, pressed her hips and lower back against the side of his truck and thrust into her.

Hard.

She gasped and stiffened, then folded her arms around his neck and used this leverage to raise and lower herself on him faster and faster, flowing down onto each of his thrusts, belly tightening, tightening…breath whimpering in his ear…nipples chafing, sizzling at the soft texture of his shirt, the rough graze of the mat of hair beneath.

His own breath was a harsh expellation of fire. He thrust into her, each drive raising the tension, the need to plunge deeper, until finally he felt her channel open to him totally, and she was a sobbing, begging bundle in his arms. Wrapping one arm hard about her waist and backing her once more into the truck, he guided the middle finger of his other hand around the cleft of her buttocks, found what he was looking for and touched her.

Again she straightened and tensed, then her entire body collapsed around him; her movements grew as short, jerky, and frantic as his own strokes into her. Then they held each other tight, bellies flat together, her breasts crushed to his chest, mouths open on each other's shoulders to muffle their cries as they spiraled into the long, drawn-out tremors of mutual release.

* * *

The garage air was cold where her skin was bare; Joe's face was hot, damp and heavy between the crook of her shoulder and her neck; her own face was warm and moist where her forehead rested against the T-shirt covering his collarbone. Her breath was a thick shudder in and out of her lungs, a harsh counterpoint to Joe's heavily serrated respirations.

"We have to stop doing this," she whispered when she could speak.

"This?"

He flexed his hips and she trembled and shut her eyes against the sensation, reaching for control.

"No." Her head moved from side to side on his shoulder, too comfortable to lift. "I mean this, out here. Especially with all of them in there."

"Probably." He ran his mouth through the moisture clinging to the side of her neck, relishing the salty flavor, the spice-scented vitality of her. "But out here is where you found my shaving kit."

Her answering laugh was breathless and amazed. "So it is."

For a moment longer they clung. Then Joe's legs started to buckle a little and Hallie unwrapped hers from around him. He tried to keep her where she was.

"Not yet," he said.

"We have to, Joe," she murmured back. "What if the kids, someone else comes?"

He nipped her ear. "Someone already came, and given a few minutes, would like to again."

She laughed—naughty, eager—and pushed back to slide down his length until her feet touched the concrete floor. It was cold beneath her socks; she hadn't even noticed kicking out of her shoes so Joe could remove her pants. "Later. I'll figure out something." It was a statement that encompassed more than the moment, more than mere physical union. It included Maura, and Mary's killer, and *later,* combined. "I promise."

"No." He stooped to retrieve her panties and trousers, rose to plant a lingering kiss on her mouth before putting her clothes in her hands. "*We'll* figure something out." That will solve everything, he added silently. "I promise."

"Okay." Hallie nodded. Watched him turn away while she stepped into her pants and put herself to rights. Noted the tear she didn't think had been in his shirt before they'd made love. Jeez Louise, who had she become where Joe Martinez was concerned? She'd never...well, but she guessed *she'd never* was in the past, because it certainly appeared she had now. And because she had, apparently torn his shirt, he'd need another one to put on before they went inside—and preferably one that was the same color.

Intent on finding him another shirt, she climbed into the truck and knelt on the seat to reach behind it, feeling for his duffel bag. Her fingers encountered and dragged out wool blankets, an extra jacket, a nylon stuff sack clanking with tools, before they stubbed painfully up against the sharp edges of something hard and metal.

"Ow, damn."

She pulled her hand out, shook it, reached in again more carefully.

"Hallie, you all right?"

The question was automatic, curious but not overly concerned. Then she heard him turn, heard him swear, his feet skid across the cement to reach her at the same moment her questing fingers knocked the top off the shoe box he kept behind the seat.

"Hallie, don't—"

"You got a clean T-shirt in here, Joe?" she asked, not hearing him.

She broke off and stared at his paling face, feeling the color drain from her own when her hand found the plastic rectangle. Slowly she brought it to light. The VHS cassette's dull black case seemed to shine with malevolence in the waning afternoon light.

Joe's mouth thinned. "I told you not to go there."

Hallie's throat tightened, her heart cracked. Hiding it all behind the facade of lieutenant sheriff, she raised her face. "Yeah? Well, I want to know what you *haven't* told me, Joe."

He looked away, a sure sign this truth would be limited at best. "I've told you everything, Hallie." He couldn't watch. How would she feel when she'd found it all? Angry? Betrayed? She would put a wall between them and he would lose both her and Maura in a wink, and for all his physical strength, nothing he could do would stop it.

Still, for all he hated the idea, it would be cowardly to turn his back; he might not want to watch, but he had to see. He repeated the assertion he doubted she'd believe. "Everything."

"Everything?" She tilted her head, regarding him from various angles, seeking out the lie.

He set his teeth and nodded. "Yes, damn it. Every freaking damned thing I'm going to tell you and that you need to know." He turned toward the steps. "It's cold out here, Hallie. You found the tape, now let's go in."

She looked at him, said coolly, deliberately, "Not yet."

His gut twisted. Funny, he thought dully, how the same phrase could be used so differently within the span of minutes. How different each use could make you feel.

"First tell me—"

"Read my damned lips." Anger, frustration, fear shortened his fuse. He brought his face within inches of hers, enunciated each word clearly. "I have told you freaking everything, Hallie. You know everything I know. Hell, with whatever you had Zeke bring into the library, you probably know more and I don't notice you sharing." He swung away from her, ran his hands through his hair. Swung back and poked a stiff finger at her. "I don't care who you are, we are, there are some truths that don't belong to you, Hallie. They're mine and I have to live with them. You don't, so back off."

She slapped his hand away, grabbed a fistful of his jacket and got in his face. "Would you if it were me?"

"It is you, Hallie." He snorted with derision, peeled her fingers off his jacket. "What the hell did you think? Who else would I risk everything to protect?" He scrubbed the heels of his hands across his eyes, stepped to a garage window to watch the snow swirl. "Judas, think about it. I didn't know about Maura, Mary was dead, that leaves you."

"Me." A quizzical statement, but not a question.

"Yeah, you." A puff of humorless laughter fogged the windowpane. "Since I was five years old the only place all roads lead is back to you."

"Wha—?" Stunned emotion stung the back of her throat, pricked suddenly behind her eyes, broke off the word before it could be uttered. She swallowed and tried to speak. Failed. Worked her tongue to moisten her mouth and tried again. "What if all my roads since I was five lead to you, too, Joe?" she asked hoarsely. "What then?"

He shook his head. "I don't know, Hallie. I just know you can't have this."

She nodded, tightening the line of her mouth, jaw and cheek, the muscles around her eyes. Ridding herself of the appearance of emotion if not the emotion itself. "Okay." She gave another nod, a flex of muscles in her throat, a tap of the videocassette against her thigh. "If that's the way it is, that's the way it is."

"Thanks." Joe turned, lifted a hand to her cheek, let it drop without touching her when she pulled her face away. "It's the way it has to be. Now let's go in."

"Yeah." A distracted response he should have recognized and reacted to the moment he heard it. "Sure. In.

Right behind you. Just help me get a couple of things. I mean—'' Idly she picked the camera off the seat, collected the microcassette recorder and the box of labeled tapes, and slid them with the videotape into the deep pockets of her trousers. Watched him make no move to stop her and nodded again. Glanced once more at the truck's seat. Shook her head as if making a decision and tossed him the condoms. ''We don't want to forget these things, do we.''

He regarded her warily. She was about to tear him apart; he could feel it. The problem was sensing the direction she'd take so he could raise his guard. ''No.''

''No,'' she agreed, apparently pleased with common ground. ''Because if nothing else, we sure have figured out how to get a damn good *time* out of each other, haven't we?''

The tone was calm, the language intentionally coarse, guaranteed to inflame Joe. And it did. He rounded the truck, caught Hallie by the shirtfront and hauled her up, eye-to-eye with him.

''What the hell do you want from me, Hallie?'' Volume and fury were controlled by sheer will. ''What the hell more can I give you?''

''Everything, Joe. I want it all. Secrets and lies. Truth and consequences. I want Mary's killer put down and I want this stalker taken out, even if they're you or Zeke or anybody else I know who looks like a suspect. I want it done. I want to know. Most of all, I want you, and that'll never happen if you don't cut the cake right here and—''

''I told you,'' he interrupted, breathing hard, ''you've already got everything I can—''

''Yeah, yeah,'' she snapped, cutting him off. ''I know. You've told me everything.'' She pushed herself out of his grasp, turned into the truck and put her hand on the seat-release lever. ''But the thing I want to know is what haven't you *shown* me?''

''Judas stinking Priest.'' He made a belated grab for the

seat. "Hallie, you've got to trust me on this one. You don't want to know this. You don't."

She swung the seat forward under his hand. "Joe, if you don't quit hiding the facts from me and we don't start workin' this together, this thing won't get solved," she told him positively.

And then she found his secrets.

Chapter 14

Or rather, they were Mary's secrets, actually.

Sorted and filed, records kept in her neat, precise script. As he'd told her about Mary's search for a breeding stud, the files were a sociologist's, a scientist's data, impartially collected and cataloged for future review.

It wasn't as though he'd kept them in plain sight. Instead, Hallie had found the containers Joe had boxed them in and lifted the shoe box and two heavy metal strongboxes into the garage's version of daylight. Joe took the shoe box from her before she had a chance to sift through its contents, and tucked the strongboxes under his arm.

"Trust me, Hallie," he said tautly. "You don't want to look through these with people here. This is somethin' you've got to wait and do where there's no one to see you punch the walls."

She studied his face, understanding all at once that this was a whole lot more to him than hide-and-seek. "Sort of like what I've got to show you."

His expression went closed; he wasn't sure how much

more he wanted to know about Mary. "What Zeke brought in?"

"Yeah."

"I'll want to punch the walls?"

"I've seen you do it over her before."

His curse was graphic, violent and self-directed. The last time he'd punched a wall over Mary was the night he'd discovered the records on her third miscarriage. His mouth twisted. He knew enough more about his late wife now that he didn't think anything further would shock him the way what he'd kept in the strongboxes would hurt Hallie. "You show me yours, I'll show you mine." The joke was as weak as his grin.

She smiled slightly and headed for the steps into the house. "We'll put them in the library."

Appropriately symbolic, Joe thought, following her. Confessions belonged in the confessional.

Especially when they were someone else's.

As though she'd heard his thoughts, Hallie stopped on the landing and looked down at him, three steps below her. Something—perhaps mischief—that he hadn't anticipated seeing, glowed in her expression, startling him, filling him, sharpening an appetite he thought he'd recently appeased.

"Got the condoms in your pocket?" she asked offhandedly—just as though she were asking him if he'd remembered to get the groceries out of the truck. "Don't want to have to send you out for them later."

If he could have reached her, he would have kissed her until she was as senseless as she made him feel. But since he couldn't reach her without dropping his boxes or knocking them both off the steps, he simply grinned up at her from his heart and patted his pocket so she could hear the foil crackle.

"Right here," he said.

She smiled back and opened the door to the blast of heat and voices that ushered them into the house.

* * *

It was a while before she and Joe had the chance to look over each other's finds. People came and went, the reunion waned and swelled.

Zeke and Hallie's mother gave them strange looks when Hallie and Joe disappeared individually to return wearing different shirts—although, to her credit, Hallie changed her entire outfit to hide the garage-floor muss stains on her trousers and simply looked like she'd decided to get out of her work clothes and into her civvies to finish out the day.

Rested and fed, Maura returned to the party with her and batted her father's nose, bounced in his arms and stole his heart all over again.

Those of Joe's siblings and old friends from the department and state police post who hadn't arrived with the earliest group arrived throughout the rest of the afternoon as the roads were cleared and opened, and shifts changed.

Joe's brother David plowed out Hallie's driveway, creating huge mounds to either side that delighted the children who donned half-dry snowsuits and went out again to play king-of-the-hill. Then the road commission beeped David and he took his borrowed road plow and left.

Hallie's father arrived to claim her mother, left after a steely-eyed exchange of glances with Joe that would have intimidated a lesser man down to his socks. Since Joe wasn't a lesser man, he was merely hounded with guilt.

Joe's-uncle-the-priest enjoyed the food, the lively, irreverent and often "blue" discussions, and blessed the gathering collectively, Maura individually, then cornered the baby's father to, as Joe's mother put it, "administer to Joe's faith." Which was another way of saying his uncle took Joe aside, offered him reconciliation, then, when Joe politely refused the offer on the grounds that he had nothing to reconcile with anyone but Maura and Hallie, spiritually and none-too-gently busted him in the chops.

Though glad to have seen them again, Joe was not sorry

to see the back of his family when they finally left—particularly after Gabriella took him aside and inquired solicitously, and with bat-her-lashes non-innocence, after his health and change of shirt.

When he told her where to go and to mind her own business, she grinned at him and said, "Aha! Thought so," as though he'd just confirmed every last one of her suspicions.

Which, of course, he probably had.

Late in the afternoon, one of the deputies ferried the captain, Crompton, Montoya, the other deputy and three of the detectives to their respective homes, the captain leaving Hallie with strict orders to "keep her apprised of the situation." About the same time, a fresh pair of deputies in uniform arrived, leaving Joe uneasy at this obvious changing of the guard; they took their orders from Frank, who'd stayed behind, then helped themselves to coffee and leftover paella. On their arrival, and as though given the nod, all but one of the state troopers said their thanks and left.

If he hadn't realized it before, the show would have made it very clear to Joe in just what high regard Hallie was held by her community of peers and underlings.

It was also clear from the new deputies' and the trooper's posturing exactly who they thought they were on hand to protect Hallie and Maura from. All three were men Joe had known for years; one had even graduated from high school with him and Hallie. They *knew* him. But apparently the years didn't matter at the moment.

The territorial affectations made Joe as angry as they made Hallie when he and Zeke did the macho thing around her, but since he couldn't really disagree with the men's assessment of the situation, he had little choice but to accept it.

He also had more pressing things to occupy his attention. Like Hallie. For some reason, he couldn't take his eyes off her. Though she was obviously distracted by thoughts of impending revelations, to Joe's mind her skin glowed the way some women's did after they'd made love, or during pregnancy. Healthy, beautiful, he could see the on-duty officers watching her, too, seeing her somehow differently than they ever had before. And he could feel himself prowling between her and them, keeping them separated from her, claiming his own.

When he realized what he was doing he felt foolish; in the next instant, when the trooper offered her a cup of coffee on his way to get one for himself, Joe knew that if he'd been a wolf, he'd have growled.

Awareness of this fact made him uneasy.

It would have been bad enough if this was all he had to deal with where Hallie was concerned, but no. She also seemed hell-bent on driving him physically, mentally, emotionally crazy: flirting with him across a room one moment, making sure to brush or somehow touch him when she walked anywhere near him the next—quite clearly staking her own claim. It was a side of her he'd never seen before. To say he liked it was an understatement. To understand the invitation was excruciating, notably because with Frank, his deputies and the troop apparently dug in for the night, Joe had no idea when or if he'd be able to accept.

The thought of whether or not he *should* give in to temptation didn't even cross his mind; he was already pretty damned sure he shouldn't, but that hadn't stopped either him or Hallie so far.

After another long private consult with Hallie, Zeke bundled Sam and Ben into heavy blankets, strapped them onto the toboggan attached behind his snowmobile and left. Then there was nothing between him, Hallie, and Mary's collection of secrets but the library door.

And, of course, Maura. But since she didn't seem particularly concerned about the content of her biological mother's logs, pictures and diaries, or Zeke's files on Mary, Hallie finally sighed, blew a raspberry on the infant's tummy that made Maura laugh and brought her into the office with them.

It had been years since Joe had voluntarily set foot inside the room. The same feeling that had swamped him then engulfed him now: paranoia, guilt, the need to repent for sins he'd never committed. Then he took a deep breath and blew it out, clearing his head of dead history to really look at the room for the first time ever.

It wasn't anywhere near as forbidding as his imagination remembered it. Painted in what he thought he'd once heard Hallie refer to as a ''light sage,'' with splashes of rose, blue and deeper green detail, it was cool and inviting. The front of the room was bounded by glass halfway up on two sides; he'd seen that from outside. What he didn't recall were the cupboards and shelves lining the same two walls beneath the windows and the desk that held Hallie's home computer setup built against the front-porch wall; the largely open area that made up the rest of the huge room contained several comfortable chairs, soft reading lights and a Scandinavian camp bed.

It was a room to retreat to, a haven for solitude—a spot that reminded him of some of the private growing-up places he and Hallie had shared. In an instant it washed away all the old memories, made him wonder why he'd always avoided this room in the past.

Perhaps because Hallie had made it easy by not inviting him into it, he admitted suddenly. Perhaps because when she was married to Zeke the door had always remained closed—his office at home, the threshold not to be crossed by anyone without the need to spill their guts and heal. Not by anyone who didn't have confessions—whether secular or spiritual—to make.

The thought that it had not been ancient demons or cowardice that had kept him on the other side of the door was oddly comforting in the moment before Hallie fired up the computer and they opened the boxes.

Hallie drew the short straw when they chose who got to go first, and Joe chose to explore Zeke's files before embarking on Mary's. That way, if they truly didn't seem linked to each other, he might find some way of talking Hallie out of scrutinizing—

Yeah, right, his mind snorted. *That'll happen.*

Mentally he shook his head; he could hope.

"What am I looking at?" he asked, pulling out the first manila folder.

"Mary was a patient of Zeke's for about four years before she died," Hallie told him. "Since she lost the second baby."

Joe inhaled, exhaled. Not surprise; sadness. He knew a few things about Mary that Hallie didn't yet. "She never told me."

"I didn't think so." Maura fussed slightly and Hallie took off the "World's Best Mom" necklace Sam and Ben had purchased for her at their grade-school Secret Santa Shop the previous Christmas, dangled it where Maura could see it and grab for it. "For what it's worth, Zeke never told me, either." She grimaced. "Well, he couldn't, could he? But so you know."

Joe nodded. "I know, Hallie."

She studied him, the incongruously colored eyes in the dark olive face, the nose that was a little too patrician for the rest of his features. The full, wide, exquisitely talented mouth that had nearly brought her to ecstasy by simply touching her breasts. The generous hands, broad shoulders, and all the other things that made up the physical aspect of Joe.

It was all this and history that made her love him.

The admission neither shocked nor intimidated as it might have last night, last week, last year, a lifetime ago. It simply made her wonder what on earth had taken her so long to grow up and recognize what should have been obvious from the moment she and Joe met. And even after she'd slept with Joe last night, felt her heart opening, acknowledging his presence—even then, she'd needed her ex-husband to point out the direction of her lifelong affections.

She'd have borne his child any number of times, with Mary in the picture or not; she knew that now. Truthfully she'd known it then, too; she—they—had simply all put a different name on it. "For Mary," they'd said. "For Mary and Joe." But the real deal was she'd have done...well, she'd *do*—anything—not for Mary but for Joe.

She swallowed the taste of shame, reading between the lines of what she'd read in Zeke's files. Perhaps Mary had had a right to her jealousies and concerns, after all. It had to be difficult to watch another woman love your husband more—and maybe better—than you thought you loved him yourself. Even if—or maybe that was *especially* if—the other woman never acted on her feelings, and was dense enough to not even be clued in to the fact that she was, and would always be, in love with your husband.

It had to be impossible, then, wondering how you could compete.

Wondering if your husband reciprocated a feeling that he, too, didn't act upon.

Hallie bobbed the "Mom" necklace out of Maura's grasp. She couldn't think about Joe and love in the same sentence just now. It would make her wonder...and really, that wasn't what this was about. This was about finding a killer, and a person who'd followed her and her kids around for at least a couple of months. A person who, for whatever reason, seemed to be out to at least disturb, if not to threaten, Joe.

And now for unknowable reasons, her, Hallie, as well.

She sucked air, blew it out, and continued. "Anyway," she said, "because Mary was family, so to speak, Zeke felt he couldn't ethically treat her and wanted to send her to someone else, maybe someone who could prescribe an antidepressant. She told him she was afraid of drugs and didn't know if she could trust anyone else." Hallie let her shoulders rise and drop. "It's a common problem, he sees it all the time. Usually with a little work, some time that asks a patient to look at herself, maybe accept things she doesn't want to about herself, he can convince her to at least see a psychiatrist or psychopharmacologist once for a consult. But Mary wouldn't change her mind."

"As…" Joe hesitated, looking for the word. "As tractable as she could appear, she was damned stubborn." *And scary,* he didn't add. But he hadn't known that when she was alive.

"She had to be stubborn," he heard Hallie say. "I don't think I'd have suffered three miscarriages before I decided to try something else."

"Yeah," Joe agreed absently, distracted by a comment he'd missed from one of Mary's sessions just before she'd found herself a stud to get her pregnant for the third time. The comment was an observation about Mary's perception of reality—or lack thereof—that rang a bell he couldn't place. "But you wouldn't consider not being able to carry your own child as something that took away your womanhood. You'd have gotten on the adoption list and waited for a baby. Or you'd have taken in strays, or worked with kids from Children's Village, or been a foster mother, or decided to adopt older kids, or found some other way to get on with things. Mary couldn't get by what her body wouldn't let her be. Her mother was always on her about that."

"About accepting herself?" Hallie was surprised. She'd gotten to know Mary's mother pretty well over the last year and a bit, and the woman hadn't impressed Hallie as the accept-who-you-are type. Rather the opposite, in fact; ready to pick on each little failure, turn it into something huge.

"No." Joe glanced up from the papers he was reading, shook his head. "Picking on her about whatever Mary couldn't do. Lose weight, she wasn't eating enough. Gain a pound so she didn't look like a stick, she'd better go on a diet. Marry a man who can get you pregnant but whose baby doesn't 'take'…'' His jaw clenched around a mirthless grin. "Well, you take it from there."

She'd rather not. "Joe, I'm sorry. I knew—you told me—but I didn't—or maybe I could have… God, what kind of friend was I, anyway?"

"The best kind," Joe said quietly. "The kind who was there all the time, no matter if I told you things or not."

"But if…"

He shook his head, hushing her with the slight compression of his mouth, and reached to remove the necklace from her hand, look at it. "We kept our marriages separate for a reason, Hallie. No sense second-guessing that reason now. The fact I could come to you and not explain anything was—is—" His jaw tightened, muscles ticked. "Until I…screwed up an-and left, you trusted me whether I said anything or not. You didn't have to be reassured about everything all the time. I could be quiet with you and know I wasn't alone." He canted his head to look her in the eye and finish, "I should have realized what I had when I had it, but I didn't. Now I hope I haven't screwed up permanently."

Then he took her hand and draped the necklace across her palm, closed her fingers over it and brought them to his mouth, brushed his lips gently across her knuckles and pushed them away.

Stunned, Hallie scanned his face, trying to decide what he'd said. "Joe—"

He ducked from her scrutiny. "Not now, Hallie. I can't because I don't know…." His mouth twisted and he shook his head as if to clear it. Dipped his fingers into the watch pocket of his jeans and drew out a pair of small keys. "For the strongboxes," he said and handed them to Hallie.

He thought his heart would stop beating while he waited for her to open them.

* * *

Together as kids they'd read the Hardy Boys books, Joe's older siblings Alfred Hitchcock's Three Investigators Mystery series, Agatha Christie, even Nancy Drew when Hallie demanded equal time for a female sleuth.

Age gave them Dick Francis, James Lee Burke, Ridley Pearson and David Lindsay, among others in common. But the years had also changed their tastes, made them no longer constantly overlap. Hallie loved a good, fast-paced, heart-wrenching romance; Joe read Dean Koontz. Hallie read Bruce Coville and Louis Sachar to the boys; Joe preferred reading Piers Anthony or Christopher Stasheff aloud whenever he baby-sat for nieces and nephews—genetic or honorary.

Neither one of them liked reading psychological or sociological profiles. Neither had ever gotten used to certain kinds of murder scenes in particular or hardened to the horror of rape, the victimization of children or other corruptions of the human condition. But they were prepared to deal with all of those things; deviants came with the job, after all. None of that readied them for dealing with what putting all their available information together showed them about Mary.

Individually opened, each Pandora's box contained its own trials and truths. Zeke's observations were as straightforward and literal as he was: notations of what Mary told him, what they discussed, typed transcripts of their sessions; the increasingly recurring comment that although he felt she needed more help than he could give her, Mary vehemently refused to see another doctor. Compared against her own stud-exploration-data files, there seemed to be a clear correlation between something Zeke interpreted point-blank, then withdrew as a personal observation that he might have misunderstood, then re-alluded to in his notes at a later date—after Mary's third miscarriage.

I think she came on to me again today. She seems to
be having a problem getting into bed with Joe, but that
doesn't quite make sense. It's not what she said, so
it's probably my imagination. I could have sworn she
said, "There's proof yours live. Give me a baby." She
didn't say it very loud and I'm not sure I heard what
I thought I heard. Listened to the tape but couldn't
make it out for sure. She's not well. I can't help her
and want to stop treating her, but when I told her that,
she said if I didn't see her in the office, she'd come
to the house. I believe she would. Don't want to risk
her coming when the boys are there.

Then there was a side note.

I'm too close to this. Ask Tim Dooley to do hypo-
thetical personality profile for cross reference.

Mary's notes for the corresponding date were uncharacteristically choppy, and obviously furious.

He won't do it. Men are such cowards. They don't get
it. They think if you cut off their hoo-ha's you've dam-
aged them. But what good are they if they can't give
you live babies? Might as well make a sperm gumbo
and use a turkey baster. So damned much ego to make
sure whatever comes out of you is theirs. My father—

The diatribe broke off without warning, picked up on the
next line, clear, simple and unemotional as you please.

A good scientist doesn't quit when a subject refuses
to cooperate. Have to move down the list to the next
candidate or the one after that. Maybe another one
from Joe's office.

"*Another* one from the office?" Puzzled, Hallie looked up at Joe. "Who was the first?"

He shook his head. "According to her earlier notes, the other one was big and looked enough like me to cover up genetic questions later. Even if you were talking one of my cousins from over in Corrections, there's none of 'em my size."

"But this looks like Zeke was right. She was coming on to him in the office."

"Yeah." Controlled, dispassionate. Taut, but not…hurt. Accepting. He couldn't do anything about it, couldn't change it, and the woman he wanted was curled on the floor opposite him about to learn things about his late wife that could seriously damage the relationship he hoped to have with her.

Hoped that somehow, despite time and circumstance, he already had with her.

They viewed the videotape together first. Filmed in color, it was bad, a journal of Mary's death shot perhaps from across the street. When he'd first seen it by himself, Joe had assumed the stalker-as-a-separate-person or the killer's accomplice had shot it. Hallie paled watching the tape, lifted Maura from her chair and held her tightly, pacing back and forth in front of the television. But she maintained her cool enough to note that no matter what happened, the camera angle never changed nor did the camera ever seem to waver. As though the shot had been set up beforehand—perhaps while Mary was inside the grocery store.

As she pointed out, the blessedly silent footage opened on the Blazer, then showed Mary stepping around the truck, opening the door, setting the groceries inside, straightening and turning to greet someone behind her. She had Joe rerun that bit again and again, getting up close to scrutinize Mary's face, see if she could learn anything that way. Then she sighed and told him to rewind it and set it aside. They'd

have to get the experts to take a look at it, use their equip-
ment to enhance every grain.

He'd done that, Joe told her, to no avail.

But of course, as Hallie told him bluntly, he'd been half
blind with rage, hadn't been working with a full deck, and
hadn't been working with her. And hey, that made all the
difference in the world.

Joe eyed her with wry amusement and more than a little
amazement, stuck his tongue in his cheek and, in the words
of some distant Southern relative of his father's, "allowed
as how she might be right."

Finished with the video, they moved on to the shoe box.

It contained the lesser evils—computer diskettes, the rest
of the early series of photos of Mary alive, several small
notebooks crammed with daily notes. As Joe had told her
yesterday—was it only yesterday?—the books weren't exactly diaries, but more like records, cryptic reports to herself on case files she'd taken too personally to leave at
work. Dates, but no names; a little description, but no faces;
no obvious case numbers, but plenty of commentary—a
few bits of which included questions to herself about various of these...clients, for want of a better term, acting as
possible sperm donors; notations to access physical and
mental-health histories for her "personal donor" files.

The books dated back years—some from even before
Mary met Joe and some from the time just prior to when
they were introduced. The entries at that point sickened
Hallie, included a description of the man she would have
recognized anywhere. As much as it had been in her power
to do so, Mary had looked Joe over, checked him out, eyed
the size of his family and decided he was the stud for her.
Then she'd done her homework, made her notes, studied
hard, found a friend who had a friend who introduced her
to Joe. Simple, particularly given the way the department
of social services and the sheriff's department had to constantly interact. Crossing Joe's path had been simple.

The whole thing was so cold, so unlike the woman Hallie thought she'd known that she wanted to deny the evidence, the written calculations right in front of her. Some people schemed, finagled, hobknobbed and married for money, power, status. Mary had married a man with a big heart from a big family she could use to make her babies. And when that plan had failed, she'd made a new plan.

Or returned to the old one.

It was all terribly sad, if you thought about it. With Maura in her arms scrunching down in search of mother's milk, Hallie didn't want to. Didn't really want to think of Mary again. But with all the stuff remaining to be sorted through, it was impossible not to think of Mary. Not with Maura at her breast. Not with Joe squatting in front of her, fists straining and relaxing against each other, regarding her through wary eyes, a man waiting for a verdict.

A man waiting to get on with it, who told her without speaking a word that once begun they had to go on with it or risk more than he could bear.

No way out except through.

So they finished it. And as Joe had warned her, it wasn't pretty.

Didn't even come close.

The strongboxes were full of photographs, videos, mementos of Hallie's life after children: a pair of Ben's bootees, a lock of Sam's hair—innocent enough on the surface until Hallie looked at the photos. Most of them came in two sets: those with Hallie in them, and those with Hallie taken out and Mary put in her place.

The older pictures had simply been cut and pasted. The more recent ones had been scanned into a computer and cut and pasted to look frighteningly real. Hallie eyed them with revulsion.

"She wanted my *life?*" she asked, turning to Joe. *"Mine?"*

"That's what it looked like to me." Joe shrugged, wanting to reach out, to protect, but not sure if she'd accept what he could offer. She'd always been pretty too damned capable of looking out for herself, after all. "She figured hers wasn't working, why not try yours."

She stared at him. For the first time in her life, she truly understood what it felt like to hate someone almost beyond reason, to be filled with contempt. But it wasn't for Joe. Nor was it, as Joe had feared it might be, for herself for having been taken in.

It was for Mary.

"And she would have…you think she would have…" She couldn't ask it. The very thought was untenable, incomprehensible.

"I think she was capable of a lot of things nobody was aware of," Joe said steadily. The admission that had nearly killed him to recognize a year ago came next. "And yes, especially after comparing this stuff against Zeke's notes, I think she might have tried. But then you came to us about the possibility of an embryo transfer and she saw things differently. Look—" He pulled a newer notebook out of the pile, flipped through a few pages, pointed out passages to Hallie. "The comments she made here—" he turned another page "—and here." More pages. "And look at how her handwriting changes. Loops and swirls, not all mincy and cramped." He shrugged. "She was happy. I don't know if it would have lasted, or what would have happened when Maura got here, if the jealousy would have started over again, maybe worse, or if she'd have been too busy with the baby…" His mouth twisted. "You want to know the truth, I hate that she was killed, but the more I learn about her, the gladder I am Maura will never come in contact with her."

"Except through what you tell her," Hallie said gently.

He nodded, feeling old and tired. "Except for that."

She touched his face, drew a finger along the line of his

jaw. "And then Mary will be the person we thought we knew before she died."

He sighed, a weight lifted from his shoulders. "Yes." He turned his head suddenly and kissed her hand. "Thank you."

"Any time, *m'ijo*," she whispered back, but not loud enough for him to hear.

Silence swelled the room for a minute. Frank stuck his head in the door to see if they wanted any help, ducked back out when they refused.

The minute passed.

"Okay," Hallie said. "We've got all sorts of information on Mary, but obviously even if she was stalking me at some point before she died, she's not the one doing it now."

"And if we assume," Joe agreed, "that you're right about the video camera that taped the murder having been set up in a stationary position, say in a vehicle across the street, then we can probably also work on the premise that your stalker and Mary's killer are one and the same."

"I don't like that assumption." Hallie felt her nipple slip out of Maura's mouth, glanced down to find the infant asleep, carefully brought the baby to her shoulder. "It doesn't make any sense. Why would somebody want me? If your original thought about Mary ending an affair with someone who didn't want it over is true and he's the person who killed her...why target me? No." She made a negative tcch sound between her teeth. "The pictures have been left for you, geared at getting to you somehow. Which has to mean *you're* the goal. The kids and I...we're just—"

"The bait?" Joe supplied, his voice ugly.

The admission was not pleasant. "Something like that."

"You don't think I thought of that?" Joe fairly exploded to his feet, prowled a restless circuit around the room. "I went over and *over* it, Hallie, damn it. Every angle. I cross-reffed her caseload against mine. I broke into the department's personnel files to see if I could find a physical match to me. I peeled apart her descriptions of the people on her list the best I could and ran 'em against every picture we got on file, including the criminal records. I—''

''Then there's something missing,'' Hallie interrupted, rising gently so she wouldn't wake Maura and heading for the door. ''Maybe if we run Zeke's files against Mary's and yours—''

She stopped short in front of the computer monitor, staring at the screen. In bold black letters on a red background were the words: ''Look to the children. I don't want to hurt them.''

Then, before she could turn around and find out if Joe had seen, too, the screen went blank, the power went out, and something crashed through the library window and thudded in a shower of glass to the floor at Hallie's feet.

Chapter 15

November 26, 10:23 p.m.

Joe was on them in an instant, frantic.

"Hallie? Are you all right? Where's Maura?"

"Here, Joe. Fine." She'd turned sideways the moment the glass shattered to protect Maura from any flying shards. Already her hands skimmed the baby's head, face, body, making sure nothing had touched her, no glass clung to her sleeper. "Maura's here. She didn't even wake up and I can't feel any glass. She's fine."

"What about you?"

Even as her hands had swept his daughter, his hands brushed Hallie down, heedless of the stinging the action caused when he encountered glass in her clothing. His fingers slid into the sticky mess she hadn't even felt on her right arm. Air hissed painfully between her teeth.

"Bad?" Joe pulled his fingers away.

"Feels like there's a piece of glass stuck in there."

"Deep?"

"Messy. I don't know."

Frank and a deputy burst through the door, weapons a dull extension of their arms in the shadowy light given off by the snow and the street lamp outside. At the front and back of the house, doors slammed open—the state trooper and the other deputy exiting to do a quick search of the area.

"What happened?"

"Power went out and something came through the window," Joe said tersely. "Baby's fine, Hallie's hurt. Don't know how bad. Get a light."

"There's a couple of six-volt lanterns and a box of candles on the front-left side of the shelf in the coat closet," Hallie supplied.

With a quick gesture, Frank dispatched the deputy. "We need units?"

"I don't—" Joe began.

Hallie cut him off. "Yes. Sweep the neighborhood. And send a unit to Zeke's. Tell 'em to try not to freak Zeke, but to make sure the area's quiet, the boys and Zeke are okay, then sit on 'em." She turned back to Joe. "Joe, did you see the computer before the power went out?"

"No."

"I had it hooked to the department's computer so we could run Zeke's and Mary's floppy files side by side with the department's from here. Someone broke the connection and put up their own message. 'Look to the children. I don't want to hurt them.'"

"Look to the—" Joe repeated, flabbergasted, then broke off when realization sank in. A single graphically succinct word hit the air and faded. "We've got to get you out of here."

She shook her head. "We've got to get *Maura* out of here. She's not part of it, I am."

"Hallie—"

"We can't risk the kids, Joe. Even if I go, it couldn't be with them."

His fists clenched, his jaw jutted, his mouth took the shape of a noiseless snarl. She was right and he hated it.

When Mary died, he thought he'd ripped the heart from his chest and thrown it away so it could never hurt him again. But in a day and a half—although in reality, she'd held it for thirty years if only he'd realized—Hallie, his best friend, his partner, the tomboy behind the catcher's pads who'd caught his sliders, curves and fastballs when they were kids, had also caught his heart when he'd pitched it, kept it safe this last year for him, along with his daughter. Sewed it back inside his chest last night, this morning, this afternoon, when he found he couldn't live without it anymore.

Didn't want to live without her.

Couldn't, he supposed, if he were honest, since she was his heart, his lungs, his memories, his self—all those vital things that made him who he was and would be.

Could be.

Gently he took Maura from Hallie's arms, settled her in the portable crib set up for her earlier. When the deputy returned with the candles and electric lanterns, he was the one who looked at the apparent mess that had been made of Hallie's arm. A lot of thin blood trails from tiny, inconsequential nicks and scratches, and one significant cut deep enough to need debriding and stitches.

He was about to ask Hallie if she had any tweezers when Frank, wielding one of the lanterns and trying to spot the cause of the broken window, swore and stooped to retrieve something from the floor: an antiriot, flat-nosed, molded PVC plastic round. Hallie, Joe, Frank and the deputy stared at the bullet. Most often used to quell protesters without killing them in Northern Ireland, it was an unusual find— to say the least—on the floor of Hallie's library. And although it packed a wallop in riot control, it was not the sort of round meant to be fired from any distance, and would have to have been fired from fairly close by in order to break the window—if it was meant to break the window at all, that is. If it was…

A nondescript shotgun round fired high would have achieved the same result less flamboyantly. Which meant either this was someone who'd chased Mary, then Joe, now Hallie quietly for a long time and who now wanted to be noticed—or just get real close—or it was someone who no longer cared about being caught. In any event, no one present liked the direction of their thoughts.

The officers who'd gone out to scout the immediate area rejoined them. Reports were quick and concise: nothing to report. No other power was out in the area. No other windows broken. Impossible to spot fresh footprints in old snow that had been footprinted aplenty by countless youngsters earlier today.

The striated flash from light bars cut across the windows as they finished their accounts. Frank redispatched the officers with a heavy torch in search of Hallie's circuit breaker, hoping the power problem might be so easily fixed. After all, last night's—or make that this morning's—phone outage had been accomplished from the inside; why not this? Especially considering all the people who'd been through the house earlier today.

Which thought gave rise to a whole other series of questions no one wanted to attempt to answer—or even to ask.

Hallie's arm continued to sting and seep. With obvious reluctance she used Frank's cell phone to call Zeke, apprised him briefly of the situation and asked if he could look after Maura—and George, too—for her while this thing played itself out. Not happy with the reasons, but resigned and more than willing to play whatever role it took to keep Maura and the boys safe, Zeke agreed—after making some sardonic comments about Hallie owing him big time for being about to have to forcibly wean yet another baby who preferred the real thing.

Hallie thanked him far too sweetly for his observations, then ended the call after first arranging to have a pair of deputies known to Zeke bring Maura to him and remain at the house, while another was dispatched to buy bottles and formula. Then Hallie asked him a few questions about the notes she'd read in his file on Mary. He was reluctant to speak about his observations, but did so, including telling Hallie a little about the profile he'd requested from Tim Dooley. Tim had suggested exactly what Hallie suspected: Mary compartmentalized the various aspects of herself, never keeping two pieces of her psyche in the same place at the same time. Without somehow being able to study all the pieces together, it would be difficult to make an accurate diagnosis; Tim's opinion had been that Mary needed more intensive treatment, perhaps a period of hospitalization for observation.

Because Mary had come to him voluntarily and asked him to keep their sessions confidential from everyone including Joe, to whom she would herself speak if necessary, Zeke had been stuck in his ethics without a paddle—especially since, other than making vague hints at impropriety, she hadn't appeared to pose a threat to herself or anyone else during the time he was seeing her. And, as seemed indicated in her journal entries, Mary's demeanor had changed dramatically with the prospect of Hallie carrying a child for her.

Which of course made little sense now that they both thought about it—particularly when Hallie had mentioned the Thompson-family photos with her image clipped out and Mary's inserted—since Hallie appeared to have been an object of Mary's envy, the person whose life she wanted to live. On the other hand, if the vagueness of Mary's journal entries was to be believed, Mary had also never thought anyone could ever possibly be willing to do anything like surrogacy for her.

Yes, it meant she couldn't carry and deliver a baby from her own body, but it also meant the possibility of having one that was entirely her own, genes and all. Since she was dead, there was no way of knowing for certain, Hallie knew, but the best possible face on the whole thing was to hope that somehow Mary's desire for children had allowed her to compromise to the point of letting someone else— Hallie—carry one for her. It was a pickle, plain and simple. Best to think good thoughts, therefore, than hold suspicions they no longer had any way to follow up on.

Just before they broke the connection, Zeke suddenly told Hallie to be careful, he'd have his friend's profile for her in the morning. She told him to take care of the kids and give the boys kisses for her, then snapped the phone closed. Then she pinched the bridge of her nose between thumb and forefinger, seizing and dissipating emotion, and turned briskly to Joe and directed him in changing Maura's clothing.

He studied her for a moment, troubled, worried about the delay in her getting her arm the attention it needed, then tightened his lips and did as he was told. She'd be far more amenable to receiving medical attention once her chicks were altogether away from her and as safe as she could make them.

Sure enough, the minute Maura was out of sight, Hallie's face crumpled and she relaxed enough to let tension and the shakes get the better of her. Joe gathered her in and jerked his head toward the door, urging Frank out of the room. He went without question, barking orders for some- one to find him a piece of wood to cover the ''stinking'' window to keep the ''stinking'' snow out.

''She could have died, Joe.'' There were no sobs, only a deeply rattled mother who never wanted her child so close to flying glass or antiriot bullets again. ''She could have been killed and I couldn't stop it. Oh, God, I'm sorry. I'm sorry.''

"Nothing happened to her, Hallie.'' He didn't know which scared him more—Maura in the way of flying glass and other things, or Hallie. He ran his lips over Hallie's hair, pressing kisses along the side of her head that hadn't been exposed to the glass. Pieces of it still clung to her T-shirt; he was careful where he put his hands. "She's safe, but we need to get these clothes off you, get rid of the glass, get you looked at.''

"You get these clothes off me, you and everybody else'll be able to look at me pretty well without taking me to Emergency, don't you think?''

The joke was weak, but humor nonetheless.

"True.'' Joe smiled, grateful for her all the way to his socks. "But you're making us both a bloody mess and you still need the glass taken out of that cut and stitches put in.''

"Okay.'' She nodded into his shoulder, sighed and stepped back. "Probably be better if we confine the glass to one room. And since you've held me, you should probably change, too.''

He tipped his head in agreement. "I'll have Frank get some stuff out of my duffel, then go up and get your things.''

"Frank going through my drawers?'' Hallie grimaced in mock horror. "He opens my underwear drawer, I'll never live it down.''

Joe eyed her, interested. Exploring her underwear drawer at some future date sounded like it could prove a mighty fascinating expedition—and one for which he'd have to be sure to make time. "How 'bout I tell 'im if he opens your underwear drawer I'll punch him out?''

Hallie patted Joe's chest. "Nice offer, but hardly necessary. Just tell him if he opens anything but the bottom two drawers to find me sweatpants and a loose shirt, I'll do the damage personally.''

Joe grinned. ''Let's hope he's a wise man, then.''

''And fast.'' Hallie winced. ''This thing hurts like a son of a gun.''

With one quick glance that took in the tightness around her eyes and mouth, the clear signs of pain that belied the few moments of banter, Joe swore once and hollered for Frank.

November 27, 2:32 a.m.

By the time they returned from getting her arm stitched, the power was back on, the window boarded up and the house secured—at Frank's request and insistence—by state troopers and deputies who'd been nowhere near the residence in the last two days.

Hallie, exhausted and whacked out a bit by the painkillers she hadn't wanted to take but on which she'd compromised by accepting a mild dose, fell asleep during the ride back, leaning against Joe in the back seat of a squad car. He woke her only enough to get her walked into the house and upstairs to bed. There he removed her boots and sweatpants, settled her into the warmth and comfort of the quilt and flannel sheets, and tucked her in, elevating her bandaged arm on extra pillows. Then he went around the other side of the bed, undressed and climbed in to spoon himself along her back and slide his arm around her, ensuring not only that her arm would stay elevated, but that he'd know if she so much as twitched.

When he was certain Hallie was once more asleep, he folded his arm underneath his pillow and finally allowed himself to drop off, too.

And to hell with what anybody downstairs might think about him sleeping up here with her.

November 27, 6:47 a.m.

Morning eased pink and gold light along the edges of the world when next Joe opened his eyes to the sensation of Hallie's bottom settling more firmly against his.

He groaned. She was hot and moist, her hips rotated, bringing him into intimate contact, separated only by a thin and wholly erotic scrap of silk.

Rational thought waned. He put his hands on her hips trying to still them. "Hallie?" he whispered.

There was no response but a murmur of excited encouragement, a shift that allowed her to release one of his hands from her hip, draw it to her breasts. His other hand she placed in blatant invitation on her mound, then reached underneath his fingers to press his sex into the silk sheath her movements created of her panties. He groaned again and his hips jerked involuntarily, embedding him more firmly against her.

The feeling was incredible, one he was definitely *not* certain how to experience now. But asleep or awake—he still wasn't sure which she was—Hallie gave him no choice. She circled his erection low and tightly with thumb and forefinger, rotated her hips, and pressed that incredible *spot* again and again until all conscious thought left him and he was pure sensation, inarticulate sounds, an explosion of white light and little death, and muscle contractions the likes of which he'd never imagined.

When the shudders finally eased, he felt Hallie turn in his arms, opened his eyes to look at her. His erection was still full, hard, and thoroughly, dryly intact.

"Well, what do you know," she said, mischief and marvel a two-pronged devil in her eyes. "It worked. I wondered if it would when I read about it, but I've never had a chance to try it."

"What was that?" Joe asked, incredulous, still caught in the aftereffects of what she'd done to him. Still amazed at how hard he remained, how ready he was to dump her on her back and love her long and well.

She winked and offered him a naughty grin. "One of the dispatchers passed a copy of *The Multi-Orgasmic Man* around the office. I was curious, so I read it. I didn't think this, uh, particular, uh, *technique* would work so quickly, but apparently, used with the right, enlightened man, it does."

"'Right'?" Ever mindful of her arm, Joe bounced her on her back and loomed over her in mock outrage. "'Enlightened'? You mean you were just toying with me, woman? I was part of an experiment?"

"Yeah, I guess so." She blinked guilelessly at him. "What, you didn't like it? You wouldn't want me to do it again?"

Amazing woman. So painfully shy with him yesterday morning, such a hedonist this one.

"Hell, yes." He bent and kissed her, deeply, warmly, thoroughly. "If that's the result, you can experiment on me any time you want, if—" He paused significantly.

She narrowed her eyes and took the bait. "If?" she asked. It was a question, not the out-and-out agreement he sought.

He grinned. Never give ground you can make them take, he thought. It was the way his Hallie had always been.

And he would worry about courting the type of disaster thinking of Hallie as his could bring later. Right now he had his beautiful blonde all to himself, eager for him to fill her. And he had his own powerful hankering to take his own sweet time doing so.

"If..." He dipped his head and his murmur was a sensual caress at her ear, his fingers gentle invaders ridding her of her underwear, sliding back up the length of her thighs. Pausing to delve her secrets, draw the wetness from her. Slipping from her channel to moisten and tease the swollen pearl above it. Leaving her in glorious agony, arching her hips upward in mute request for more when he glided his fingers higher up her body still, along the line of her belly, tracing each breast without actually touching either, drawing a line through the hollow between them. He watched them pebble painfully tight, plump high toward his mouth above Hallie's ribs, begging for attention. "If..."

"Joe, please," Hallie pleaded, reaching to draw his head down. "You're making them crazy. You're making them hurt. They're full. Please, *please.* They have no baby to— oh—" Disgusted. She might be needy, but *he* didn't need to have *her* spell out what Maura being gone meant. "Never mind. If what?"

He bent to flick his tongue across one nipple, then the other; chuckled when she moaned and arched into that small caress. For all her ability to find his vulnerabilities and milk them for all she was worth, sometimes she could be so transparent.

"If—" he whispered again, against her mouth, teasing. She fumed vocally when he pulled away from her and reached for a condom, forgave him immediately when he presented it to her like a gift on his return, and unwrapped it at the instant.

It was his turn to suck air and sigh when she clothed him in it. To take a minute to collect his thoughts.

"If you let me experiment with you in return."

"Oh, well." She spread her arms and legs wide, leaving herself entirely open to him. "Absolutely. Experiment away. Just bear in mind that if you torture me, however pleasantly, I will be forced to torture you back."

"I look forward to it," he muttered. Then he rolled one of her nipples with his thumb, opened his mouth over her other breast and laved it with his tongue until she hooked her fingers in his hair and demanded relief.

He gave it with relish, stroking and suckling, alternating back and forth between them to relieve the ache, then working his way down her body, demonstrating his own "techniques" until she was liquid, mindless—a hot volcano at the point of constant eruption, the epicenter of an emotional earthquake; a collection of recurrent aftershocks that exploded again and again when she finally sobbed her need and succeeded in dragging Joe up her body.

He entered her gladly, scooped her into his arms and took her mouth—once, twice; hungry, bruising, passionate. The third time he brought his mouth down, she whispered it against his lips so he wasn't sure he heard it.

"I love you, Joe."

He almost tried to pull back, to question at that point, but Hallie didn't let him. Instead she wrapped her arms around him, opened her mouth to his and gave herself up to him. To silent screams of pleasure and the deep-seated tremors of passion and the unspoken wiping out of last night's terrors. And Joe, experiencing his own sudden and desperate need to affirm life, assure himself of Hallie's life, his unwritten claim on it and her, pounded with her into sweet oblivion.

When it was done, they spoke little, instead remaining joined, holding tight, communicating with sighs and caresses and kisses. Wondering, though neither would acknowledge it, if this was all there would be. Wondering if it would be enough.

Determined, without words, to make it so.

And so, more than once that morning, the springs of Hallie's bed squeaked under the assault of life claimed, life affirmed. And neither one of them cared who waited downstairs for them.

Or who heard.

November 27, 2:48 p.m.

"Later" came with its attendant concerns, but not before Hallie managed to bring Joe to near-hysterical laughter and a plea for mercy when she finally explained to him where Sam's and Ben's fascination with Mary's mother's throat frog came from yesterday.

It was, as she pointed out, a simple misunderstanding of phraseology to be blamed on Hallie's mother, who'd always asked her wiggly grandsons if they didn't have frogs in their pants when they couldn't sit still. The euphemism had stuck—unfortunately—and had been used by grandma and grandsons alike throughout potty training, becoming something of a family joke between Zeke and Hallie. When she set about demonstrating—in supremely adult fashion—what their innocent, too-literal, ever-curious minds must have been unable to imagine, Joe's laughter turned into other sounds—gasps and groans and harsh-throated demands—as his body verified yet again his insatiable desire for Hallie.

But that was earlier, before they'd dressed and come downstairs.

Before they'd reentered the world of broken glass and stalkers and PVC bullets and files that cross-checked nowhere.

"We're looking in the wrong direction." After four hours of fruitless record combing, Hallie jammed her hands through her hair, frustrated. "Even if there's nothing connecting directly with me, there's got to be a link somewhere between you, Mary and the killer, at least. Something you missed or forgot about. Something Mary hid someplace else. Something that's not *here.*"

"You'd think." Joe pushed away from the computer keyboard, stretching full length in his chair to unkink muscles held in one position too long. "I looked everywhere I could think of. No safe deposit box, no storage or bus-locker keys. No home safe or anything left for safekeeping at her mother's—or at least nothing Clara would admit to. Hell, the only reason I found what I found is because Mary saved every stinking shoe box that ever came through the door and you wanted her buried in those damned matching shoes.''

''You looked—''

''Yes,'' he interrupted before she could finish. ''I did. I pulled every blasted box out of every damned closet and dumped it. Her personal credit-card bills, motel receipts, phone bills, checkbook records—everything's here.''

''Can't be,'' Hallie stated positively.

Joe gave her flat-eyed exasperation. ''Is.''

''When it was time to do the deed, where'd she meet her lover?'' Hallie asked with deliberate callousness. ''Car, house, motel, hotel, cabin in the woods?''

She rose to pace. It was well past time to nurse Maura again and she was feeling more than a smidge uncomfortable. If she didn't get some relief soon, she'd turn into one unhappy momma with a problem to express.

Literally.

She sighed. That was the real problem with nursing. Your entire life focused on the needs of your infant—which while occasionally inconvenient was not a relationship Hallie would exchange for the world—and one relatively small, but highly vulnerable area of your body. And unfortunately right now the ache in that area was distracting her from the task at hand.

She felt Joe watching her, glanced at him to find him wearing what could only be described as a smirk of male satisfaction, as though he'd read the direction of her thoughts in her expression. He raised a brow and smiled *come hither*. She swore and turned her back, pulling her bra straps away from her chest.

''Need any help?'' Joe inquired innocently.

Hallie glared at him. ''No, thank you.''

''All right,'' he said.

''Go soak your head, Martinez,'' she advised him.

''Come with me,'' he suggested.

Across the room seated at the round library table covered with Zeke's session records, Frank cleared his throat.

"Case," he reminded Hallie when she turned her glare on him. "You were going somewhere with stuff Joe—or one of us—" he added diplomatically when Joe eyed him pointedly "—might have missed."

"I was?" Hallie asked, trying to think. Damn Joe anyway. Knowing that she loved him made her brain soggy. "Oh, yes." She brightened, relieved when the direction of her interrupted query came back to her.

"We still haven't figured out who he was, whether or not Mary used her maiden name when she met him—any of that. Like, did he do the registering? Did they pay cash? What kind of records would she keep on sperm donors who were willing to personally deliver?"

She paced away as less palatable thoughts occurred to her. Ran them through her mind and edited them as carefully as she could before presenting them to Joe. "How would she find out her...subject was fertile and disease free? What kind of access did she have to medical histories that we're not seeing here? I mean, Joe—" She turned and spread her hands, an investigator at a loss. "All we've got here are nondescript data entries that, given Zeke's characterization of her, could be phony. We've got no names, no specifics. Heck, for all we know without doing a DNA trace, her third miscarriage really was yours and she pretended to herself it wasn't." She stabbed the air with a finger. "You found her private records and got into her work files, Joe, but something's not here."

His dark olive complexion paled slightly. "I suppose." He considered for a long moment, shook his head. "I don't know, Hallie. Maybe..." Another headshake, as if to clear it of images he couldn't reconcile. "I suppose we could have the lab go through the video frame by frame, see if there's anything in it that wasn't obvious that we might have missed.'' He hesitated again. ''Has Zeke gotten the stalker profile back from his friend yet?''

Hallie glanced at the clock. ''Should have by now.'' The sensation of fullness in the area of her chest increased. She needed to get out of here—gracefully—if it was the last thing she did. She crossed her arms, tapped her foot and eyed Joe. ''Why don't you call Zeke. Have him fax it over. I'll go...'' She hesitated, at a loss for an excuse. ''I'll go make a fresh pot of coffee and bring us some.''

''Coffee?'' Joe asked, skeptical. ''You don't drink coffee. At least not when you're nursing.''

''Bring it to us?'' Frank asked. ''Since when? What happened to all that hooey you're always spouting about equal rights meaning equal trips to the coffeemaker for men and women?''

''Oh, stuff a sock in it,'' Hallie told them, very much on her dignity. ''Do you want the darned stuff or not?''

''Absolutely,'' Frank said.

''Might never get me an offer like this again,'' Joe agreed.

Rolling her eyes and giving her head a disgusted when-will-men-ever-grow-up shake, Hallie departed the scene, head high.

Grinning, Joe watched her go, then reached for the phone. It rang beneath his fingers before he could lift the receiver.

It was Zeke. Talk about great minds, coincidences and all that rot.

''I got the profile,'' Hallie's ex said without preamble. ''I'll fax a copy, but...'' He hesitated, clearly uncertain how to broach what came next.

''Give me a preview?'' Joe asked carefully.

''Who's around?''

''Frank, four troopers who were nowhere near the house the last couple of days.''

''Male or female?''

Joe pulled the receiver away from his ear, eyed it as though he could send an expression of wordless curiosity and exasperation through the wires to his former friend. Then put it back to his ear. ''Judas, Zeke, male. What the hell's going on with you?''

Zeke sighed. ''Tim thinks your doer could be a woman looking for revenge for something that might have occurred at least a year before Mary was killed.''

Chapter 16

Everything inside Joe went cold. He stared at the computer screen in front of him. If Zeke was right, no wonder the files wouldn't add up.

"Say that again."

"You heard me the first time," Zeke said, obviously irritated—perhaps with himself as much as with Joe or anyone else. "He said both the stalker and the killer are probably one woman. The murder was a little more violent than most women might pull, but the rest of the profile fits. The little hints and misdirections left for you. The kinds of pictures taken—women are a lot more patient about setting up revenge than men. That's why your poisoners are usually women. They can wait it out and not give it away. But if the woman is military or either former law or on-the-job law, that could explain her choice of weapons and her use of violence."

Zeke paused, measured his interpretation of Tim's opinions. "It can also explain the message to watch after the kids. She wants to hurt you and maybe Hallie by default, but even though she took pictures of 'em to get your attention, she doesn't want the kids in the way when it goes down.''

"I see." Joe was numb. He should ask another question, but he couldn't think what to ask. A woman, not a man. And one who'd been willing to kill Mary—and film it—and was already going after Hallie to get to him. The answer was there someplace, if only he could think.

He forced his attention back to the moment. "You said, 'When it goes down.' Does that mean…? No." He shook his head. Wrong direction. "Does, ah, what's-his-name, Tim, think there's a time frame on this?"

Zeke's silence was angry, palpable. "Yeah."

"When?"

Another silence, this one brief. "Given the way she seems to be upping the stakes, Tim thinks probably within the next couple of days at the most. Sooner, more likely. Possibly it'll coincide with some anniversary." There was a pause, then the neutral question, "Wasn't it just about exactly a year ago Mary was killed?"

For an instant Joe's heart and lungs seemed to stop. Then he swallowed, nodded even though Zeke couldn't see him. "A year today." He hadn't precisely forgotten, but he had lost track of the date these past two days with Hallie.

"That's what I thought."

"Look, Zeke—" Joe's mind whirled suddenly with possibilities he had to check out. "Fax that report. I gotta go. There's somethin' I've gotta look at."

"You'd better take care of Hallie," Zeke told him seriously, "or the next person out for your head'll be me. I don't want to spend the next nine or ten months dippin' bottles in chocolate frosting trying to get your kid to eat."

"Chocolate frosting works?"

"Until she figures out she's been duped, sucks all the frosting off and spits out the nipple."

Joe's chuckle was bloodless. "Tell the little twerp to behave. And don't tell Hallie about the frosting, okay?''

"Take care of her, Martinez, or all bets are off."

"Yeah," Joe agreed tightly. "I will."

Then he cradled the receiver with extreme gentleness and turned to Frank. "You follow that?"

"Your half, which wasn't much."

"Zeke's friend thinks the person we're looking for is a woman. Maybe someone on the job."

"No." Frank's denial was automatic. Bad cops happened, but it wasn't something he liked to consider. Not here within the ranks of their own everybody-knows-everybody community, at least.

Joe stared at him, offering no quarter. It took three minutes, but Frank backed down.

"Damn," he muttered. "Judas *damn*." Then, "We switch genders, that give you any better idea who we're looking for?"

"Not yet." Joe grimaced, a man who'd made a chauvinistic assumption he regretted more than anything else he'd done in his life. "I went through all my cases last year, but I dumped any with women in 'em. Never looked at any with cops. Didn't seem to fit." Another twist of his lips. "Maybe I didn't want 'em to."

Frank nodded. "Yeah."

For a moment they stared at each other, two men in sync at last for the sake of a partner whose life might literally have been endangered by their blind spots. Joe rose, jaw working. Frank got up with him and grabbed his jacket.

"Where to?"

"Department," Joe said. "Take a look at some old files. Anything dated around this time."

"Hallie?"

"Tell your guys where we're going and why, tell 'em to tell Hallie. Zeke's fax oughtta be here any minute anyway. She'll see what's up." He turned to go after his own jacket, turned back. "Oh, and tell 'em to sit on her. Keep her here, don't let her pull rank on them."

Frank's response was a sarcastic, "Oh, absolutely. That'll work."

"It had better," Joe said grimly. Then he grinned slightly. "Besides, she'll take it better coming from them than she would from either of us. She'll pay attention, won't take it out on them because they're only following orders."

"There is that," Frank agreed. "But will it work?"

Joe eyed him, deadly serious. "When we get to the department, I'll call here and beg if I have to. Tell her to hook up to the department and I'll send her what we're looking at while we're looking at it."

"We can do that?" Frank asked, preceding him into the hallway.

Joe pulled his jacket off the peg beside the front door. "If we can't, but the public can, our tax dollars are goin' for squat."

Impatiently he waited for Frank to leave instructions with the troopers on duty, then they both beat a hasty retreat before Hallie's bathroom door could open.

November 27, 5:09 p.m.

Fuming at having been left behind by "the boys," Hallie did everything she could think of to coerce her keepers into letting her chase after Joe and Frank, or to at least *take* her to the department after them. Immune to her orders by virtue of the fact that she had no jurisdiction over them, they gave her mild refusals, called her ma'am, and generally did their job better than Joe could have imagined possible.

Forced to wait—something she'd developed an unwilling talent for, given how busy the boys were at various times of the year—she used her time to best advantage, studying Zeke's fax, going over the reports she already had, shaking out the boxes to see if there was anything any of them might have missed. A rattle in one of Zeke's cardboard file boxes caught her attention. She shook it again; again the rattle, but nothing fell out. Quickly she examined the box, opening and folding back the joins. Sure enough, hidden behind a fold of cardboard lay an unlabeled green three-and-a-half-inch high-density floppy diskette.

Probably nothing, she cautioned herself, when excitement churned her stomach. Probably blank; one of Zeke's that fell in and got stuck. Her competitive streak raised its head. She *wanted* it to be something. Teach ''the boys'' about leaving her behind while they went off to solve cases without her. Especially if, in being left behind, she managed to solve this case herself.

Jeez Louise. She rolled her eyes and sighed at herself. Was that petty of her or what?

Smiling for the first time since she'd found Joe—and Frank, blast his ever-lovin' hide—gone, she slid the disk into the floppy drive and ran a quick directory. Names—surnames, Hallie guessed—scrolled up the screen. Patient files, she decided, disappointed. A diskette from Zeke's private-office PC that had somehow gotten mixed into the hard copies he'd given her. No Martinez on the list, so probably nothing to do with Mary. Although why Zeke would leave an unlabeled diskette full of patient files lying about—and then *lose* it—was something she couldn't fathom. He might be loose about some things—especially when it came to Sam and Ben—but he was thoroughly button-down when it came to protecting his patients' rights to privacy.

She pulled the floppy from the drive, tapped it thoughtfully. Maybe this was something Zeke meant for her to find and look at ''by accident.'' Something he'd discovered but couldn't ethically share with her. Something he'd found a way to have her discover behind his back but that would give him plausible deniability.

Speculation got you nothing but a heavy conscience and ulcers. She picked up the phone. She'd just ask the source. Then, if the disk wasn't his, she'd open the files with a clear conscience and see if they were Mary's.

November 27, 5:18 p.m.

So far as Zeke knew, the floppy wasn't his. Couldn't be, he said. He kept his personal files on tape.

Within five minutes of hanging up, Hallie knew the diskette had belonged to Mary. Knew where and how Joe's late wife had managed to get medical histories she didn't have access to through her own work: somehow she'd used her sessions with Zeke to gain entrance to his records, copy what she wanted and get out without him being the wiser.

No doubt easy to do when you and your husband were best friend's with your therapist and his ex-wife. Especially if you pretended to be distraught and in need of the ''moment alone'' Zeke's notes said Mary had often requested, and he, trusting her, had given it. Wanting to rule out physical causes for whatever might ail them, Zeke often suggested his patients go for full medical work-ups when they first started seeing him. Physical histories were attached to his records. If the first five names on the disk were any indication, Mary trolled Zeke's tapes for single, healthy men whose lab work was up-to-date and on file.

There were fifteen names. Hallie went through them all once quickly, then went back through them all slowly. Ten names rang bells, five were unknown to her. One of the ten who rang bells was listed as deceased, on November 27, two years previously. Odd coincidence, that. Same date Mary had died, a year later.

When Hallie read the rest of the entry, a glimmer of light dawned. Not enough to draw a conclusion, but a place to plant suspicion.

Tomas Guttierez, six-foot-six, two hundred sixty pounds, Mexican, age twenty-seven, was also listed as the sperm donor for Mary's third pregnancy.

Sheriff's department, November 27, 5:20 p.m.

Joe paced. Frank paced. Even run on fast computers with a specific set of dates and restrictions as to gender, cross-referencing the fifteen years' worth of case files with Joe's name on them took longer than either of them liked. Particularly since, not really wanting to believe an officer could be involved, they made sure to look at *all* of Joe's files that involved women.

At a desk nearby, another technician ran the tape of Mary's murder again and again, blowing up frames and pieces of frames, examining them, moving on. With nothing to do but wait, Joe watched the footage he could have played from memory. At 6:15 p.m. the tape starts rolling; 6:19 p.m. Mary enters the frame; 6:20 p.m. she turns and smiles as someone apparently calls her name and approaches.

At six-twenty and twenty seconds, she's no longer smiling. Continues to face the camera while tossing her purse and car keys onto the front seat of the Blazer. Six-twenty-two she says something, possibly telling her attacker to just take the vehicle and go. Six-twenty-two and forty seconds, the first real fear crosses her face. Six-twenty-three she holds out her hands, trying to protect herself or bargain or both. Six-twenty-three and thirty-two seconds, her mouth forms the word "No!" then she folds and falls as the bullets enter her body.

Six-twenty-four through six-twenty-six, the film runs on the empty, blood-splattered Blazer. Then the camera jiggles, is lifted, and pans down to sit on Mary's face, waiting, apparently, for the life to go out of her eyes. At six-twenty-nine the tape goes blank. End of story.

The end, Joe thought bitterly, of another life.

He doubted now that he and Mary would have been able to stay married, that she'd have been able to keep up the facade forever, but "dead" didn't solve anything. Dead didn't let you resolve, after the fact, what she'd done to you and others.

He stared at the frames being blown up, the ones that

established with frightening accuracy Mary's time of death: November 27, 6:28 p.m.

A nauseating thought occurred to him. He turned to the computer tech.

"Can you narrow that search to one specific date and *time?*"

The tech shrugged. "If it's in your reports, I can."

"Try November 27—" He broke off when someone across the room called his name.

"Hey, Sarge—" His old rank. "Phone. It's Lieutenant Thompson."

"Tell her I'll call her back. I'm on to something. I can't talk right now."

A brief silence. Then, "She says to tell you it's urgent."

Torn, Joe looked at the phone, then back at the computer screen. "Take a message. Or no, better yet—"

He eyed Frank who shook his head. "Oh, no."

"Let Frank talk to her."

"Thanks a bunch," Frank muttered, but went.

In the end Joe wound up talking to Hallie just as, Frank muttered when he'd handed him the phone, they'd known darn well he would.

"What you got?" Joe demanded, sounding harrassed.

"Talk nice," Hallie suggested tartly. "I might tell you."

He sighed. Hallie felt the sound, the breath clear to her toes. He had something, she could feel it. The same way they'd always been in sync as partners, they were in sync now only more so. Flesh and bone so.

And, at the very least where Maura was concerned, heart and soul so, too.

"Sorry," he said. "I've got something here I don't like, but I don't have all the pieces—"

"Would a name and date help?"

The tiredness went out of Joe's voice in a flash. "I got a date and a time," he said carefully.

"November 27?" Hallie asked.

"Give me the name," Joe said.

November 27, 5:37 p.m.

Hallie hung up the phone with justified satisfaction. Between what Joe was looking into and what she'd just given him—when he'd finally accepted the phone from Frank, that is—she was pretty sure it was all over now but the identification and the capture. She could *feel* it.

What was it they said about counting your chickens before you caught them and made sure they were chickens?

Not enough apparently, because that's exactly what she did: counted her uncaught chickens, mentally beheaded them, plucked them, and readied them for the grill. Which was really a bad idea considering that it was just as she'd finished painting these virtual chickens with her equally virtual homemade barbecue sauce that the doorbell rang and the virtual version of hell broke loose.

Shouldn't-haves never having stopped her before, Hallie answered the door before any of the troopers could reach it. Crompton and Montoya stood on the porch.

"L.T.," Crompton said by way of greeting.

Hallie eyed them. "What's up?"

"Sergeant Nillson radioed, requested Deputy Crompton and me to bring you and meet them at Mr. Martinez's house," Montoya said.

Behind Hallie an exasperated officer swore and tried to get between her and the door. Hallie glared at him; he backed two steps away.

She returned her attention to Montoya. "He say why?"

Crompton shook his head. "Just said they found something more Mr. Martinez wants you to look at."

"I see," Hallie said. And she almost, but not quite, could.

What she almost saw she didn't like. The parts she couldn't see, she liked even less. *No way out but through,* she thought. But first she'd find out if she couldn't go around.

"I just spoke with both Joe and Frank at the department not ten minutes ago. Things have changed since then?"

Montoya shrugged. "I don't know, ma'am. We just do what they tell us."

"I understand." Hallie chewed the inside of her cheek. "Come in and wait. Let me give 'em a call, make sure we don't have our wires crossed."

Crompton put a foot across the threshold; Montoya hesitated.

"If it's all the same to you, Lieutenant, we'll wait for you in the car."

Crompton looked at her, grimaced and sighed. "What she said, L.T.," he agreed reluctantly.

Hallie placed the call quickly. According to dispatch, Joe and Frank had indeed left the department only moments before. No, he didn't know where they were en route to, but yes, they had left in quite a hurry.

Good enough, Hallie thought. Then she put down her not terribly dainty size ten-and-a-half, wide, and informed the troopers in her way that, orders or no, if they did not move of their own choice, she would move them herself and don't think she wouldn't.

With tremendous reluctance the troopers moved. But only as far as the kitchen where they decided which two of them would stay and which two would follow wherever she led. The Martinez house, she told them, irritated, then suggested they go on ahead and meet her there. Which, surprisingly, they did.

Officers dispatched, she grabbed her jacket, then almost in afterthought, retrieved her Beretta 9-mm and ammunition from her bedroom safe, put on her shoulder holster, covered the rig with her jacket, lifted Joe's keys from the hook in the kitchen and joined Crompton and Montoya in the car.

*Backtrack to county computer and video lab November 27,
5:33 p.m.*

Joe stared at the screens, jaw working, muscles tight.

The name Hallie had given him haunted his memory the
way any shooting would; the photo of Tomas Guttierez was
spookier still. Physically like Joe enough to have been a
cousin. Mary's lover—or whatever she would have called
him; "subject," perhaps—Guttierez, had died two years
ago today at approximately 6:28 p.m. in a shootout with
Detective Sergeant Martinez of the Cuyahoga County sheriff's department. Guttierez, who'd been in therapy with Dr.
Ezekiel Thompson trying to work out layoff-related depression. Who'd unintentionally destroyed his girlfriend's
daughter in a drunken rage. Who'd taken his girlfriend hostage. Who'd given Joe no choice but to put him down. And
whose girlfriend fit all the characteristics described in the
profile.

Tomas Guttierez was Cat Montoya's boyfriend.

He should have seen it, he was sure. How, he didn't
know, but something should have clicked. After all, it had
been there on the tape in full view all this time. Right there
in the corner, the date, the time running, the instant of the
shooting, the clocking of death. He looked at the screen. It
wasn't absolute; there was still a chance it wasn't Montoya,
but in his gut he was sure.

Now that he saw it, it was so damned obvious. Montoya
had had access to the house two days in a row—both days
when things had gone wrong. She had access to the neighborhood; she lived a block and a half from Hallie. She'd
been back in the county and working for the sheriff's department for not quite three months, was it? And hell, she'd
practically told him everything herself yesterday. Upping
the stakes, playing tag with the devil.

He looked at Frank. "Montoya," he said.

"You sure?"

"You looked at the same evidence I did," Joe said tightly. "You tell me."

Frank eyed the screens, made the same mental trek Joe had made. Scrubbed his knuckles across his mouth. "Sometimes I hate this job."

"Yeah," Joe agreed. "But we still gotta do it."

Frank made a sound of regret. "I'll find out if she's on duty. See if we can locate her the easy way first."

"However we do it," Joe said grimly, heading for the door, "it better be fast. If she's working a pattern, we've got an hour."

Fast on his heels, Frank held out his watch. "Less."

Martinez residence November 27, 5:50 p.m.

The house was dark and cool, smelled empty in spite of being recently dusted and vacuumed. Hallie waved the troopers off and let herself and the deputies in, turned on lights and upped the heat.

"Now what?" Crompton asked.

"Now we wait," Montoya said calmly.

Hallie eyed the deputy curiously. There was something in the way she spoke that raised the hackles on Hallie's neck. Not with fear, but caution.

"Nuts," Crompton was saying. "It's dinnertime. My blood sugar. You know I gotta eat regular, Cat. We shoulda stopped for somethin' on the way over."

"Sounded important we get the lieutenant here," Montoya reminded him. "Now she's here, you can go get something, bring it back."

Crompton jumped on it. "You sure?" He turned to Hallie. "L.T.?"

Hallie slid a covert glance at Montoya. Now she remembered what hadn't clicked earlier. Tomas Guttierez had been Montoya's boyfriend, the man Joe had been forced to shoot when he'd threatened a neighborhood. Montoya had made Joe's life hell pressing internal investigations to end his career. Instead, she'd been the one to quit the state police and leave the area. It was possible she'd returned last year not long before Mary was killed, then left again. Certainly she'd come back again recently enough to hire in with the county, move into a house not far from Hallie's own and be able and available to take all the pictures of Hallie and the kids she wanted to take.

"L.T.?" Crompton repeated. "It's all right if I go?"

"Yeah, sure, Leroy." Hallie nodded, reached into her pocket for her wallet, withdrew a couple of bills. "Bring me back a burger or something, too, would you? I forgot to eat before I left."

"Will do. Cat, you want anything?"

Hallie watched impatience flare and skitter across Montoya's face, saw her eyes flick to her watch. Then self-control returned.

"No, thanks, Leroy. I'm not hungry."

Crompton grinned, headed for the door. "You always say that, then you always steal mine. I'll bring you something anyway." The door closed quietly behind him.

Montoya glanced at Hallie. "He's a bit of a hypochondriac, but he's a good partner."

"I'll bet he is."

"He and his wife take people in just like that, no questions. Make 'em family." She walked around the house, looking things over, touching what had been Mary's as though she knew they'd belonged to a beaten rival. "You ever had a partner like that, Lieutenant? One who doesn't ask who you were or who you are, just accepts *that* you are?"

Hallie smiled. "Yeah, I have. I've known him all my life, though, so I suppose he doesn't really count."

Montoya lifted the glass from an anniversary clock, put the works in motion, set it by her watch, re-covered it. "I suppose," she agreed absently.

Hallie looked at the clock. Something about time rang a chime in her mind and faded.

"What are we doing here, Cat?"

Montoya turned, faintly surprised. "Lieutenant?"

"What are we doing here?"

Montoya shrugged lightly. "Waiting," she said. "Did I forget to tell you?"

"Waiting for what?"

Montoya viewed her, puzzled. "The right time, of course. Six-twenty-three to six-twenty-eight. After Mr. Martinez gets here and before Leroy comes back."

Frank's unmarked car November 27, 5:50 p.m.

Swearing violently, Joe snapped Frank's cell phone closed and pitched it onto the dashboard.

"She's not at the house," Frank guessed.

"She's on her way to *my* house," Joe snapped. "With Montoya."

"Sh—" Frank bit off the word. "How'd Montoya get her away from the troops?"

"Brought her partner along to verify the story. Let a couple of the troops follow. Calm as you please."

"You think she wants to kill Hallie?"

"I don't know who or what the hell she wants. Just step on it or let me drive."

Martinez residence 6:10 p.m.

"What happens after Joe gets here?" Hallie asked.

Montoya shrugged. "Then we play the game."

"The game?"

"Yes." Montoya nodded. "The same one he played with my boyfriend at my house two years ago. Only this time we do it at his house and we see who stands up in the end."

"You mean when he had to put down your boyfriend?"

She gave a clipped nod of response.

Hallie opened her jacket, showed her the Beretta. "I won't let you hurt him."

Montoya lifted but didn't point the weapon she'd managed to unholster without Hallie noticing. "I know that, Lieutenant."

"He won't let you hurt me, either."

Montoya's smile was tight. "I know that, too."

"Then what are we doing here, Cat? The real reason. Besides waiting."

The other woman shrugged—tiredly, Hallie thought. "I just need to know if he knew before he shot Tomas. I used to be sure he did. After two days of being in on you looking for me, I'm not sure anymore. Seems like maybe he didn't. But then maybe it doesn't matter, either."

"Knew what?" Hallie kept her voice soft, neutral, an encouraging whisper without judgment behind it.

"Knew his wife screwed my boyfriend to get herself pregnant. I thought he knew. I thought that's why he managed to be first on the scene the day I found out. That's what Tomas and I were fighting about when my little girl got hit by that ricochet from my service pistol. Mary Martinez. Tomas wanted to leave me for her. I figured her husband must have found out, too, and come to confront Tomas. I thought that's why he didn't try harder not to shoot Tomas. I thought maybe it just made a good excuse. If anybody got to kill Tomas, it should have been me."

Hallie eyed her, appalled, trying not to show it. "Joe didn't know it was your boyfriend Mary had the affair with until about forty-five minutes ago," she said. "He didn't know she'd had an affair at all until I made him look through her closet for shoes she could be buried in."

"God help me," Montoya whispered. "That's what I was afraid of."

Then she glanced at the anniversary clock, cocked her head to listen to the timer on her watch. Eye- and ear-tracked the sound of a car bouncing over a curb and screeching to a snow-crusty halt at the foot of Joe's front porch steps. Listened to the sound of men crunching and stamping onto the porch, the slam-bang of the front door opening, Joe yelling, "Hallie?" and sounding desperate when he did it.

Then Montoya smiled briefly at Hallie, brought her pistol to the center of her chest and, before Hallie could reach her, steadied it with both hands and fired.

Shucking off her jacket, Hallie dropped to her knees beside her deputy, pressed the garment into the pumping wound. "Don't you die, damn you, Montoya. Not yet."

"Better now than later, Lieutenant," Montoya gasped. Her eyes widened and fixed on the ceiling. "It doesn't even hurt anymore," she said. Then the blood pumping from the wound in her chest slowed and stopped, respiration ceased, eyes glazed.

The digital watch on her wrist read 6:27 p.m.

The gunshot drove Joe wild with fear. He drew his weapon and moved forward with as much caution as he could muster.

"Hallie?" His voice cracked and he didn't care who heard. "Hallie. *Dios, m'ija,* answer me! Please!"

"Here, Joe. In the living room. Cat's dead."

He rounded the corner, stopped at the sight of Hallie on her knees closing Montoya's eyes.

"What—?"

Hallie's eyes and face were wet when she looked at him. "That day you killed him, she thought you knew about Tomas and Mary. That's what they were arguing about. She found out about the affair. She thought you had, too—that you came and killed him on purpose. When she found out you didn't even know…she shot herself, Joe. Just like that. Time of death—6:27 p.m. I was here. I can tell the M.E.—" Her words broke and a sound suspiciously like a sob hiccuped out of her.

Joe knelt and folded his arms around her, pressed her face to his chest even as he buried his in her neck. "Shh, Hallie. It's all right. It'll be all right."

"Eventually." Hallie's voice was watery and muffled.

"Yeah," Joe agreed, wondering if his heart would ever beat properly again, if he'd ever stop hearing the shot he thought might have taken Hallie. "Eventually."

Around them Frank marshaled state troopers and deputies called to the scene, the arrival of the medical examiner, the return of Crompton who had to be told about his partner. The anniversary clock ticked, the digits on Montoya's watch turned over. Silence and grief were palpable entities: not only would the sheriff's department bury one of their own, but she'd considered taking another of theirs with her. It was a merciless, difficult scene. Unable to look anymore, Hallie turned away.

She ached both physically and emotionally to hold Maura, to wrap her in the special comforting bond that existed between mother and nursing infant—only one of the many bonds that indirectly but inevitably and irrevocably for all time tied her to Joe. She looked at him, chest suddenly aching, words she wanted—needed—to say to him dried on her tongue. If things had gone differently today...

But they hadn't. Joe was all right. The boys and Zeke had made especially sure that Maura was all right. She, herself, was all right—or would be eventually. She risked another glance at Cat. Time would dull the ache of this betrayal, of this loss, and *Life* with a capital *L* would tap-dance on. But not yet. Not yet.

Behind her, as though he'd read her mind, Joe touched her shoulder. "Looking at her won't bring her back," he said quietly.

She ducked her face, brushed her cheek against his hand. "I know." Looked up at him and said softly, "I need to hold Maura, Joe. Just really..." She hesitated, feeling the tears rising behind her eyes, burning in her throat. "I just really need to see the boys and hold her."

He shut his eyes, wanting much the same thing himself, except the person he needed to hold was Hallie. He drew her out of the way of the activity in the living room and into the relative privacy of the tiny dining room. "You got room in there for me, too, Hallie? Room to let me hold you?" He didn't want to ask, but he couldn't hold the question back.

She smiled up at him tremulously, everything she was, mirrored in her eyes. "As much room as you want, Joe. As long as you want it. My house and my bed are yours."

"What about your heart?" This wasn't the time or the place to ask, but he couldn't, didn't, stop himself. "Can I have that, too?"

She eyed him, surprised. "You've had it for thirty years, Joe. I'm not takin' it back now it's been riding around in your back pocket or tossed under the seat of your truck. Thing's probably never been washed and—"

He hauled her into his arms, bent his head and kissed her to shut her up. To taste her. To make sure of her life. To blot out the fear he'd felt coming through the door.

To stake a claim on "forever" that until now he wasn't sure he'd have. When he lifted his head, her mouth was tender, her eyes soft, her being gentle in his arms.

"I love you. Halleluia Thompson," he said. "Will you take me home with you and raise my daughter and maybe after we give it some time, be my wife?"

"How much time?"

Joe grinned. "Enough," he said. "Just enough."

Epilogue

Eighteen months later, May 3, 1:55 a.m.

Except for the dim light she left on for him in the kitchen, the house was dark when Joe came in at the end of his shift. He'd been back with the department a little over a year now, after deciding that bounty hunting and married life didn't mix.

The county had been dubious about having both him and Hallie in the same department, but since she'd become a shift commander and he was currently working evenings—performing penance, he was certain, for the time he'd been away—as a deputy rather than a detective, things were going smoothly.

Things would have gone smoothly in any event, Joe thought, because there was no way he intended to mess up what he had with Hallie.

Somewhere off in the shadows of the front hall, George's nails clicked across the floor in greeting. Joe took off his shoes and switched off the kitchen light, picked his way carefully through the front hall, stooping to scratch the dog in passing.

"How'd it go tonight, George? All quiet?"

The dog groaned and stretched, accommodating himself to the better placement of Joe's fingers on his ribs. Joe chuckled softly.

"Good. Glad to hear it."

Shoes in hand, he tiptoed up the stairs, opened and shut the baby gate, then turned left at the landing to go first to the farthest bedroom where Sam and Ben slept, lightly snoring in the moonlight. They'd grown over the past eighteen months, and their opinions with them; but they'd forgiven him his year-long desertion the instant he assured them he had no plans whatever to remove Mary's child from their household. When he'd asked for their mother's hand in marriage, Sam had politely asked if he didn't want the rest of her, too, and Ben, as literal as ever, had wondered which hand he wanted. They'd both stood up for him and Hallie three months later, on the day Hallie's adoption of Maura was finalized.

Next he peeked into Maura's room, stepped softly across the floor to pull the blanket up over the twenty-one-month-old who seemed to think she was every bit as old as her big brothers, and who had gone on her first climbing expedition to prove it at the age of ten months when she'd tossed all of her stuffed animals out of her crib, hauled herself onto the dresser at the head of her crib and gleefully shouted her first word, "Jump!"

Fortunately Sam—oh, he of the chocolate frosted idea—had heard her and thwarted the expedition in true hero fashion before anyone else could arrive: quietly, firmly and in no uncertain terms. Joe shuddered to think what might have happened if Ben was the one who'd heard her first. Zeke's and Hallie's younger son was equally as protective of his little sister as his brother, but he also had a tendency to encourage her adventurousness. Instead of removing her from the dresser before she could "Jump!" into the pool of her toys the way she'd learned to jump into mom's or dad's arms at the community swimming pool for lessons, Ben would probably have told her to wait a minute, dragged over her bean bag chair and allowed her to practice "Jump!"-ing into his arms so he'd be able to do it at the pool.

Needless to say all climb-on-able stuffed toys had been removed from her bed, the dresser placed elsewhere and "Jump!" was a word reserved for the swimming pool when daddy was in front of her period. Her most recent favorite phrase was "Me, too" as in "me, too, go," or "me, too, not…" whatever Ben and Sam were doing.

Particularly Ben.

The last bedroom was far and away Joe's favorite. Smiling at the lump Hallie made in the bed, he shed his clothes, then glanced at the crib where the newest Martinez slept, butt in the air. Lord, the woman did make the prettiest babies he'd ever seen, bar none. He lingered for a moment, watching his six-week-old son sleep the sleep of the recently fed, then breathed a deep sign of contentment and rounded the bed to join Hallie.

She rolled toward his weight, sinking the soundless mattress and box spring of their new bed. "Joe?"

He leaned in to give her a kiss. "Who else you got crawlin' into this bed at two in the morning?"

"You mean besides your son?" Her voice was sleepy, laugh-filled.

Joe glanced across at the crib. "He givin' you problems again?"

"Nothing I can't handle."

"Maybe I should just get him up and have a talk with him anyway." Being on second shift, he liked having middle-of-the-night chats with his offspring. That was when they were usually their funniest and most talkative.

"Joe Martinez," his wife warned him, "you wake that baby and I won't tell you what my doctor said today."

Anticipation flooded his loins. He forgot about waking the baby immediately. Antonio was six weeks old; the wait was over. "He say we're good to go?"

"'Good to go'?" Mock furious, she flung her pillow at him. "Good to *go?* Is that how you think about us? The honeymoon's over, we've got four kids, so no more romance? I'm just 'good to go'?" Huffy, she gave him her back. "Well, you can just think two or three times about *that,* José Guillermo Martinez, because that's how long it'll be before you have—"

He scooped her over into his arms and smothered the rest of her huff in a kiss that teased and coaxed, that made hot, dark, laughter-filled promises. She stiffened her lips, pushed halfheartedly against his shoulders for a moment—just long enough to give him a silent piece of her mind. Then she sighed and surrendered, closed her arms around his neck and opened her mouth under his, drawing him in and meeting him promise for promise until he was lost. When he was groaning into her mouth she pulled her head away.

"Promise me something?" she asked.

"Everything," he swore. "Anything."

"Don't let my mother go the frog-in-the-pants route with Tonio without making sure he understands the other version first, too?"

Shaking with silent laughter, Joe folded her against his chest, buried his mouth next to her ear. "I promise."

"Good." She sighed, contented, and traced his mouth. "I love you, Joe."

"M'ija," he whispered back, stretching out beside her and opening her pajamas to find her breasts with hands and mouth. "My darling. My heart. *Te amo.*"

Then they were silent except for the breathless, muffled sounds of parents, mindful of sleeping children, loving each other.

And getting really "good to go."

* * * * * *

SILH/HR/0010c

  Taurus

You may feel unmotivated and not so sure where your life is heading; don't despair, changes are just around the corner. Financial matters improve and you may receive something material from an unusual source.

Gemini

There are many positive aspects around you and by being confident you can succeed in all you desire, making this an excellent month. A friend has news that sets you thinking about how loyal someone close is.

 Cancer

You could be fighting to find some personal space as the demands from work and socially get too much. Sift out the important and allow the rest to drop away, leaving you time to refresh.

Leo

You should be revelling in the attention you are receiving as a result of recent achievements but deep down you feel that someone close is not being as supportive as you would like. Whatever their motives, now could be truthtime.

  Virgo

Romance is highlighted and you will feel pleased with the way a special relationship is going. Finances are looking good and you may splash out later in the month.

Look out for more
Silhouette Stars next month

2 FREE

books and a surprise gift!

We would like to take this opportunity to thank you for reading this Silhouette® book by offering you the chance to take TWO more specially selected titles from the Sensation™ series absolutely FREE! We're also making this offer to introduce you to the benefits of the Reader Service™—

- ★ FREE home delivery
- ★ FREE gifts and competitions
- ★ FREE monthly Newsletter
- ★ Exclusive Reader Service discounts
- ★ Books available before they're in the shops

Accepting these FREE books and gift places you under no obligation to buy, you may cancel at any time, even after receiving your free shipment. Simply complete your details below and return the entire page to the address below. *You don't even need a stamp!*

YES! Please send me 2 free Sensation books and a surprise gift. I understand that unless you hear from me, I will receive 4 superb new titles every month for just £2.70 each, postage and packing free. I am under no obligation to purchase any books and may cancel my subscription at any time. The free books and gift will be mine to keep in any case.

S0ZEA

Ms/Mrs/Miss/Mr ....Initials.................................
                                                    BLOCK CAPITALS PLEASE
Surname ....

Address ....

....

....Postcode..................................

Send this whole page to:
UK: FREEPOST CN81, Croydon, CR9 3WZ
EIRE: PO Box 4546, Kilcock, County Kildare (stamp required)